A large dark shape loomed through a hazy black cloud, standing twice as tall as Urza. Its incredibly bloated body expanded and contracted with an over-exaggerated breathing motion. One arm nearly dragging the ground ended with razored claws. The other looked stunted, but in actuality it had been replaced by a type of slender cannon that spewed the dangerous substance. Urza swept back, avoiding a new stream of fiery gel and focusing mana into a lightning strike. A blue-white arc leapt from his fingers and smashed into the negator's carapace of hard, glossy black skin. The energy danced over the outer form, all of it drawn over to the Phyrexian's left hip where it entered. The glossy carapace split down the out-side of the left leg. Corrupted flesh sizzled and burned as the lightning was somehow channeled down into the ground and away from anything vital.

This negator was immune to natural fire and resistant to lightning. The two creatures Urza had found time to summon early on had met with fiery deaths, and now the 'walker was losing too much mental strength to tap more mana. It was a hard realization for Urza Planeswalker to admit. He was losing this fight.

A World of Magic

THE BROTHERS' WAR
Jeff Grubb

RATH AND STORM
A MAGIC: THE GATHERING Anthology
Edited By Peter Archer

PLANESWALKER
Lynn Abbey

TIME STREAMS
J. Robert King

BLOODLINES
Loren Coleman

THE COLORS OF MAGIC
A MAGIC: THE GATHERING Anthology
Edited By Jess Lebow

BLOODLINES
ARTIFACTS CYCLE · BOOK IV

Loren Coleman

Wizards
OF THE COAST

BLOODLINES
©1999 Wizards of the Coast, Inc.
All Rights Reserved.

Cover art by Kev Walker
First Printing: August 1999
Library of Congress Catalog Card Number: 98-88156

9 8 7 6 5 4 3 2 1

ISBN: 0-7869-1380-0

T21380-620

U.S., CANADA, ASIA,
PACIFIC, & LATIN AMERICA
Wizards of the Coast, Inc.
P.O. Box 707
Renton, WA 98057-0707
+1-800-324-6496

EUROPEAN HEADQUARTERS
Wizards of the Coast, Belgium
P.B. 2031
2600 Berchem
Belgium
+32-70-23-32-77

Visit our website at **www.wizards.com**

ACKNOWLEDGMENTS

I would like to offer my warmest appreciation for the following people, many of whom worked beyond the regular call of duty on this book:

My family, Heather, Talon, Conner, and Alexia for their patience.

Dean Wesley Smith, Kristine Kathryn Rusch, and Michael A. Stackpole for their advice and support. My agent, Don Maass, for his efforts.

Peter Adkison and Richard Garfield, who brought us MAGIC: THE GATHERING. Peter Archer and Mary Kirchoff, who definitely fit under the above category. Jeff Grubb and Rob King, for setting the bar high with wonderful books before mine. And definitely Jess Lebow, who was always available for questions and assistance and who I'm sure often stood between me and the storm.

Preface

The Legacy

Barrin paused in the classroom's open doorway, his charitable mood fading.

Barely an hour returned to the Tolarian Academy, the master mage had decided to walk a quick tour of the main building before retiring, a habit he formed over his many years as the academy's chief administrator. Tonight it possessed the added benefit of giving Rayne a chance to finish her own unpacking. Her private apartment was not far down Scholar's Row from his own, and when she finished, he thought, they might linger over a second exchange of goodnights

Seeing light spilling down the tiled hallway, Barrin decided to offer assistance to what was certainly tutors up late preparing the next day's lessons. Students, of course, obeyed a strict curfew, and the academy's full scholars rarely, if ever, required such late-night preparations. Rayne was likely to be waiting for him—a slight twinge against his conscience—but he knew that in his place she also would be checking in to offer advice. Besides, adding his personal touch helped to keep Barrin in contact with the daily functions of the academy. This had been, after all, his first real leave of absence.

The first thing Barrin noticed was that someone had punched a new door into the classroom. The rough hole in the previously complete wall stood open, not even framed, and at odds with the smooth plaster and elegant woodwork finishes put on academy facilities. A curiosity turned slightly alarming when he recognized the room beyond contained Urza's primary laboratory. That alarm lasted mere seconds, as Urza himself walked from the back room followed by the silver golem Karn. Both of them carried books and scrolls which they added to a growing pile surrounding the lectern. Barrin frowned over the activity. His scowl deepened as he realized that Urza was too distracted to have yet noticed the mage's presence—a fact which should have been instantly registered by the planeswalker's preternatural senses. A distracted Urza could be a most dangerous thing.

The man standing in front of Barrin was known throughout history as the defiler of Argoth and the harbinger of the Ice Age, though Urza himself could not—or would not—admit with one hundred percent certainty that the global catastrophe resulted from his efforts. Barrin was inclined to give the planeswalker the benefit of the doubt, especially since his track record had improved since coming back to Tolaria after the last major disaster, but benefit of the doubt was one thing, careless blind faith was another. The master mage was feeling a bit unnerved by the sight of the deeply focused Urza. As he approached the lectern, Barrin recognized in the 'walker's intense stare and disconnected manner that same fanatical drive that motivated and created the last set of cataclysmic events. He knew that Urza was again obsessing on his personal crusade: Phyrexia.

Those creatures had once been the ancient Dominarian race of the Thran—who at the height of their achievements had mastered a level of artifice unknown to anyone since—save perhaps Urza himself. Then some kind of war tore the Thran from their advanced ways and sent them hurtling down a darker path toward wicked corruption. They were forced to leave Dominaria for an artificially created plane—nine spheres nested inside one another turning blacker and more torturous the closer they get to the center—and after a time they emerged from their exile as the twisted, hideous abominations that have plagued Urza for millennia. For the loss of his brother, for the death of his one-time traveling companion Xantcha, for replacing that which was human with corrupted artifice the realm of Phyrexia had earned its place as Urza's enemy, one planeswalker against nine nested spheres of malignant, venomous force. His vendetta had nearly cost him his life—existence rather—several times over. So far, others had paid that price for him.

Though obsession was doubly dangerous in a being so powerful, Barrin could understand Urza's pain and nearly forgive the planeswalker his costly mistakes. Barrin believed in Urza's war on Phyrexia, believed that they would return to Dominaria (had seen them with his own eyes), and that without Urza and the efforts of the Tolarian Academy there would be little in the way of stopping them. For that reason Barrin had helped create the

Weatherlight, the skyship that would presumably be the ultimate weapon against the day of invasion. Barrin always doubted the veracity of such an assertion, but Urza had stood adamant—convinced.

If this weapon was capable of defending Dominaria from invasion, why was Urza again demonstrating the distracted intensity which Barrin had learned to recognize and fear?

Karn noticed the mage's approach first, his deep-set eyes widening with recognition. The silver golem certainly would have spoken a greeting if Barrin had not been prepared and spoke first. Seldom it was that Barrin could take Urza by surprise, and usually he learned something from it—never too old to be a student.

"I had not heard of your return, Urza. Welcome back."

Urza had disappeared six months ago, after helping to settle the refugees from Serra's Realm across Dominaria and returning only once with a handful of new students and three new scholars, including Rayne.

Urza did not bother to turn around. He simply reformed the patterns of energy which made up his body so that suddenly he faced Barrin. He was obviously too preoccupied for the more subtle nuances which gave the illusion of his still being of normal mortal flesh.

"Barrin," he greeted neutrally, "I expected you back three days ago."

How are you? How was your leave? Such courtesies were left as far behind the planeswalker as normal life.

"My chances for time away from the academy come seldom. We—I decided to take a few extra days at Angelwood. It's not difficult to lose track of time on Tolaria."

The planeswalker did not even bother to feign chagrin

4

at the reference to the island's temporally-shattered areas where time flowed at different speeds, by-products of the catastrophic failure of Urza's earlier experiments with time travel. Angelwood was a moderate slow-time environment where the enhanced sunlight and frequent but gentle rains created a paradise of lakes and shaded glades. It was a favorite among academy staff for sabbaticals, though the time differential worked against those desiring an extended term away from work. Meeting Rayne during his vacation had seemed to shorten it even more, the time passing so quickly in conversation and shared meals.

She was a rarity in many ways, not the least of which being that she was one of perhaps a few dozen adult scholars ever admitted to Tolaria. Phyrexians planted sleeper agents all over Dominaria but always as adults—never children. Security at the academy usually demanded that new students be admitted when they were in their young teens. Senior students were promoted to tutors, and then they could advance to scholars and eventually might serve as chancellor, one of the eight academy administrators. Rayne's natural talent for artifice had won her admission and instant status as a tutor. Four months later Barrin had signed papers promoting her to full scholar, but it wasn't until their chance meeting at Angelwood that the mage had truly learned to appreciate her. She had long black hair that accented her delicate features, and she possessed an impressive mind and commanded a strong yet subtle presence. Barrin couldn't explain such feelings to the planeswalker. Urza, Barrin doubted, would not understand. Caught up in his obsession, the 'walker barely recognized the civilities of friendship.

Not so Karn.

"It is good to see you again, Master Barrin," the silver golem rumbled out of his cavernous chest, putting an end to the awkward pause that followed Urza's lack of response.

To Barrin, Karn still sounded a bit despondent. Ever since Jhoira's decision to leave Tolaria, the golem had been unable to hide his melancholy. Jhoira had been the golem's best friend for several decades, and even though the silver man claimed to understand why she left, time did not heal his wounds.

"Did you enjoy Angelwood?" he asked.

Barrin smiled, as much for Karn's courtesy as for the fond memories of the last few weeks. "Very much, Karn. Thank you."

"Good," Urza said brusquely, "because we have some hard work ahead of us, important work." He waved Karn off. "I will need several new desks, Karn, and a large worktable."

The silver golem nodded perfunctorily to Urza, offered Barrin a grim smile, and then trudged off to fulfill Urza's request.

"So important that it could not wait for tomorrow?" asked Barrin, now resigning himself to a long evening.

"We have delayed too long already." Urza glanced toward the classroom's main sketchboard, covered with a script Barrin recognized as a meld of ancient Thran and the modern Argivian used as the Academy standard. "I've proceeded as far as I am able alone. Completing the Legacy will require the facilities of the entire academy if we are to have our defenses readied against the Phyrexian invasion."

Urza paused, nodded as if agreeing with himself, and then turned away from Barrin and the conversation. He picked up a large roll of plans and moved to the wall, unrolling and pinning them up against a fresh sponge-wood board. They described an apparatus of titanic size and complexity.

"I will annex this room until the new labs are built." He studied the plans with a critical eye. "I wish I could find Serra and ask her some more questions."

Thrown off by the abrupt changes of topic, Barrin stared at the planeswalker for a moment, then just shook his head. "New labs?" he asked. "Urza, why should we—"

The planeswalker interrupted without turning. "The existing ones are fine and will certainly be utilized, but cannot accommodate the needs of the Lens and Matrix."

So much for clarification.

"Urza?" Barrin began but was again cut off.

"I know that the auxiliary lenses will capture ambient mana." Urza traced a long finger over one area of the plans he studied. "Filters, perhaps? To separate the mana before focusing?"

"Urza."

"Filters, yes certainly. She must have used them. Even Serra's Realm was not purely white mana. She mentioned that total purity was not possible. The question is can the Matrix focus one source of mana in alteration of the more basic—"

"Urza!"

In the large open classroom, designed with an ear toward acoustics, Barrin's shout rang out like a thunderclap. Urza turned slowly from the board and his new plans, whatever they were for, to face the mage. The planeswalker's eyes sparked with fire, and Barrin recognized them as the twin powerstones over which Urza had fought his brother over three millennia ago. They surfaced in times of weakness or intensity (when the planeswalker was too distracted to maintain the illusion of normal eyes). Barrin possessed no doubts that this was one of the latter.

"The *Weatherlight*," Barrin said simply, naming the sky-borne vessel the academy had worked so hard to create, a warship capable of traveling between the planes of the multiverse. "The *Weatherlight* was supposed to be your ultimate weapon. It is the core of our defense, the one thing that the Phyrexians will be hard-pressed to match."

Urza smiled, a bit sadly. "I was overconfident," he said. "The *Weatherlight* can inspire hope with the wondrous feats already at its command, and it will hurt Phyrexia badly in limited engagements, but it will not win the war on its own." He paused, his eyes regaining their illusion of being still human. "Barrin, you were there—in Serra's Realm. That was one battle, and we nearly lost it. Alone, the *Weatherlight* would have fallen. We still have work to do."

"It was under powered," the mage said, playing at contrariness and defending the *Weatherlight* to keep Urza talking.

"It was inadequate," Urza said with great weight, putting an end to the argument. "The *Weatherlight* is the core of the Legacy, not its entirety. Indeed, it may buy us the time we need to complete our defense. As you once pointed out, we cannot assume I will always be present to direct the battle against Phyrexia. The Phyrexians still hunt me with their negators. Other planeswalkers present a threat as well, and there are always unforeseen . . . occurrences." Urza possibly alluded to the years he spent as a prisoner of Yavimaya. "Fate might yet intervene, and though I tend to believe that even fate will not dare gainsay my claim to oppose this evil, I will not rely on that fact. Plans must be set down against the future to finish the *Weatherlight*."

Barrin considered the *Weatherlight* as she already sailed. The airship had fantastic speed, powerful armaments, and the ability to travel between planes. What more was there? True, Barrin concentrated on magic over artifice, but in the decades he had spent with Urza he'd picked up a feeling for the craft. The *Weatherlight* was, in his opinion, already the ultimate artifact, with design mated to purpose. Perhaps they could add a few trappings—install some minor features. Wouldn't it be better to begin looking elsewhere for answers?

When he put those thoughts into words, Urza readily disillusioned him. "The *Weatherlight* is more than any regular artifact, defined by its purpose and static in its function. It lives." As if realizing the implication of his words, he quickly amended the concept. "Not as you live, of course, nor even Karn, but it shares one thing in common with you both—the ability to *evolve*, to grow beyond its current form and ability. The Legacy will be a series of artifacts, crafted over the years, that can be introduced to the *Weatherlight* at a later date. Before you ask why we did not incorporate such features into the vessel from the beginning," he said, forestalling Barrin's question, "it is because of time constraints and secrecy. There are features I have not even conceptualized yet that will eventually be crafted, I am sure. Even were we able to add all possible features to the ship now, its power signature would stand out like a blinding beacon, drawing Phyrexia after it. As it is, the *Weatherlight* will be hard to track until nearer the moment of its final purpose."

The scope of the project left Barrin nearly dumbfounded. "What is that purpose?" he asked, caught up in the vision and expecting now the grand revelation.

Instead, Urza admitted, "I don't know."

Barrin blinked back his surprise.

"The *Weatherlight* is the grandest artifact ever conceived." Urza flapped his arms, once, in a very human gesture of frustration. "As I envision it, the vessel will be able to evolve and do almost anything imaginable. What is that to be? Who will imagine it? When will the invasion come? Where? What will be the key to its ultimate defeat?" His voice rose, its edge of frustration and frenzy cutting apart Barrin's earlier confidence. "Questions! Only questions. I have no answers, not yet." He took a few seconds to regain control of himself. "This is why the bloodlines will be so important."

Again, Urza had jumped three steps ahead in his thinking, apparently assuming Barrin to be gifted with sight that allowed him to peer into another's mind.

" 'Bloodlines'?" the master mage asked, doubt touching his voice as if unsure he had heard correctly. It was not the kind of term to encourage confidence and peace of mind.

"Of course, bloodlines," Urza said, exasperated. "The second half of the Legacy. A *human component*. Haven't you been listening? We can't say for sure that I will be present for the invasion. There must be someone for the masses to follow who will understand how to beat Phyrexia, someone who will know how to use the

Weatherlight in order to save Dominaria." He gestured back to the sketchboard where flowing Thran script mingled with Argivian. "Within the bloodlines we will discover the inheritor of my Legacy, and in the meantime the project will provide us with warriors with which to stand against Phyrexia and its agents." He stepped closer to the board, his voice softening and taking on messianic tones. "They will be Dominaria's soldiers. One among them will be its salvation."

"You expect to train a successor then?"

The administrator within Barrin took over, considering the years, decades perhaps, that it would take for Urza to even locate enough suitable candidates, especially if he wanted to form an army from such a program's detritus. The sheer logistics for such a limited return did not seem prudent.

"Not train," Urza said, dismissing the idea with the easiest shake of his head. "Not as such. What I have in mind will require of a candidate too many specific traits that could never be learned, even in the time given some mortals here on Tolaria." He turned from the board, fixing his hard gaze on Barrin. "Our new army and the heir to the Legacy must be bred."

BOOK I

The Human Component

(3385351 A.R.)

The difference in designs between demon and man is often that razor-thin line which divides the intentions of one from the other. No one has demonstrated that principle to me better than Urza. When forced to descend to the level of one's enemy, that fine blade may be the only path remaining back to sanity.

—Barrin, Master Mage of Tolaria

Chapter 1

Gatha gazed out one of the nearby teardrop windows, his arms crossed defiantly over his chest as Barrin answered questions for a batch of new students. Smoke-tinted glass stained the outside world a dull gray, physically expressive of Gatha's own darkening mood as Barrin continued to make him wait. Rain spattered off the window's upper curve, at times hard and insistent and then fading to a light drizzle. The latest buildings for Urza's new laboratories had been completed just in time. Tolaria's stormy season had begun.

"We've been over this before," Master Barrin explained in answer to a question Gatha had ignored. The mage's voice remained patient, though at a glance the senior student noticed a tightening around Barrin's hard green eyes which forewarned of a darkening mood. "The magic presents no direct influence on the developing child. It is a procedure used prior to conception, to accent the traits which the child already stands to inherit from its natural parents."

He was still discussing the Bloodlines project: Urza's controversial plan to develop some kind of master warrior.

It was now six years into its first generation of subjects. Gatha shrugged aside concern for Barrin's argument and began tapping his foot to illustrate his impatience.

Like sheep with their shepherd—in Gatha's judgment—the new students flocked around Barrin at the front of the workshop. The space had been cleared and cleaned by the senior student in preparation for this orientation class. Except for the half-built gestate cradle pushed into one forward corner, it was the same as every lecture hall in the main academy buildings. Gatha might have found better uses for his time, though a request from Barrin was never to be ignored, and there was something to be said for any recognition by the academy's chief administrator. The senior student held his silence and his place, occupying himself by studying the latest arrivals to Tolaria. The group was one short of a full dozen. Their eyes burned brightly with interest over the tour of the new labs and the information imparted by the master mage. Many of them aspired to be the next prodigy, of course—the next Teferi or Jhoira—or like Gatha himself. At the island academy such visions of personal grandeur were expected, even encouraged, if one owned the talent. A few students fell outside such a generality, though. They glanced about, troubled and nervous. Gatha labeled these ones right away as the next set of 'able hands.' They might work on the major projects, even on the Legacy itself, but always under the exacting direction of others, tools in the hands of masters like Barrin, Rayne, and one day soon, himself.

One such student raised a nervous hand. He was whipcord thin with hair the color of rhubarb and a nose which battled and defeated the rest of his face for attention.

"The plans for these 'Metathran' we've heard discussed in the hallways and amphitheaters." His reedy voice grew in strength and confidence as he progressed. "Simulacra given true life through focused mana? Forced development, probably through overlaid patterns cloned off desired predecessors?" He glanced around for support, found it wanting. "A slave race?" he asked, confidence finally waning and telling in his restless stance.

Gutsy, Gatha decided at once, awarding the junior student credit for calling Barrin on the morality of Urza's newest plans. Strong opening, near-brilliant supposition but ultimately dumb.

The senior student looked back to the window, catching a light reflection of his own face in the tinted glass and of course unable to ignore the triangular tattoos decorating his forehead. It was a debatable honor to be given an artificial set of the Keldon triple widow's peaks. The marks were placed on his entire family after his father served as military liaison to a Keldon warhost hired to fight for Argive.

He turned his attention back to the group of new students. Gatha looked at the gutsy inquisitor who had engaged Barrin. The younger student dwelled too heavily on the methods, not enough on the potential. He would amount to little. Urza Planeswalker supported the plan, and therefore it would happen. It became now, to Gatha's way of thinking, a question of who would lead and so be recognized by the chancellors for promotion to tutor status. Anything else was a waste of a student's time.

Barrin, however, seemed able to dip forever into a well of patience when it came to the newer students. "Timein, isn't it?" he asked, favoring the student by remembering his name.

Gatha shrugged off any concern for competition. The other's scarecrow build guaranteed some measure of easy recall.

"We were speaking of the Bloodlines project, dealing with human generations. These 'Metathran' you ask about are, as you said, *simulacra*," Barrin continued. "Still, I won't disagree with the idea that we are raising new *philosophical* issues at the academy," he said, switching his address to the entire class. "You've all had your first classes in Phyrexian physiology and psychology by now, so you have some idea of what we are up against. We'll need the Metathran to fight them, and no," he returned to Timein on a more personal note, "they will not be slaves. Gatha," he called out, "what is the second criteria of Metathran psychology?"

Caught in the midst of his personal reflection, Gatha started. A hot flush raced from the back of his neck up over his scalp—a discomfiture which lasted all of three seconds. He swallowed away the dryness in his mouth his brief embarrassment had brought. Eyes were upon him now, and he managed to look both contemplative and studious as he turned back to the assemblage. Gatha did not mind an audience.

"To restrict their mental functions to areas of personal survival and martial ability," he recited verbatim from Urza's text, adding his own dramatic touch to the quotation, "with a *limited* concept of self and society." He traced one finger along his jaw, then smoothed a pleat along the front of his white robes. "In effect, they are a type of golem."

Nodding his approval of Gatha's conclusion, Barrin's steady gaze still conveyed a measure of warning to the senior student that he should pay more attention. "Like any artifact, the Metathran will obey its programmed instructions. As with the *Weatherlight*, they are instruments of our defense."

No one raised another question, though the shuffling gestures of several students—Timein among them—suggested that the issue was not completely answered to their satisfaction.

Barrin seized upon the opportunity to end the session. With one hand he tugged at the golden mantle to his robes, straightening it, and with the other he waved toward the workshop's door.

"That will be all for today. Return to your regular classes." They moved toward the door. "Gatha, you will remain, please."

As the students filed out, Gatha caught mixed looks of curiosity, admiration and jealousy from the new students. He drew strength from those stares and glares. Such expressions meant that his name was known, as he wanted it. Only Timein offered nothing for him at all, glancing over with a simple expression of frank appraisal, as if he were weighing Gatha's worth by observation alone. Gatha smiled back, tight-lipped and challenging.

"What do you think?" Barrin asked when the room cleared and Gatha had shut the door.

It was a purposefully vague question, meant to elicit more than basic information but also something as to how Gatha himself thought. The student did not mind, confident in his own ability.

"A verbose way of saying that the ends justify the means," he said, immediately seizing upon the earlier drama in which he'd had a part. "Most of them are still trying to untangle the argument."

The hints of a smile tugged at the corners of Barrin's mouth, though not necessarily one of encouragement or humor. "You think you see more clearly than they do?" No hints of approval or disapproval in his tone.

In place of answering, Gatha walked over to the half-completed gestate cradle. One of the new modular designs that Urza had requested, its sledge-shaped body would be capable of full growth support for the Metathran soldier created within, if the artificers worked out the majority of the design problems, that is.

"I've read the academy histories," he finally answered, circumspect. He reached out to place a hand upon the slick metal casing, noticing a touch of oil to its surface. Being able to touch a thing always made it seem more real. "I have yet to find even one project that has advanced this far along that was not carried through to completion." A polite way of saying that arguments were pointless at this late stage.

Barrin nodded and then headed over toward the door. He paused, hand on the knob. "Coming?" he asked.

Gatha quickly fell into step behind the mage master.

"Your achievements have not gone unnoticed," he said as they walked down a long hall, past doors leading off to other workshops. The labs still smelled of new construction, raw wood and finishing paint. "You have made certain of that. Still, self-promotion aside, you excel in your studies of the magics and your natural grasp of artifice is impressive as well." He pulled a key from within the folds of his robes and used it to unlock a door at the end of the hall.

This new workshop had been modified and outfitted for immediate use. Blue metal file drawers had been mounted into one wall. Metal tables sat in the center of the room with trays of instruments, some obviously magic in nature but most of pure artifice, arranged on top of it. The room was well lit and spotless, but it was very cold. Their breath clouded in front of them. Gatha shivered involuntarily, one hand clutching at the front of his blue tunic trying to draw it tighter against his skin.

Barrin closed the door behind them and locked it. He gave Gatha another frank look of appraisal, eerily reminiscent of Timein's earlier expression. The student bore up under the scrutiny, for the first time feeling a bit awkward. Finally, Barrin awarded him with a reluctant nod.

"I'm adding to your duties," he said, moving to the file drawers. The master mage threw a catch on one of them, then leaned his weight outward as if pulling it open against great weight.

Gatha sucked in a cold breath and held it. Resting in the drawer, on a long plate of metal, was a blue-skinned humanoid of impressive height and elongated skull. Dark blue glyphs—magical sigils perhaps?—decorated the naked body, reminding Gatha of his own tattoos. There was an elegance to the sexless, lean-muscled creature. The master mage did not need to tell Gatha that he looked upon his first Metathran. Part of Urza's newest labs were obviously functional.

He looked to Barrin, found the elder man staring at him levelly.

"What do you think?" the mage asked again.

What did he think? Gatha recognized immediately that he had achieved the next step in his education here

21

on Tolaria. He was being trusted with a new responsibility and his next break would come from his own ingenuity and his ability to make things happen.

Gatha let out his breath and smiled. "Where do I begin?"

*   *   *   *   *

Rayne bent farther forward, leaning far out over the lens to inspect for flaws. Tall and lithe, she reached nearly to the middle of the four foot radius device. The muscles along the backs of her legs tightened and quivered, holding her from smashing through the delicate item. Silk bands tied back the wide sleeves of her flowing robes to prevent even their light brush on the lens's surface. Hardly daring to breathe, wary of fogging the area over which she worked, she continued her search.

The sapphire tint to the material partly reflected her own image, making detection of a flaw harder than if it had been clear crystal backed by a deliberate pattern. She studied her own raven-black hair, her thin nose, and her long slender eyebrows in the reflection. There, near the single curl of hair that tucked down in front of her ear was a mar in the lens's otherwise perfect reflection.

She rotated the special magnifying glass that a student had created for her over into her field of vision. The glass clipped comfortably to her forearm and moved about on a pliant, telescoping arm. It was light enough to almost be ignored and left both of her hands free in case they were needed. She couldn't be sure if Gatha had put a touch of magic into the glass or not, but it cut the glare and allowed her to focus on the most minute object.

Now it showed her the lens's flaw in great detail, a large irregularity in the lattice structure.

"Ruined." She straightened up cautiously, still treating the lens with extreme care. It represented too much work to rate anything less.

Karn moved forward, the silver golem's massive frame dwarfing Rayne. He had waited quietly against the wall for three hours. "The crystal lattice again?" he asked, his voice soft and deep.

Rayne smiled at him, recognizing his regular attempt at courtesy now that she had disengaged from her study.

"Yes, Karn. Over five hundred student-hours, all told, ruined by a microscopic defect." A flawed artifact, she turned her back on it. There was no wishing it to perfection. "Place it on the rack, please. Urza will want to inspect it himself, though I know the flaw is too large."

A scholar of artifice at the academy, Rayne normally commanded enough authority on such projects to make her own decisions—but never when it came to Urza. The planeswalker always double-checked her work when it involved his own projects.

With a delicate care belying his great strength, Karn used a large, grooved fork to grasp the lens securely by its edge rather than the plane. He hefted it, pivoted and slid it carefully into a storage rack next to two others that had also failed to meet standards.

Rayne had already moved on to a new activity. Her private shop always held at least three different ongoing projects, not counting students' work that she had to check over in order to gauge and track their progression. The room smelled of oiled leather and metal. Tables appeared cluttered with tools and parts; though in truth, the *clutter* was actually a complicated but well-ordered system of easy access sorted by probability of use. Most residents of the academy failed to grasp the concept. A few of her better students had picked up on the system. It was also the one time she believed that she'd impressed Urza Planeswalker. On his one visit after her assignment to a Legacy artifact, he had walked in and actually said, "Very nice," in reference to the layout. He never touched one tool, but four of his assistants were sent over that day to study the shop design.

At a table, Rayne puzzled over a new clockwork engine built from Thran metal. The living metal kept growing, binding up joints and gears if not perfectly balanced for the expansion. She flipped the magnifying glass back into her line of sight, staring through it while working on the smooth, intricate pieces. Behind her, Karn finished moving the lens and then resumed his patient vigil

"Barrin will be late again, will he not?" She paused to correct her own Argivian. "Won't he?"

"I do not know, Mistress Rayne." Rayne stopped working and glanced back at the silver man. With a slight hitch to his shoulders, surely a learned trait, Karn elaborated. "He did not communicate such to me, but he did seem very involved in studying Gatha's recent accomplishments."

Gatha was one of Barrin's best pupils. "But as much a curse, that one," she said aloud, a touch of dry humor to her voice. First there was Teferi and Jhoira, and now Gatha. "Why do the brightest ones always bring with them so much trouble?" She glanced back to Karn. "What did he do this time?"

The golem cast his gaze away. "There was an incident at the labs, something to do with enhancing certain traits among the Metathran. Gatha experimented with the Eugenics Matrix without the permission of Urza or Barrin. The facts bore him out, but the result was," the golem paused, "messy."

Rayne shook her head, as much over the trouble surrounding Gatha's lack of caution as the problem the engine presented her. Everything rests on the details, she thought in relation to both problems. It would help if she knew what the engine's ultimate purpose was, but Urza had left her in the dark. Part of the Legacy, perhaps, or another refinement to the Metathran labs. Rayne felt frustrated working like this. It would be more frustrating, she imagined, to be saddled with Barrin's problems.

"Bring me a stool please, Karn. It will be another late night."

Conversation waned as she worked further into the delicate engine. What more was there to say? They both knew Urza to be a hard taskmaster at times. Barrin followed because he believed in Urza, in the 'walker's vision for defending Dominaria. Rayne's vision was more limited to her own work, the creation and maintenance of artifice. In matters of greater scale, she trusted Barrin's judgment. If the master mage thought his presence elsewhere important enough to remain away, then she could do no less than keep working as well.

* * * * *

The vault sat at the heart of Urza's labs, a domed room of titanic proportions devoted to the creation and full gestation of Metathran warriors. The grand arches that buttressed the lower walls allowed better than thirty feet of head clearance. Enchanted globes set into the walls filled the cavernous room with soft light. Conspicuously missing were the gestate cradles. Barrin had ordered Gatha and others to remove the devices before Rayne's students were brought in to fit a new lens into one of the mechanisms. The mage doubted that such a precaution was really necessary. Most students knew the labs were already functioning to some degree, but Urza's orders stood.

The students worked high above the floor on scaffolding set next to one large pillar, junior students steadying the platforms or passing up tools as they were called for by their seniors. Voices and the sounds of work echoed around the vault. Rayne stood out in the open floor, her hands tucked into the opposing sleeves of her robes, supervising her students with a critical eye that missed nothing. Barrin did not approach her yet. An earlier nod and brief smile told him that she knew of his presence. Now he awaited some signal that her attention was no longer required on the work in progress. As he would with any scholar of the academy, Barrin allowed her full authority over the area in which she worked. Besides, the master mage needed a few extra minutes to muster his courage.

Soon the students had finished their task, and they sealed the pillar where the lens had been placed. Rayne waited while the students disassembled the scaffolding and were beginning to remove tools and equipment from the vault, then turned toward Barrin and awarded him with a full, warm smile for his patience. Barrin's legs felt weak, but they managed to carry him forward. As always, he was struck by her delicate beauty, porcelain skin and slender frame—not the usual image of an artificer.

"Hello, my dear," she said, reaching out with one hand to accept his embrace.

He folded her into a quick hug, for a second oblivious to the nearby students. "Greetings," he paused, now a touch self-conscious about the nearby onlookers.

Rayne sensed more in the undercurrents of his voice, no matter that he had tried to hide both his distress and nervousness. She frowned lightly, curious.

"There is news?" she asked, deliberately trailing off the question to allow him an easy time of response.

Nodding, the mage met her searching, dark brown eyes. "Gatha completed the latest tests, and Urza is less than happy with the results." He took a deep breath, tasting the chill air of the large chamber. "All indications point toward forty generations, he says, in order to develop the heir to the Legacy. We are unsure, so far, how many subjects we can hope to raise in fast-time environments, but the island's shattered time streams might work for us. How Urza is calculating this is anyone's guess."

Rayne gave the lightest of shrugs. "Numbers do not lie," she said simply.

Barrin caught the implication: Numbers do not lie, but Urza might. The master mage pushed that disturbing thought from his mind. There was a time and a place to have that discussion, but the planeswalker who founded the Tolarian Academy was not the subject Barrin had come to talk about.

"My new quarters in the slow-time area are complete," he said without further preamble. "Close enough to complete anyway, for me to take up residence."

The possibility had been considered years ago, and preparations were made in case a large facility in extreme slow time was necessary. The Legacy, especially the Bloodlines project, required an overseer other than Urza—one whose presence was considered more dependable. Drinking of the island's slow-time waters, the proverbial fountain of youth, arrested aging, but forty generations demanded more extreme measures. The island's temporal anomalies offered the solution. Some of the best and brightest would move into slow-time areas, those who would coordinate the various projects and keep the Legacy focused over the centuries. Barrin would be first among them. They would be in slow time for twelve hundred years relative to the rest of Dominaria but only thirty or so subjective to the person.

"I've already ordered my assistants to begin moving my offices and labs," he finished weakly.

Rayne stepped back, arms folding protectively across her body. "So soon," she said, hugging herself tightly. She looked up, apparently ready to say something but then shook her head. "This is goodbye then?" she asked calmly.

"That depends on you." It bothered him, the idea of living out such an extended and isolated life in slow time. It bothered him more when he considered that this move could take him away from Rayne forever. It was that thought, more than anything, that had driven him forward on this course. "You could come with me."

Was that a flash of joy in her eyes? Barrin couldn't be sure.

"I could?" she said, part question, part statement.

"Yes," he said, verbally stumbling forward. "I would like you—I am asking you to join me. I am asking you to marry me."

Now Barrin felt the cold sweat standing out on his forehead. Rayne stared back as if not comprehending what he had just asked of her. He felt several long heartbeats marking the seconds.

"There is nothing else for it then," Rayne said, smiling beautifully. "Of course I will."

"Yes?" Barrin asked, marveling at Rayne's acceptance.

He flushed suddenly warm in pleasant shock then smiled and gathered Rayne in for another hug. They embraced each other heavily, and Barrin counted himself fortunate to have found such a person to share his life. It was a good omen, perhaps—certainly good fortune— which Barrin was not about to dismiss for all his other concerns.

He felt immortal in a way that a slow-time life could never provide.

Chapter 2

Croag began to awaken from a long slumber of rest and preservation, the member of Phyrexia's Inner Circle beginning to stir within his bath of soothing, glistening oil. The insinuating fluid seeped through microscopic ducts into his semblance of skin—gray-sheened and stretched tight over ropy wire-braided muscles and a cleft skull. Small on an otherwise large frame, the skull looked out with eye sockets currently capped by protective shields. Teeth bared in frozen maniacal grin, Croag consumed more of the life-sustaining oil through gaps in his sharpened teeth. One skeletal hand of razor-sharp fingers and corded with muscles of metallic fiber rose from the glistening oil. It screeched against the bath's metal rim and finally locked around a scarred lip. Oil ran down along the Phyrexian's arm, dripping back into the pool from the sharp spiked point protruding from what must have been the monster's elbow.

In his state of semi-consciousness, Croag heard several thunderous whispers which reverberated through his skull and brought with them pleasant memories: the scents of smelted iron and fresh oil. A dark shape loomed out of his dreams, black against a night that lacked both moon and stars. The landscape was lit by sparks from the venting of countless forges, and far above, burning cinders rained down from a metallic sky. The shape grew in size, striding across the plane until all grew insignificant by comparison. The dark leviathan stopped, recognizing Croag among the infinite reaches of his mind.

This night Yawgmoth had come to speak with him.

It was the dark god of Phyrexia, creator of their plane and architect of their improved bodies. In all the multiverse, there was none so perfect in form as he. From his slumber over the millennia, the Ineffable spoke to the Inner Circle and made his will known. Croag easily recalled the one time the dark one actually woke, and the grand terror that physically shook the nine spheres of Phyrexia until all recognized his power and were bent to the task of remolding the Dominarian Nexus with Phyrexia at its center.

A querulous rumble shook Croag, still locked in a dream. The council member trembled before the display of power. *Urza Planeswalker lives*, the dark god confirmed.

Eyes of molten red flashed out of the darkness in anger and disapproval. Their searing heat threatened to cripple Croag's body. Compleat though they might be, even a member of the Inner Council could not stand before their enraged god. *Report*, thundered the Phyrexian lord.

Croag understood his master's anger. Urza Planeswalker had been born in the shadow of Phyrexia, mastering the powers of a very unique powerstone left behind in the mountain portal of Koilos. He had also managed to somehow lock away the Dominarian Nexus, preventing any

Phyrexian reprisal and thwarting the full inception of the Dark One's plans for over three millennia.

Insult to this injury came when Urza launched his own attack on Phyrexia. Many members of the Inner Circle were lost in that attack, and many more were later returned to the vats—rendered, decanted, and compleated again according to a better plan. Four Spheres Urza fought his way through, showing the Phyrexians where they were weak and nearly waking the Ineffable himself. Urza was eventually driven back and pursued by negators. They were to destroy the planeswalker and be rid of him forever.

Somehow Urza managed to escape, time and again, always leaving behind the ruined corpses and burned out shells of the negators for the Phyrexians to reclaim and study for faults. He led the Phyrexians into Serra's Realm, an artificial plane constructed by another planeswalker and devoted to pure white mana which threatened the existence of any Phyrexian. Distracted by so tempting a target, here the negators lost Urza's trail. Serra's Realm fell prey instead. Assaults against the abominable plane finally drove Serra away, and then the Phyrexians' corrupting influence worked to turn the realm into a dark mockery of what it once had been, until Urza reappeared, challenging the corruption that had finally made the artificial plane habitable by Phyrexians sensitive to white mana.

Not a single detail was forgotten or omitted in Croag's report to his dark lord. Indeed, the Phyrexian was powerless to withhold anything from his master. His mind was simply drained of all information—relevant or not. When finally finished, the member of Phyrexia's Inner

Circle waited for judgment, knowing it could come either swift and terrible or prolonged and cruel—all at the whim of their god.

The raging thunder that was the Ineffable's ire for Urza Planeswalker spent itself inside Croag's dreams. Tendrils of furious, molten energy slashed at his frame, and darkness squeezed upon his mind. The death scent of scorched oil permeated his body, but this was not punishment or condemnation, and Yawgmoth spared his subject his full fury. Then, under control once more, the Phyrexians' self-made god left Croag with other images from his own mind.

The Inner Council member was shown plans for Rath. The ceaseless spread of manufactured tan flowstone as it swept over the limitless horizon and would one day sweep over Dominaria itself. It was to be the staging ground for the coming invasion. He was told of the evincar, the one who must one day rule Rath and work the will of Phyrexia. This one would come of its own time, and until then Croag would be responsible for administrating the duties of evincar or finding someone who could.

Lastly, the half-conscious completed Phyrexian was shown the penalty he would suffer if plans did not proceed according to schedule. Interference from Urza Planeswalker would not be tolerated. If he failed, his flesh and metal components would be disassembled by the hunched-over, skittering creatures known as birth priests. The raw material of his artificially perfected body would be stripped down and reused. Nothing would remain of Croag, his name burnt from the minds of all Phyrexians.

Croag chattered his understanding.

The dark god retreated from Croag's mind. Smoke left in his wake dispersed on the hot winds of forge bellows, but the stench of burning metal never completely vanishing.

Beneath the surface of the bath, Croag came fully awake. His eyeshields dilated open, revealing large sockets that immediately filled with oil. His vision glowed amber from the cold-burning lights above the surface of the pool. It swallowed large amounts of the fluid. Tightening his grip on the bath's outside edge, Croag hauled himself upright, breaking through the surface and immediately calling to his servants.

The dark god had given him a task.

* * * * *

The pain distracted Davvol. As best he could, the Coracin native compartmentalized the agony of the mechanically-taloned hand locked with vice-like strength around the back of his neck. He ignored the tremors of his own traitorous muscles, and with a focus of will, he cast his mind forward from his body. For a brief second he stood there, looking back into his own eyes— black orbs with just a touch of steel-gray in the center. He cringed away from their lack of compassion and the obvious signs of illness in his pasty, corpse-like flesh.

The creature standing next to him, holding him in its grip, was hardly better to look at. Its body was a meld of machine and flesh, with one real arm and one of metal framework and corded muscle grafted back into place. Grillwork replaced its mouth and covered the bony ridges of what must have once been ears. Davvol extended his consciousness to touch the thoughts of the creature before him. Interspersed between the hate and contempt which ruled most of the Phyrexian's thoughts, it only knew of its own purpose. It was a speaker, one of the few who could speak Coracin's language.

Free from his body's entrapment, Davvol's mind now drifted through the antechamber of his world's most sacred temple. Usually lit by torch alone, it now stood illuminated by strange smokeless lights brought by the Phyrexians. The temple was an ancient ruin of rough stonework with one set of metal doors that took up the entire northern wall of the antechamber. To Davvol's knowledge, and that was saying something, no one had been past those doors to view the *Gift of the Gods* in over three thousand years. Even the antechamber was forbidden to all except the most powerful of Coracin's leaders. Twelve years as his nation's historian had once allowed Davvol the right to visit this supposedly hallowed place. Here he had taken his mental powers to new strengths. Then his forced retirement stole that privilege from him, until today.

Now he visited the temple again. Two score Coracin leaders were held in attendance by half as many black-armored soldiers. The speaker, the soldiers and another larger Phyrexian who appeared to be in charge stood across from the captive Coracin heads of state. This large Phyrexian was the one who could save Davvol's life—the one who could protect him from his own diseased body. The Phyrexians traveled across worlds. They could exchange the weaker flesh for metal and machine. They would do so because they needed him, could use him elsewhere, just like they relied on him today. Among the

Coracin, even those rare ones with mental abilities similar to his own, Davvol was unique. Because his body had begun failing him so early on, he had spent the entirety of his thirty-four years of mature life developing his mind until none could match his strength. His mind was all he'd ever had.

Flares of black and red energy sparked at the edge of his consciousness. He saw the wards that guarded the doors react to his disembodied presence. His mental intrusion however was not quite enough to trip any alarms or traps. He entered another chamber, and there it was, the so-called *Gift of the Gods* that had sat at the heart of the temple for millennia: a machine, spiderlike in that its slab body would move forward on six articulated legs was obviously made of metal.

It gleamed as if age could not touch it in this vault. Davvol marveled at its physical timelessness. He studied the head, thrust forward from the slab body, savage in its likeness of natural physiology. The speaker had shown him a picture of it, calling it an engine of some kind—a Thran war machine brought here long ago. Yes, that is what it was, a war machine sitting at the center of Coracin's lip-service religion. This was what his leaders fought now to protect for themselves.

"It's there," he said, returning to his body with the speed of a single thought. He winced from the painful pressure applied by the speaker's mechanical hand. "Two sets of doors. The engine sits in the second chamber approximately thirty paces inward from this point."

The larger Phyrexian, the one showing less flesh and so obviously in charge of the situation, screeched something to the speaker—the sound of tortured metal and popping rivets. The hand released Davvol, and he slumped to his knees in weakness.

"Which one can defeat the wards?" the speaker asked. Its Coracin language translation came out harsh and rudimentary but understandable.

Davvol coughed wetly then rose shakily to his feet. The answer was already within his mind. Many people knew who among them was the keeper of that secret, and he felt no shame in giving that up. He had been a welcome member of the ruling elite once, before his physical appearance and health began to deteriorate. His perfect memory had been an asset, giving him a handle over administrative tasks few could match. He had given his mind over to his countrymen in hopes that they, in turn, could find a cure for his diseased body, but these people had been unable to heal him. They had stopped trying once he was expelled. Now they shunned him on the street as if his body's state was a fault he could control.

The fault was theirs.

"That one," he said, pointing out the correct man. The man shivered in fright, and the eyes of thirty nine other Coracin leaders cast venomous daggers at Davvol.

The speaker chattered and hissed back to the other. After a moment, "That one we have interviewed before. He was most resistant. Remove the knowledge from his mind."

A chill shook Davvol as the Phyrexian asked for the first thing he would be unable to deliver. "That may prove difficult," he began, and hastened when the speaker reached out for him. "What I mean is that my talent cannot root around in another's mind. I can read only surface thoughts, generalities." He swallowed hard, tasting a metallic sting at the back of his throat. "He would try to sabotage my efforts. He should open the wards himself."

"He refused earlier even when tortured," the speaker said.

Davvol pulled himself erect. "Yes, I'm sure he cherishes the solemnity of his position." He walked over to the other man. "It's only an artifact he guards—a machine." Something so easy to give up in return for life, thought Davvol. "I'm sure there is something he cherishes more, perhaps something he is more afraid for than his own life."

The elder man stared back. His expression twisted between loathing and hatred, and then he spit into Davvol's face.

Davvol did not flinch or move to wipe away the spittle. He felt it trail slowly down his left cheek. It didn't matter, he promised himself. The image was there in his mind—the other man's weakness. This insult only proved to him how little he still owed these people. He turned back to his Phyrexian masters.

"He has a daughter."

Chapter 3

Gatha stood in the Grand Vault, as it had now been formally named, the focal point for the creation of Metathran warriors. It was also the central hub to the various labs and workshops in which the bulk of the work for the Bloodlines project—and to a lesser extent the ongoing Legacy project—was accomplished. He still could not help admitting to being impressed by its sheer magnitude—the arches, the central pillars that housed most of Rayne's mana-focusing lenses, the *space*—Urza certainly did not think small. Neither did the young tutor.

Gatha paced a short path alongside one of the gestating cradles, its curved nose sticking out of the large socket into which it had been plugged until full gestation of the Metathran warrior was achieved. This one was *his* warrior, one of those which would owe its existence— not exactly a life—to Gatha. His hard-soled boots beat a slow rhythm against the polished stone floor. One hand trailed along the side of the cradle, over rough gear teeth and the alternating smoothness of polished metal and glass viewports that looked into a dark interior. He did not attend the "birth" of them all, but this one might be special. He would know soon.

Timein found him there. "Master Gatha," the younger man said by way of address, voice devoid of any emotion. The senior student waited for acknowledgement before continuing.

Gatha glanced over and nodded curtly. Six subjective years had done little for Timein except to sharpen the student's mind. Still a tall and gangly body that looked ready to fall apart in a strong breeze and an adam's apple that almost split through the skin on his neck, at least his voice had lost the reedy tenor of youth. Timein began to bring him up to date on some of the minor experiments being conducted in real time, leafing through a stack of reports he carried in his knobby hands. As he listened Gatha compared and admired his own features in the reflection of a cradle viewport.

Eight years, again subjective, had brought Gatha into the comfortable stages of manhood nearing thirty. He now wore a trimmed goatee that he reached up to stroke while listening to Timein's report. He had filled out physically, and his mind had never been so brilliant. A tutor, one of the youngest ever, though he fell shy of Teferi's mark by a solid two years. Master of time, he considered himself. He felt himself second only to the Master Mage Barrin and Chancellor Rayne, who lived in the more extreme slow time and rarely ventured forth. Eight subjective years, passing in between moderate slow-time environments and real time, while for Dominaria forty-two years had passed. In the moderate fast-time envelopes, where much of his actual work was accomplished by students, over seventy years of research and production had accrued. Preoccupied with their own relative immortality and the fate of Dominaria as real time progressed, most other tutors and scholars underused the fast-time outposts. Gatha prided himself on never wasting opportunity.

"Results of recessive gene enhancements, post-birth, *negative*." Timein's voice barked out the word, bordering on disrespect and definitely capturing Gatha's full attention. "*Surviving* subjects show high rate of mutation, considered inadequate for further bloodline development."

Wheeling, Gatha strode over to Timein and snatched the report. It still smelled of fresh ink, and his thumb smeared one of the red circles that highlighted various figures. Gatha's strong hands wrinkled the parchment, clutching it tightly. Teeth clenched hard enough for his jaw to ache, he read down the list of three years' relative work—wasted. The red circles were no doubt Timein's notations, calling attention to numbers that supported the student's own predictions of four months ago. Gatha spared the student a quick glance, but Timein had settled a careful mask into place. The preparedness of the student allowed Gatha to place an easier handle on his own rage.

"What do you make of this, Timein?"

Gatha had learned years ago that Timein did not volunteer information, not to him at least. Though a promising sorcerer, Timein made no secret of the fact that he disapproved of the Bloodlines project. The trouble he occasionally stirred made it easy for Gatha to sidetrack the younger man's own studies, keeping him junior through extended assignment in slow time. It helped, more often than not, having an assistant nearly as brilliant as himself. Also, Gatha was not about to let Timein remain in real time where the sorcerer could conceivably age and learn faster and be promoted over him. That wouldn't do at all.

Timein merely shrugged. "I made my opinion known months ago, Master Gatha." A not-so-subtle method of reminding the academy tutor that Timein's *opinion* had also been right. "I imagine Masters Urza and Barrin will not care to hear that this tampering *post-birth* exceeded their guidelines."

Ah, a threat—Gatha smiled at the challenge. As he had noticed years ago, Timein simply did not know when to stop while ahead.

Waving over a junior artificer who worked on a nearby cradle, Gatha ignored his young charge. "This cradle," he said, kicking at the device that held his latest Metathran experimentation, "is to be unplugged at once and the subject delivered to my workshop."

If the other experiments had failed as badly as the report suggested, a similar procedure used during this Metathran warrior's gestation would prove similar. Autopsy would provide that answer and perhaps a suggestion for new paths.

The artificer turned back toward her workspace.

"Do it now," Gatha ordered, though he knew standard practice for artificers as ordered by Chancellor Rayne was to always keep an orderly space. Likely, the girl was going to set about putting tools away or some such bother. "The subject is within hours, perhaps minutes, of full gestation. I do not want it brought to full term." Damn the standard procedures.

Timein had evidently caught the nuances of Gatha's early termination of the Metathran gestation, connecting the tutor's displeasure with the report he now held. Gatha noticed the gaze of frustration and sorrow which his apprentice directed toward the failed experiment. He almost laughed, wondering what Timein's reaction would be if privy to Gatha's more recent alterations, most of those with the tacit permission of Urza Planeswalker. To recapture his attention, Gatha held up the report Timein had furnished and slowly ripped it down its length.

"This report," he said with a quiet hardness, words underscored by the tearing sound, "has obviously been exaggerated to the point of error. I will visit these labs myself." The report was in two pieces now. Gatha folded them together and proceeded to tear again, this time across the shorter axis. "Timein, you will take the rest of the reports to my office and compile all data." He quartered, refolded, and tore the report again. "Let me know what Barrin's people are working on as well."

The fragments of the report went into an outer pocket. Gatha frowned at the smudge of red ink staining his thumb. He reached over and rubbed it out against the dark blue border of Timein's sleeve.

The student mage could only stare in dumbfounded silence. When Gatha nodded a dismissal, Timein blinked away most of his shock and then turned to do as he had been bid. In Timein's years on Tolaria, Gatha doubted the apprentice sorcerer had ever seen data purposefully destroyed. The shock value, seeing it wash over that gaunt face, had been exquisite.

"It doesn't matter," Gatha whispered after the departing figure.

The report concentrated on the past. Only the present, the *now*, mattered. Behind him, the echoing clangs of a cradle being unplugged from the central machinery ran out, echoing in the cavernous theater. *Now*, Gatha had other projects to begin.

* * * * *

Karn discovered himself actually stalling. The silver golem had been asked to summon Gatha into the presence of Barrin and Urza and had already managed to be sidetracked by two other errands.

In the timelock, passing into the slow-time area where Gatha had settled his own quarters and a modest workspace, Karn had paused to study the device. Without a cushioning effect a human body could not withstand the transition of extreme temporal changes. The instant alteration in blood flow that occurred on the cusp, one part of the body extremely slower than the other, made for radical embolisms and instant hemorrhaging. Here, in the timelock, slow-time waters were pumped out of the same well that served Gatha's facilities. They were then misted into a series of chambers, which stood just outside the radical change in temporal flux. The density of mist in each chamber stepped up the farther one penetrated, preparing the body for slow time. The water was then reclaimed and returned to the water table via another shaft. It was very efficient, a variation on the first device built by Jhoira, who had noticed water's tendency to retain the temporal qualities of its original environment and so could be used to alter time in small areas.

Jhoira. She was rarely far from Karn's thoughts, his first true friend after the golem gained sentience. He had thought her dead once, only to regain her companionship and then lose it again as she moved on to a life that did not include Tolaria. He saw her occasionally, perhaps once every decade, but for Jhoira time had already mended the wounds of separation. Karn could expect no such relief. Ironic, that with Tolaria's ongoing mastery over temporal mechanics, he had yet to find a way to distance himself from a pain better than fifty years old.

After his emergence into the slow-time environment, Karn stopped by the side of a small, fragrant flower garden to pick a chrysanthemum. Its deep purple reminding him of Jhoira's darker hair, and its sweet scent the light perfumed oil she had worn on occasion. Finally the golem admitted to himself that his delays were moving further from the realm of plausibility and toward the denial of his task. He abruptly handed the flower to a passing female student and set off for Gatha's tower without an answer to her look of surprise. Stopping to smell the flowers simply was not a cure for his pain or a fair delay in his mission.

Still, memories of Jhoira were not so easily set aside. Drawn to make human contact, the golem could not help establishing relationships with those around him even though he recognized each one as another potential loss—more pain to deal with.

Gatha had set up a stasis field in his small workshop where failed Metathran warriors could be brought and kept in isolation while he ran his own tests. Four subjects currently crowded that field, two of them so deformed as to look more animal than humanoid. A third was hunched over, misshapen but recognizable. The fourth looked perfect in every regard, right down to the blue skin and Thran script that appeared as tattoos but were actually natural marks—never two identical. These creations would remain in stasis indefinitely. The alternative was to destroy a failed subject since the regular stasis fields were used to store *viable* warriors for use during the time of a Phyrexian invasion. Karn couldn't say for sure that destruction wouldn't be preferable, and therein lay another problem. Gatha didn't care. The tutor was brilliant but reckless. Karn had compared him to Teferi at first, but Teferi had been a spoiled boy who grew out of his troubles and into a responsible wizard. This Karn did not say to Gatha but hoped it would be implied.

"Don't look so glum, Karn," Gatha said as he noticed the golem's arrival. "You're too bright to be gloomy." Gatha chuckled at his own joke, then glanced back to the warriors. "I've been expecting you. Barrin's unhappy again, I take it."

"He wants to see you right away."

Gatha returned to his observation of the Metathran, shaking his head either at Barrin's summons or something to do with the fourth warrior subject. There it was again. A lack of any real concern for anything but what he focused on at the moment, and here every moment cost severe delays in real time where Barrin and Urza waited.

"Look at him," Gatha said. "Perfectly formed. Beautiful." He ran one hand back over his head to smooth back his own hair. Karn had noticed in the recent years that Gatha preferred to display his own tattoos, as if this somehow related him to the Metathran warriors and their own markings. "And completely psychotic. It can attack when angry or pleased, or it might simply curl up and become catatonic for days."

"And those others?" the golem asked, nodding toward the malformed warriors. He watched the young tutor's face for any sign of misgivings but found none.

"Older subjects." Gatha dismissed them with a wave of his hand, then reached up to stroke his goatee. "No, this one is the closest I've come yet to my goal. My fast-time laboratories will be concentrating on data from its gestation for several subjective years."

"No," Karn told him. "They won't." He hated to be the one to bring such news to Gatha, but Master Barrin had been direct: If Gatha did not respond immediately to a summons, Karn should deliver the news himself. "Your fast-time labs are being diverted to other projects. Bloodlines work, but under another tutor and this time overseen by an academy scholar."

This grabbed the tutor's attention as nothing else could. "Barrin's orders?" Gatha did not bother to hide his anger, even when Karn confirmed it with a slow nod. "We'll see about that."

He grabbed up his cloak and strode immediately for the door, leaving the golem to follow or not as he pleased. Karn trailed behind, feeling miserable. He received only slight justification in the obvious foresight of Barrin's orders. Apparently the only way to motivate Gatha was to deliver such blows.

* * * * *

Barrin and Urza had commandeered a classroom which could seat one hundred students comfortably. It was the closest empty room at hand when Urza had reappeared. The planeswalker spent so little time on Tolaria these days, hounded by Phyrexian negators and not wanting to lead them back. The *Weatherlight* visited less often for the same reason.

Occasionally, some cases at the academy still required Urza's presence, and Gatha was certainly one of them. The rogue tutor stood alone in the dead space that separated where Urza and Barrin sat from the first level of seating where Karn now waited. A thin, placating smile on his face, Gatha affected an air of someone wronged at great trouble and personal expense—a child, convinced in his own superiority and put upon only for his smaller size and fewer years.

On the surface, the young tutor bore up under the rebuke admirably. Standing in silence, a slight flush to his skin and the hard cast to his eyes were the only signs of his inner feelings. Hands clasped behind his back, he simply nodded to every point made by Barrin and bowed to Urza's final demand.

"You must adhere religiously to the guidelines as set down for the Bloodlines project and exercise more discretion when it comes to the presentation of your work." Urza waited, then prompted for a reply. "Is that understood?" he asked.

"Yes, Master Urza. Of course." He was unable to hide the spark of anger that still smoldered behind his narrowly focused eyes. "My fast-time laboratories. Without them—"

"Without them," Barrin interrupted, voice hard, "you will be forced to slow down and adhere to the guidelines we've set. Your third generation subjects tend toward anger and brutality, even in their early years, and your rate of mutations are far above the average."

Urza rubbed at his chin with his right hand. "Anger and brutality are fine, each in its place, but these are unfocused." He shook his head. "Most third generation subjects show an increased lack of emotional focus. That's a step backward, and you're leading in that direction. We need to discover what is setting us back. We'll commit more generations to the fast-time pockets, try to generate data at better rates. If we solve this problem, you *may* get those labs back." He waited, and this time Gatha volunteered a curt nod. "That is all."

Gatha bowed his leave from the two of them. He did not look at Karn at all on his way out, a fact the golem did not miss.

The silver man made as if to leave, unsure of whether or not to follow. In the end he waited, and Barrin set Karn's obvious problems aside for now.

"He will ignore us, Urza." said Barrin. "He'll be more circumspect, for a while, but nothing will slow Gatha down except to further strip him of resources."

Urza, as was typically the 'walker's way, concentrated more on his own concerns. He shuffled a paper from out of a nearby stack, glancing over the report. "Why the step backward?" he asked again to the room in general. He glanced up. "You have more to say about Gatha?"

"He's incorrigible," Barrin snapped, "drunk on power and his own genius and now bitter that we've interfered with his fast pace plans. We'll regret every day that we do not curtail him."

"You once thought the same about Teferi." Urza actually allowed a touch of humor to his voice. He continued to scan the report.

Barrin shook his head forcefully. "Teferi deserved a good switching, but he did not destroy lives. Urza, this man is out of our control, and it is affecting the work of other students and tutors, raising again the same moral issues I've wanted to avoid—*we've* wanted to avoid—in the past. Gatha takes too many chances."

Urza evidenced no reaction, unimpressed by the dramatics. The mage sighed, feeling his years. He tried a new tack.

"Do you know how many of his failures are stacking up in the stasis chambers? Some of our newest students, those born on Tolaria, are now trying to discover magical ways to cure deformities we've left for them as a Legacy."

"Gatha is responsible for several of what few breakthroughs we've had augmenting the bloodlines," Urza argued calmly. He lifted his gaze to find Barrin's. "You know what he did to help bring the Metathran labs on schedule."

Yes, Barrin knew. He had assigned Gatha the work, hoping that getting his hands dirty might knock the indifferent edge off of the boy. Instead, Gatha had acquired a taste for it. He dressed in dark clothing these days, not the precise Argivian uniform he had when he arrived at the academy, the better to hide bloodstains Barrin felt sure.

"The Metathran are our own sin, but you've convinced me of their necessity. The bloodlines, though, involve and affect real lives." Barrin swallowed, trying to coax life back to his cotton-dry mouth. "Don't remind me that they are all volunteers, because this goes beyond that." He glanced toward Karn and then continued. "He's introducing Phyrexian material into the main Eugenics Matrix," he said matter-of-factly.

Now Urza paid attention. "How did you find that out?" he asked sharply.

Barrin stammered at the 'walker's reaction, his scalp prickling. The Eugenics Matrix was a Thran artifact that Urza recovered and modified and was the key to genetic manipulation. The Matrix and the simpler devices based on it offered the only real chance for success on the Bloodlines project. They also represented the opportunity for terrible abuse. All new procedures were supposed to be cleared by Urza or Barrin. The mage had heard unconfirmed rumors only but had hoped to shock a reaction out of the planeswalker never thinking that, if true, Gatha could be operating with permission.

"You knew?" he asked in a hoarse whisper.

"How else would Gatha get hold of *Thran* genetic material?" Urza stressed the different name, though of course they were one and the same. Noticing Barrin's frown of confusion, he said, "Acquired from more recent incarnations, of course, but as descendents of the Thran we can hope to reacquire their better traits." He brushed the semantics aside with a quick wave. "Where did you hear this?"

"Karn," Barrin answered, nodding to the silver golem. "He brought some rumors to my attention which led back to Gatha." He noticed the golem's start. Karn began to speak, and then with a confused expression, obviously decided against it. "I'm still investigating," the mage finished.

"Then you may stop investigating," Urza said simply. Noticing Barrin's look of dawning horror, he continued. "Nothing is more important than the Legacy. We agreed to that years ago, yes?" He waited for Barrin's reluctant nod. "It *does* matter that they are volunteers. I would not burden you with such troubles here on Tolaria if they were not. I must have the heir to the Legacy." Urza's eyes burned away, and in his illusionary mask of a young face the twin powerstones shown out in their stead. "Someone who can empathize with the Phyrexians enough to out-guess them—to understand how to employ the Legacy to defeat them, possibly inside Phyrexia itself. Once Karn has joined with—"

"Speaking of whom," Barrin interrupted as soon as Karn's name was mentioned, talking over Urza's next few words. "Karn, would you mind finding Rayne? She's visiting some of the real-time labs. Let her know I'll be late and help out if she needs anything."

"Of course, Master Barrin."

Karn bowed stiffly from the waste, the relief in his voice telling how happy he was to finally have an order. The golem exited through the same door Gatha had used.

Urza had turned back to the report he held as soon as Barrin mentioned Rayne, his intensity of the moment before forgotten just as easily as it had come. This was not the first time Barrin had noticed that Urza seemed uncomfortable around the idea of the mage being married. It nettled him slightly and led him to wonder at the 'walker's odd manners.

"She *does* worry, sometimes," the mage said by way of explaining Karn's mission.

Looking up from the report, Urza nodded. "I'm sure."

To the swamps of Urborg with Urza's indifference! This chance upon him, Barrin said, "I am married, you know. Her name is Rayne."

"I know that." Urza's expression did not change.

"Do you disapprove?" Barrin asked directly.

"What makes you think I do?" Again no expression, but there was a hint of curiosity in his tone.

Barrin leaned forward onto the table they shared. "You avoid her, even the mention of her. I've noticed before that you take special pains to prevent encounters." He paused. "I'm sure she notices too, though she will never say so."

The 'walker nodded. "So you think I disapprove. Barrin . . ." His voice trailed off as if he were trying to organize his thoughts or was deciding what not to say. "Barrin, my own experience in relationships does not . . . I do not claim to have a clear understanding of mortal events. I try to leave well enough alone where my concerns are not needed and my presence is possibly disruptive."

It was a plausible answer—slightly evasive—but plausible. "You do approve?" Barrin asked, fishing for a straight answer for once. He held Urza's gaze, as if he could will the truth from the 'walker.

"Life must endure, Barrin," Urza finally said. "That more than anything defines our purpose on Tolaria." He paused, then, "I think you have done well. I certainly would not have chosen any other mate for you."

Barrin should have known better, hoping for an easy answer.

Urza stood, gathering up the reports he had been reading. The perfunctory way he went about collecting his papers might have signaled an end to their conversation, and Barrin was willing to let it go. Ending a conversation on a positive note for once would be nice.

Urza was of another mind. "Why did you want Karn to leave the room?" he asked, pausing half way to the door.

The 'walker was not *always* obtuse to the mortal events around him. Barrin nodded. "You were about to say that Karn would be joined with the *Weatherlight*, weren't you? And right in front of him."

The planeswalker stared back, waiting.

Barrin shook his head. "Urza, he isn't a cog or a gear. Karn is a sentient being, capable of making decisions which affect his life. I doubt you've even noticed, but . . ." The mage trailed off, drawing a strange parallel between Karn's obvious personal troubles and the previously discussed problems with the bloodlines. Could one be *too* empathic? Or have too perfect of a memory?

Urza shrugged indifference to Barrin, either missing or more likely not caring that the mage had interrupted himself. He hovered in the doorway. "The *Weatherlight* will require a governing mind when it comes time for its grand purpose, as directed by the heir. Karn is perfect for that task. He will complete the *Weatherlight*." With that, he walked from the room.

The planeswalker's use of the term *complete* ran a chill through the mage. That was how the Phyrexians described the replacement of flesh with artifice, as the *compleation* of the body. Barrin slid into a nearby chair, his strength deserting him. In all the years he had known Urza, Barrin could not remember hearing the planeswalker use the term in a similar context.

Ever.

Chapter 4

Leaving the kingdom of Zhalfir in its wake, hardly a dark smudge set against the graying coastline, the *Weatherlight's* crew checked all horizons and called them clear. Karn glanced back toward the ship's stern. A colorful sunset framed the aft end of the ship. Ilsa Braven, the vessel's current captain, commanded from the quarterdeck, and she bellowed commands which would not be heard again on the *Weatherlight* for some time.

"Rig the ship for sky. Take her up."

Crewmen shifted the sail rigging, and engineers brought the ship's magical engines up to power. Slowly, the sleek vessel rose from the embrace of blue-gray waters and into a sky washed pale red by the dying sun. The skyship's sharp bowsprit whistled as it cleaved the air. The sails remained full—billowed by magical energies which wrapped themselves about the sky-borne vessel. Most of the sailors and students aboard would agree that this was one of the best moments—when the freedom the *Weatherlight* offered was palpable especially to those who rode the open deck.

Karn did not revel in that moment, though this would be the final flight of the *Weatherlight* before security issues forced it to remain in the role of a simple ocean-bound vessel. He remembered other times well enough when he had enjoyed his time on the ship—pleasant moments on deck or down in the heart of the vessel where the silver golem could physically link with the *Weatherlight's* powerstone engine and command the ship's flight with a level of precision no human crew could hope to match. Those were heady times in the golem's life, good times indeed, now lost.

Over the last ten years Tolaria had begun to feel like a prison to Karn. His constant movement between the different temporal zones made him uneasy, unable to really know any of the students anymore. They were lost in a mayfly life while the silver man stepped into slow time to assist Rayne, Barrin, or Gatha.

Against his better judgment, Karn remained Gatha's friend—the tutor's only friend, it seemed. Other academy staff avoided him. Many of the students who worked under the tutor were afraid of him. Gatha did not seem to mind the lack of human contact, content in his work and a periodic acquaintance with Karn. That Karn needed something more came to a head when, during one of those visits to slow time, the golem missed one of Jhoira's rare appearances on Tolaria. The silver golem did not hold resentment for Gatha's summons, but it did cast him into a personal depression which only Barrin and Rayne had noticed and finally worked him through with a few kind words and gestures.

It was Gatha's continued use of Phyrexian material in the bloodlines that finally convinced Karn to seek a leave of absence from Tolaria. So many of his subjects were born malformed, and nearly all of them, so far, turned malevolent to some degree as they matured relatively quickly in fast-time environments. The golem had found himself unable to reconcile his friendship with Gatha and the revulsion he felt toward the man's practices. Karn remembered the years of fighting against the small Phyrexian community that had once infested Tolaria. He remembered the terrible creatures that repeatedly rose in newer, more hideous forms and the many good lives lost because of them. He easily recalled their grotesque features—artifice and flesh intermingled—and the caustic scent of the slime and oil that they called blood. He could still hear the screeching cacophony of noise that was their speech and screams. Worst of all, he remembered his own empathy for the black nightmares—that tiny spark within him which recognized Phyrexians as kindred.

Karn knew of the black powerstone which gave him true life—Xantcha's Heart. It had been first tied to the life of Urza's former companion, a Phyrexian newt who turned against her old masters and old world. It had retained its powers after she gave her life to defeat the Phyrexian Gix, and so Urza had bound it to the golem and brought about his first sentient artifact. The powerstone responded to Phyrexians still. The principle of similarity, Barrin had called it, trying to relieve Karn's anxiety with an explanation. Like must recognize like, but Karn had felt that same spark of empathy for Gatha's creations, and it frightened him. He did not want such feelings confusing his true friendships with good people like Jhoira, Barrin and Rayne. Upon hearing that Rayne and the forest spirit Multani would lead an embassy to Yavimaya on the *Weatherlight's* next tour, its final flight, Karn volunteered to help crew the vessel in hopes of reliving a few of those better days and so reclaim some hold on the present, except that hadn't worked.

Karn heard the *Weatherlight's* call to him even now. That deep hum of power that bled up through the polished wooden deck—a sound so bass it was felt more than heard. It was different this time; missing were the other people who had made those times alive for the silver golem, mostly Teferi and Jhoira. Always back to Jhoira, for whom, Karn admitted now, he had made this entire trip. He wanted to talk to his first and best friend, but neither she nor Teferi had been in Zhalfir—the ship's first port of call—and no one had been able to say where they might have gone off to and whether alone or together.

There would be no absolution on this journey, only the hard, cruel truth the golem now faced standing alone on the ship's deck. He had tried to run away, but his past would never allow that. It followed him, tormenting and tireless. Right then Karn wished it all away.

Never once did he consider what such a wish might cost him.

* * * * *

Multani moved to the edge of the quarterdeck, away from the tight knot of academy observers whom Captain Braven had invited up into her domain for landing. The nature spirit gripped the rail. He could feel the life in the ship, a life which was still as much a part of Yavimaya as a being of its own essence, much like himself.

Even from a distance, Multani would fail to pass for a human or one of the more humanoid races. His trunk exactly that, a medium-sized bole too thick and cylindrical to remind one of a body. His arms and legs were thick branches, very knobby at the joints and his fingers and toes rootlike extremities. Barklike skin covered the backs of his hands, forearms, and the tops of his feet, and his face seemed to *sprout* from the top of his trunk. Hair the color and texture of spring moss fell back from his scalp and upper shoulders, the mane tumbling halfway down his back. He had chlorophyll eyes, green irises staining veins into the white, and a leaf-shaped pattern tattooing the left side of his woodgrain face. He was created from the essence of Yavimaya, the sentient forest packaged in humanoid form.

Now, after better than a century away, he was leading a Tolarian embassy and Llanowar ambassador back to his homeland.

Blue-green waters rolled up to a thin outer arc of beaches which alternated between light yellow to reddish browns and the intermittent green of coastal growth. The beach territory quickly faded toward pale washes of rainbow color as the *Weatherlight* moved inland. That was new. The forest green had once stretched from one side of the island to another, before Yavimaya had begun some . . . changes. The interior remained a dense canopy of greens, interrupted only by a few dark mountain peaks. The canopy rippled in places, as if by an intense wind that no one else could feel.

He felt the forest's anticipation and just a trace of concern for allowing so many outsiders access to its lands. The nature spirit sent back a soothing call.

"It's wondrous," Rofellos said, the Llanowar elf bounding up to the rail beside him.

The young warrior's dark, unruly hair fell in a tangled cascade down his back. He leapt up onto the narrow rail, leaning far over with one arm looped casually through nearby rigging. The bottom hem of his leather tunic waved in the moderate breeze created by the ship's passing. His sword dangled from a rough leather belt—an item he never set aside no matter the company or situation.

Multani had moved aside to avoid the others, especially Rayne with whom he had already spent so much of this voyage in conference, but Rofellos, for all his energy and rough ways, was welcome. He was one of Gaea's forest-born, though more violent than most, but then the same could be said of most Llanowar elves. That was the reason Yavimaya had asked the Llanowar warrior clans send an ambassador. Perhaps the Llanowar might learn from Yavimaya something more of harmonious living.

Respectful as always to Multani's slightest comment or movement, Rofellos jumped back down to the deck. "I'm sorry, Multani. I didn't mean to disturb you."

So close to home, Multani doubted that much could truly disturb him. Soon, he promised himself, he would know the forest's soothing touch again.

"Do not worry, Rofellos, Yavimaya welcomes you.

Rofellos drew himself up proudly at the recognition, whether from Yavimaya or Multani himself the nature spirit couldn't be sure. In reality, it didn't matter. Perhaps Rofellos could not fully appreciate the unique creation which was Yavimaya yet, but certainly he stood in slight awe of the nature spirit. Multani watched the elf carefully as, still racing the wind at a good clip, the *Weatherlight* flew over the island perimeter.

The elf started only slightly. "No beaches?" He grinned, obviously enthralled by the prospect. "No sand or rocks," he said in wonder, "only Yavimaya."

"You will find no sand," Multani promised. "None safe."

Below them the beaches had been consumed by a tangle of thick, thorny rootwork. The roots extended out from the small copses of coastal growth, then curled and bunched as they ran across the open space and finally dived into the ocean shallows. A few last tips stuck out like huge spikes, as if to impale landing ships. When Rofellos mentioned this, the nature spirit nodded.

"They are meant to do just that. You see years of patient growth at work here. Though Yavimaya's defenses will tend to spread from the heart outward, an initial perimeter guard was deemed of great importance."

The elf forced on himself a moment to consider this, a sign of extreme patience in a Llanowar. Finally he asked, "Does Yavimaya tell you this?"

"I simply know it to be true. Yavimaya speaks through me. It has no need of speaking *to* me."

As the coastal root network and isolated copses fell away, the *Weatherlight* crossed over what had appeared at first to be painted desert. The air chilled and quickly turned to an intense cold. The nearby humans chattered excitedly, and Rofellos continued to stare over the side, oblivious to the temperature. Multani shivered in his physical shell, turning his face upward to stretch toward the sun's warming rays.

"More roots, thinner ones, blanketing the ground." The elf fell silent for a few seconds. "Writhing over . . . are those dunes?"

"Trees," Multani whispered without looking. "The boles of ancient trees, centuries old, which Yavimaya shaped and then recently fell here in perfect order so that no gap remains. The ground here reflects no heat. The warmth is pulled into the decomposing trees so that the root desert may grow faster." The spirit looked ahead, at the high cliff of wood that barred their path. "Captain Braven, you may rise above those trees, but slow your speed. Your landing area is near."

The captain barked out the appropriate orders.

"We are not traveling into the Heart of Yavimaya?" Rofellos asked.

Multani tensed at Rofellos's choice of words. He obviously knew nothing of what he asked, merely reflecting some of Multani's earlier statement. The true Heart of Yavimaya would never be known to the Llanowar. Likely, it would never be known by Multani, so protected it was by the sentient forest. Though it was forbidden even to him, Multani knew a slightly jealous protection of his homelands.

"For our purposes," he said simply, "the borderlands will be close enough."

*　*　*　*　*

The vessel settled down in a clearing of dark grasses dotted with small, lavender-cupped flowers. The field rippled under the same unfelt breeze that had earlier shaken treetops in the distance. Trees which reached hundreds of feet into the air surrounded them, visibly impressing many of the students. Multani recognized it as new growth raised in the last few years. Several of the larger hills around would be partially decomposed trees from the ancient growth, brought down by Yavimaya for the raw material.

The Tolarians went about their routine of making the vessel fast. Sails were reefed, and the telescoping circular gangplank hauled out and dropped down over the side.

Multani winced at the harsh clanging sounds as the staircase unfolded. He move toward it once secured, but Rofellos ignored it completely. With a wild shout for his own bravery, the elf vaulted over the lower gunwale and slid down the outer curve of the hull. At the last moment he kicked outward, breaking his fall with an easy tumble across the grass. He rose only to one knee, though, suddenly transfixed by the rippling motion of the sward. Multani could only guess at the other's sense of wonder as he descended to the ground.

The air was vibrant with life, singing Gaea's song as wind shook the tops of trees and whistled past sharp grasses. Pollen, which Multani had never scented before, distracted him, every taste calling an instant explanation from Yavimaya. The earth felt spongy beneath his bare, rootlike feet, and he found it hard to control the urge to dig his toes down into the rich soil and taste his homeland again. Yavimaya withheld him, waiting on the others.

The elves appeared as if by magic. One instant they were absent and only the forest sounds surrounded the clearing. In the next, all forest sound but the distant fall of a tree disappeared, and a dozen lithe bodies appeared at the clearing's edge. They moved into the clearing with cautious grace, as if unwilling to leave the protection of the forest. All were of fair hair and skin, with features so delicate they appeared fragile. Rayne moved up to Multani's side, and the nature spirit stepped away to distance himself from her.

"Yavimaya welcomes you," a female elf said in traditional greeting to Rayne and the other humans. Her voice was light and musically cast.

Rayne smiled warmly. "We are here on behalf of the Tolarian Academy—"

"To request some rare hardwoods for the crafting of your artifacts," the elf completed for her. "For Urza Planeswalker." She smiled with shy amusement at Rayne's apparent confusion. "Yavimaya was present for all your discussions with Multani, of course."

Multani nodded his own greeting. "Long life, Shahira," he answered: A typical elven salutation. Yavimaya stirring at the edge of his mind, Multani turned back to Rayne. "The forest will provide you with your request for materials. Some of the hardwoods will take a few days' effort to grow."

As if to underscore his statement, the rolling creak of twisted wood resounded about them followed by the staccato snapping of limbs being stripped away. Within the forest, only much closer this time, one of the trees toppled, then another, this one at the edge of the clearing. Multani did not bother looking, having expected the pruning. Three more trees fell in quick succession, the canopy rippling with movement.

Frowning in thought, Rayne studied the surrounding forest. "Decay?" she asked.

Multani looked sharply to Rayne, insulted but tempering any outward show. Surprisingly enough, though, it was Rofellos who answered first.

"The cycle of life," the young warrior elf said, brushing the back of his hand across the rippling grasses. "Accelerated, but natural."

Rayne's dark eyes widened with amazement. Bending low, she examined the strange movement of the field. "The grass and flowers, they are dying off and regrowing so fast they sprout from the withering shell of their former incarnation. It creates the illusion of wind."

Multani had never doubted Rayne's intelligence. "*Decay* implies failure," he said formally. "Nothing happens here that Yavimaya does not approve and control." He nodded in the direction of the latest felling. "The forest is in a state of accelerated growth cycles," he explained. "Building up the forest's store of raw matter from which we may draw new strengths. Phyrexia is not the enemy of Urza Planeswalker alone."

The Tolarian artificer nodded her agreement. "It is good to know we have allies," Rayne said, "and tell Yavimaya we appreciate the offerings."

Smiling tightly, Multani reminded himself that Rayne could not be expected to learn of the forest's ways as fast as she might learn about artifice. He allowed himself a light laugh at her expense.

"You should have listened more closely to Shahira, Mistress Rayne," he said. "You just told the forest yourself."

* * * * *

Rofellos glanced about quickly, still feeling eyes upon him. The thrill had worn off hours ago—the persistent gaze that followed his every move, crawling over his skin with a gossamer touch. His hand stayed near his sword hilt, fingers twitching as he scanned trees and ground and sniffed the air. Danger surrounded him, stretching his nerves taught.

The young elf had taken to the treeline with Multani's permission, eager to explore the land that would be his home for years, maybe decades, to come. He'd rolled in leaves far different from those he'd ever seen, raced miles of near invisible trails never before run by a Llanowar, and used some crushed berries to paint a simple hunting mask across his eyes. It was the way Llanowars claimed land, making it theirs through intimate knowledge. A warrior race, Llanowars often lived or died on the honing of their instincts. Rofellos was not about to allow his stay in Yavimaya blunt those senses. Ambassador he might be, but first and foremost he was a warrior. Yavimaya, he felt certain, recognized that in him and approved.

Right now his instincts warned him of a threat—a watcher—someone dogging his tracks and a better tracker than he. Multani? Possibly. If so the humor of the situation was now lost on the wild elf. His grin was feral as his eyes darted among possible hiding places. Always the feeling that he merely had to turn a bit faster, look slightly harder, and the presence would resolve into the figure of his tormentor.

Now came a brush at the back of his neck. Rofellos spun about, sword drawn and flashing in a high-lined attack. He checked himself a split second before slicing into the tree that stood behind him.

"Who's there?" he called loudly, instantly regretting it. You never gave yourself away so easily, except this was supposed to be friendly land. Silence greeted him.

Rofellos backed up a step and then another. He glanced frantically into the canopy above him and deeper into the undergrowth—nothing. Spinning about again, he set off at the strong pace he could keep up for a day and night and half a day again if need be. He would run this presence into the ground.

With every step the disembodied gaze followed, nagging at the back of his mind.

Chapter 5

Davvol stepped through the doorway of dark energy, followed closely by the speaker sent to summon him from his work. He quickly fell to his knees as the heat rolled over him, and scorched air burned down into his lungs a caustic and oily brand. Flaring eruptions from the mile-high furnaces lit up the eternal night sky of Phyrexia's Fourth Sphere a hellish red-orange, spewing tons of ash into the air. High above, a tangle of pipes and mechanisms which formed the underside of the third plane rained down a light mist of oil. The metal rooftop on which Davvol rested radiated a near-blistering heat of its own, working its way through Davvol's armor and forcing him to stand or roast against the oven-temperature plating.

Another Phyrexian moved nearby in the shadows cast by a large gout of flame and oily smoke. It looked the part of a monster of Coracin fable—skeletal arms and skull, and that terrible grin of sharpened metallic teeth. Its clothes fell over it as a funeral shroud, seemingly tattered and ruined. When it moved closer, Davvol noticed the cloth's writhing movement as the tattered ribbons constantly shifted to cover a new portion of the Phyrexian's body. Instantly he knew that cloth to be alive and integral to the Phyrexian. No doubt this was the most powerful creature he had ever stood witness to. What a magnificent creation! Davvol trembled, his strength giving out, and he fell to his hands and knees before its power.

The new Phyrexian hissed and screeched something in its own tongue to the speaker. "I am Croag of the Inner Circle," the speaker translated into Davvol's language, though with a tortured squelch behind every word. "You do not approve of our world, Davvol?"

Davvol forced himself to his knees alone, hands already blistered with burns imparted by the searing metal floor. Pain can be controlled, he thought, cursing his weaker flesh. Fear can be controlled.

"I look upon your world as perfection," he answered, "but my body is weak." He remembered the Phyrexian term that would describe flawed meat, not yet augmented by artifice. "Incompleat."

At least his body was no longer dying. The Phyrexians had done that for him, though little more in his forty years of service. They gave him only enough to keep him alive, allowing him to live out a Coracin native's full years while he helped seeker teams find and uncover treasure troves of lost artifice.

More hissing and screeches. "I have chosen you to serve the Ineffable's plans. You will come with me."

Croag lifted his thin arm, braced with metal straps and cords, and summoned another Phyrexian from the shadows behind him. The new beast carried another portal, its fingers already setting stones into place to direct the channel that could step between worlds. It placed a rod upon the ground, and a doorway rose from it.

Davvol swallowed against the dryness cutting into his throat. The Ineffable had summoned him? The Phyrexian dark god himself? Never before had Davvol been allowed past the Second Sphere of Phyrexia, and here the Fourth almost killed him. Was Croag leading him to the next sphere? If his death was sought, why not rend him down into the vats? How had he earned such torture? Davvol rose on shaky footing to stumble after Croag, the last vestiges of his courage prompting him onward. There was nowhere to run, not here and never from the Phyrexians. They owned him and had made that clear from the start, though they had yet to honor any part of their promises to compleat him. They kept him alive but only that. Croag disappeared into the new doorway, and Davvol followed, nearly passing out with the final step he took in between portals . . . and planes.

By comparison, Davvol stepped from the Fourth Sphere of Phyrexia into paradise. He, Croag, and the speaker stood on what appeared to be the rim of an extinct volcano. A sharp wind billowed out Davvol's smoldering cape and rustled Croag's living garments with a rasping sound. Its chill touch brought back to mind the blistering pain in his hands, but Davvol set his teeth against the agony while surveying the alien landscape. No sun stood in these overcast skies and likely never did. Blanketed from one horizon to the other, the gray cloud cover glowed evenly with a muted light. Red and orange lightning crackled and leapt in the skies, cavorting to the accompaniment of booming thunder.

The ground around them was a dull, tan sandstone, fused and smooth as if from intense heat. It flowed out for as far as he could see, interrupted only by the mountain chain that trailed back from the volcano. In a few places nearby, Davvol saw the facsimile of boulders, noticing they were little more than sculpted bubbles in the seamless flow of ground. Down inside the caldera, as if raised up from an old eruption, stood a magnificent tower fortress.

"What is this place?" he finally asked.

"This is Rath." The speaker waited for more of Croag's grinding screeches. "It is the instrument of the Dark Lord, a new plane, set in the Dominarian Nexus, from which we will complete his task."

Davvol stood on a new artificial plane, still in its infancy by the look of it. He brought his hands together in contemplation, fingertips almost touching but mindful of his burns. Turning about, Davvol contemplated the entirety of Rath. His eyes, steel within black, searched the horizon for further signs of life but found none.

"I am required here?" he asked.

"You will oversee and accelerate the schedule of Rath's expansion," the speaker said for Croag. "You will hold it in stewardship until the Ineffable names an evincar to rule." Croag must have seen something in Davvol's face, for another series of noises spat from the speaker. "This does not please you?"

Davvol studiously blanked his face. No matter his personal feelings, he knew better than to try the Phyrexian's humor. "It pleases me greatly," he said, lying only slightly, wounded that they had not simply named him evincar. With greater authority might have come stronger steps toward his own compleation. Still, what they offered impressed him, and hadn't his memory for details proven its worth long ago in an administrative position? "By expansion, you mean—"

Croag's chattering interrupted him, and the speaker quickly translated. "Rath is still growing." It pointed down to the caldera fortress. "The Stronghold taps into Rath's lava furnaces. Flowstone is created which continues to expand the borders of this plane, pushing back the energy envelope. Flowstone production must increase, and you must control any dissident troubles."

Davvol glanced around. "Dissidents?"

"A city of slave labor beneath the Stronghold." The speaker pointed to the smudge of forestland Davvol had noticed before. "They were brought over from Dominaria long ago."

The Coracin native thought to ask more about this but then realized that it no longer mattered. The situation would be as he observed it, time enough for questions later. What truly mattered would be the resources at his disposal. Already his mind worked at several plans for optimizing production.

With a strong gust of wind snapping his cape out behind him, he folded his hands carefully together and asked, "What may I draw upon to complete this job?"

"The flowstone," was Croag's first, not entirely helpful, answer. "Also Phyrexian troops, for keeping order, and the negators."

He would have negators at his command? Davvol had seen the terrible powers wielded by Phyrexia's elite hunters only once, and that had been enough. Terrible, sinister designs, compleated for the hunt and destruction of Phyrexia's enemies. Negators, troops, and slave labor, the power swam in his head. He glanced down into the caldera. The Stronghold was his to occupy. The Phyrexians withheld the merger of flesh and artifice he craved, but here they had given him a world to rule. Certainly that could only bring opportunities later. He nodded to himself, eager to get to work. The Phyrexians would know his worth; nothing would be left to chance.

"Negators," he said. "I wouldn't have thought the locals strong enough to warrant them, but they are most welcome."

There was a pause for translation, and then Croag shook his cleft skull in a human gesture of the negative. He chattered a new flurry of squeals and hisses. A clammy hand clutched at Davvol's heart, forewarning him that whatever the negators were for, the problem would not be so simple as he'd wished.

"The negators are not for you to control the Vec," the speaker said. "They are for the protection of Rath itself, for the destruction of the only one who might upset the Dark One's plans.

"You, Davvol, are to assist me. You will hunt down and destroy Urza Planeswalker."

*   *   *   *   *

In the Stronghold, Croag walked unattended through the wide hall that led to the throne room. The lower steel bands of his robes brushed the flowstone floor on occasion, smearing a glistening band of light oil wherever they touched. A set of pipes followed the corridor at shoulder level, radiating heat. His hidden footfalls, eerily silent, left behind only scratches and pits in the floor. The doors to the throne room were of thick metal, set on tracks that led back into the tan walls. They rolled away to the accompaniment of a dry metal grinding. A sound which angered Croag, telling of the neglect by Rath's current steward.

Davvol, he had left behind, the member of Phyrexia's Inner Council preferring to come alone. The Coracin native would be singularly useful in the administration of Rath, but he was weak—meat—and would only be a liability in this encounter. Nothing could be allowed to threaten Croag's newest plans, not even Koralld.

"I have been expecting you, Croag, yesss," Koralld hissed when Croag stepped into the dimly lit throne room.

A Phyrexian overseer, Koralld had been brought to Rath to steward the expansion of the artificial plane—he had failed. The overseer sat on the room's large metal throne, hunching back into the seat of authority as if physical contact would improve his ability to hold the position. His legs remained tensed, the fibrous muscle that showed between the gaps of his armored skin coiled and bunched. His articulated hands grasped the arms of the throne, each finger ending in a razor-sharp talon. He had mandibles instead of teeth, and each one dripped a viscous substance that would burn meat and pollute blood. A single eye stared out from the middle of a large, armored skull.

Croag worked his way farther into the room but kept an appreciable distance from Koralld. The overseer was not about to go easily.

"Rath is still behind schedule. You failed."

Failure carried only one sentence with Phyrexians. Failure implied imperfection. Imperfection had to be corrected.

Koralld tilted his head to one side. A serpentine tongue flicked out to clean the metal tipped mandibles.

"You bring a full meat body to replace me, no. I do not think that is ssso."

From the floor to both sides of Croag the flowstone softened and bulged up in two large cylinders. These quickly hardened into spears and drove unerringly toward Croag's body. They were too slow. Koralld's mastery over the flowstone, while impressive for its control, lacked any real power. Croag's skeletal arms flashed out in blurring speed, smashing aside the lances that shattered into stone fragments and chips.

This was only the prelude to an attack, however. The chamber lights flickered out, plunging the throne room into darkness as Koralld sprang for Croag. The Inner Circle member slashed out blindly, his razor-tipped fingers slicing easily into Koralld's carapace even as the overseer smashed into him.

Croag's robe of steel bands absorbed a great deal of the impact, allowing him to keep to his feet and slip away from the enraged Koralld. Croag's eyes burned brightly now, filling the normally empty eye sockets of his skull with an unfocused, reddish light. The darkness retreated before his compleated eyesight. There was the actual throne of Rath and the doors, he picked out the broken cylinders of flowstone and the broken pieces scattered about but no Koralld.

Where would he go? Croag turned a slow circle, his steel bands rubbing together. He had to be here. Koralld's only opportunity was to kill Croag here and now and so prove his superiority—earn his ascendance.

Ascendance!

Koralld fell from his overhead holds even as Croag snapped his attention to the ceiling. The member of Phyrexia's Inner Council saw the handholds crafted into the stone above, prepared no doubt for this occasion. In the same blinding motion he had shown himself capable of before, Croag shot his arms up to bear the brunt of Koralld's attack. The other Phyrexian's claws ripped past the steel bands this time, digging down into the wire-cord muscles. The overseer bit in with mandibles to pierce his victim's shoulder. Croag's right arm fell useless, the shoulder flaring in a deep pain as Koralld's venom disrupted the mixture of glistening oil and serum that all members of the Inner Council relied upon for blood. The overseer's attack then turned against him, as his own weight tore the mandibles from Croag's shoulder. He scrambled to get his feet beneath him, landing awkwardly.

Here Croag struck back, snapping forward to sink his own polished steel teeth into Koralld's. No poisonous discharge, but it held Koralld fast and left him unable to use his best weapon. Croag's left hand flashed outward and then in, talons piercing the overseer's right arm and driving farther into his body to pin it in place. Steel bands snapped at Croag's mental command, some whipping out to wrap around legs and the overseer's one free arm. Others snapped back and forth, flailing at the trapped Phyrexian, their razor edges methodically scoring and slicing past Koralld's armored skin.

The lesser Phyrexian screamed his rage and pain, thrashing about desperately for release. Croag's eyes burned more sharply now, their unfocused fire coalescing into twin coals that began to sear into the side of Koralld's head. There was a second pulse and a third. Each time the searing rays burned deeper. On the fourth, Koralld quit struggling and simply hung in Croag's deadly embrace, feeble tremors shaking his body. On the sixth pulse, the overseer's scream gave out, and the tremors stopped.

Croag was not finished. The Phyrexian kept up his efforts, fiery pulses boring into Koralld's head while the razor bands sliced deeper. He waited until his artifice-bonded cells repaired themselves and he regained use of his right arm. Croag brought up both hands to crush Koralld's carapace skull. Flesh brains pulped out.

"You did not think, Koralld," the Phyrexian finally said, responding to the overseer's comment before the attack.

He threw aside the ruined skull and walked toward the throne while the steel bands of his robe reknitted themselves. No, Rath needed something else besides an overseer's hard-handed rule. Davvol? Was he the key to the upkeep of Rath and the destruction of Urza Planeswalker? Perhaps. Davvol's mental powers suited him for administration, and perhaps a fresh outlook might solve the puzzle of how to kill the planeswalker. Croag certainly needed to find some answers. He had not forgotten his master's commands or the punishment that awaited him if he failed. At least Davvol would be much easier to control.

Croag knew complacency to be a common downfall of even the most powerful Phyrexians. Could Davvol be dangerous? The Phyrexian Inner Council member could not see how. Davvol had yet to show any ambition except in the matter of his compleation. *That* could never be allowed to happen—not fully. Davvol would be kept alive so long as he proved useful, so long as he was kept motivated, and what mortal did not fear death?

In the darkness of the Stronghold, Croag seated himself upon Rath's throne.

Chapter 6

Barrin stepped into the workshop, noticing first the disarray of tools left out on the workbenches. Timein stood nearby, staring out one of the gray-blue tinted windows. A slight chill crawled over the nape of the mage's neck. Timein's posture and position reminded Barrin of a time eight subjective years ago—sixty-five in actual Dominarian years—when he had first offered Gatha a position in the Metathran experiments. Barrin doubted it to be coincidental that Timein had requested their meeting here in the very same workshop Barrin had then held his orientations on the bloodlines. Timein had specifically wanted this room—wanted Barrin to remember.

"I'm here, Timein."

The student sorcerer turned around slowly, awarded Barrin a bow of respect. "Thank you for your time, sir. You will find the papers on the edge of that first table."

The mage did not look immediately. He instead met Timein's placid gaze and tried to discern what could be so important that the senior student had deliberately bypassed the usual administrative chain to come directly to the academy's chief administrator.

"If you wish to register a complaint, you should do so through proper channels. Working under Gatha can't be easy for any—"

"I will register no complaint concerning Tutor Gatha," Timein interrupted, though his voice remained respectful, "but I do have a discovery I believe should be placed directly into your hands."

Barrin thought he knew Timein better than to expect grandstanding, so he shrugged him the benefit of his doubt and picked up the stack of papers set nearby. The top page looked to be pasted back together from several pieces that had been deliberately ripped. Barrin did not recognize the report and glanced back to the young sorcerer.

"Who did this?" he demanded.

Timein stood mute. That told Barrin enough. So much for the idea of accurate records. He began reading.

The first page was not the only one that looked as if it had been pasted back together or fished from the trash. By the time he had read a fourth of the way through the pile, Barrin was seated and arranging certain papers over the cluttered desk for ease of referral. All told, the stack covered about forty years of real-time research into the problem currently facing the bloodlines—the growing lack of empathy for Dominaria and an embrasure of their darker . . . elements.

"You can prove this?" were Barrin's first words.

Timein nodded. "In the next room."

A few junior students waited there, escorts for a sullen, elderly man who frowned at Timein's entrance and glared hostility at Barrin. The man's head had an elongated curve going back over his shoulders.

"This is Rha'ud. He's a bloodlines subject raised in fast time."

That explained the skull's elongation to Barrin. Several subjects had evidenced a few unusual physical characteristics after some of Gatha's experiments. They were also known for a natural hostile approach to anyone associated with the academy.

"Why are you here, Rha'ud?" Barrin asked softly, feeling for the other man. "You were not compelled?" Barrin ignored Timein's wounded glance.

Rha'ud shook his head once. "This one," a nod to Timein, "said he might be able to help my little girl. She don't get along so well with others." He swallowed. "With anyone."

The mage let it go, not wanting to parade over the man's pride. "Let's hope he can," he said.

Timein brought out a small box and removed from it a stone streaked with cobalt and milky white. Some areas sparkled green or red from less obvious mineral deposits.

"A Fellwar Stone," Timein explained. It was a naturally occurring stone capable of channeling the five types of mana.

He placed it on the table, close to the elder man, and cast an incantation over it. The stone rolled toward Rha'ud, once, twice, then fell still. The young sorcerer picked it up and placed it closer to one of the escorts. The stone began rolling at once and was prevented from falling off the table only by Timein's quick grab. He nodded to the students.

"Thank you." They got up and left the room, Rha'ud between them.

"That doesn't prove much, Timein." Barrin waited, sure the student would explain himself.

"Just a quick demonstration," the younger man said. "The stone will roll slower and turn less often depending on the generation. It barely trembled for Rha'ud's daughter." He placed the Fellwar Stone back in its box. "I'm using a variation on the laws of contagion. If a person has memories for the lands of Dominaria they are drawn to anything of a similar type. Using wood, the spell will work only for those with an affinity for nature—green mana. A hot coal or piece of obsidian likewise for the mountains or red mana. I promise you, Master Barrin, that the bloodlines are developing without an affinity for any part of Dominaria. The fast-time labs we are using to accelerate the turn of human generations do not allow them to gain memories of the land."

"These are not mages," Barrin said, troubled and looking for an argument, "and if they were it is a matter of bringing them outside—"

"A person's connection to the lands of Dominaria means more than his ability to draw upon the mana he possesses," Timein interrupted again. "I can prove to you that that connection directly affects the person's natural empathy for the world around him. How far back a lack of such ties causes irreversible harm is uncertain, but theory suggests that it could be at birth or even conception or *over generations*."

Barrin stood speechless. He paused, his gaze meeting Timein's, while considering the implications. "The entire project could be in danger of permanent contamination. Is that what you are saying?"

Timein simply nodded.

The mage sighed. "All right, Timein, I'm convinced, but we'll have to turn this over to a larger workforce at once for independent verification and study of possible treatments, and I'll have to tell Urza." He was certain the 'walker would not be pleased about these findings or the destroyed reports. Barrin would *not* tolerate such blatant disregard for protocol, especially when lives were affected.

The sorcerer braced himself up at the mention of Urza Planeswalker. "He will be back to Tolaria soon? I heard he had just visited."

"Yes, but we have another problem that requires immediate action. In fact, it's ironic that the bloodlines problem is so similar to Karn's."

This appeared to catch Timein off guard. The younger man frowned. "Karn? How can he suffer from a lack of memories of the land?"

"His problem is just the opposite. He suffers from an *infinite memory*. It is paralyzing him, though slowly, over the course of decades." Barrin shook his head in implied pity. "Rayne and I have noticed it affecting his performance in any task requiring human interaction, and he will continue to grow increasingly inflexible as time passes."

"Did Urza have any ideas?" There was no questioning Timein's concern.

Barrin shrugged. "I don't think so, not yet. He simply said that the situation would have to be dealt with 'decisively.' " The mage braced Timein with his gaze. "I'm telling you because I'll want you to work with Rayne and myself on this. Perhaps your empathy research can help."

Timein nodded gravely, accepting the charge. "If it can't?"

"The solution will be entirely in the hands of Urza Planeswalker."

Loren Coleman

* * * * *

The workshop was one of the larger ones, with an overhead gallery for students to observe the progress below. Several tables stood upon the floor. Racks of tools and equipment lined the walls. The room smelled of aged wood, leather, and oil. Rayne thought the room much bigger than required for so simple an alteration, and the gallery remained clear, which surprised her; the academy was still a place of instruction, for all its preoccupation these days with the Legacy. Only Barrin stood solitary in attendance above, and she suspected her husband of turning away the idle curious for the sake of the patient. Rayne approved and nodded her support to Barrin.

She stood at Karn's left shoulder; the large silver golem lay down upon the centermost and largest table in the shop. Turning her gaze back from the gallery, Rayne placed a gentle hand on Karn's thick arm.

"It will be all right," he said, his voice a soft rumble, stealing her thought for him.

No one else in the room cared for nor actually needed Karn's comforting assurances. Urza stood at the table's other side, discussing some finer points of Thran metal with Gatha who managed to at least look curious whether or not he actually was. Rayne doubted it. Gatha was here on the order of her husband. He had helped design "the cage" and consulted with Urza on the magics that would be employed.

"Learn some compassion for the lives he touches," was Barrin's private comment to Rayne, though both doubted it would happen. Even after two years, Gatha still chafed at the new restrictions to his own work. He complained about the "insignificant duties" placed upon him such as teaching classes and filling out extra paperwork to ensure that no more research was "misrouted." His single appeal to Urza had met with stony silence, and there was no higher court.

Urza moved to Karn's head and without preamble reached beneath the neck to unfasten the clasp. Even for the planeswalker this took some doing, trying to manipulate the intricate lock hidden inside a small cavity. It was designed to be difficult, and the combination was known only to six people, including Karn himself. The lock released with an audible snap. Urza lifted, and the golem's entire head swung forward to rest with his face touching his chest. Rayne noticed that the assembly was not hinged, but the silver metal itself seemed to bend and fold to allow the movement. Karn shuddered once and then went completely stiff as Rayne reached in and removed the black powerstone that gave the golem life.

The Heart of Xantcha. Rayne never before had the chance to examine it. It was the size of a grapefruit and perfectly black, where most powerstones were constructed of a clearer crystal. Rayne thought that she could feel the power that resided within the stone, imagined it as Karn's spectral voice asking for help. A single tear welled up in the corner of her eye, but there was nothing she could do for her friend. Urza Planeswalker had decreed it would be so—Karn's recallable memory would be capped at twenty years, to prevent the golem's slow failure toward compelled dormancy.

Rayne glanced back up to the gallery, wondering how her husband must be feeling over the results of his insight. She saw that a single person had joined Barrin.

It was Timein, the sorcerer whose latest work had suggested that a subject's empathy for Dominaria was better than ninety percent based on the ties developed over the first eighteen years of life. His evaluation of Urza's plan—before discovering the use it would be put toward—could find no reason why a "floating memory" of twenty years would not adequately duplicate the formative years repeatedly over the lifetime of a subject. She wondered if foreknowledge of Urza's plans might have changed his answer—if only in presentation.

They all shared responsibility, everyone now present. Rayne possibly the more so as it had been her initial theory that the increasing pressure of growing Thran metal against the powerstone might somehow be used to restrict memory recall. That theory had held up despite numerous student attempts to break it, despite her own best attempts as well, once she realized the single flaw that Urza had decided Karn could live with and probably be the better for. Despite the research, no one could say how this procedure might affect the golem's mind.

In the meantime, design of the cage had gone forward. The planeswalker now lifted it from a nearby box. A two-part shell, it looked delicate but was stronger than any other known metal. The basket had been fashioned from a pattern of whorls and segmented braces which perfectly enclosed the heart of Xantcha. Rayne set the powerstone inside one half, and when Urza closed the basket it magically fused into a solid piece. A full-year's growth of the metal would squeeze the stone and begin to suppress Karn's older memories. Over two centuries of accumulated experience and knowledge would be lost to time's press in as little as a single decade, after which

Karn's memories would fade as any regular person's might, locked away but with a full recall capacity of only twenty years. It was hardly a young man's lifetime, but according to Urza, "More than adequate."

Rayne winced as Urza replaced the powerstone—no more concern showing in the 'walker's eyes than for any other artifact. Rayne glanced away. There were worse things than death, certainly, and so far Urza Planeswalker seemed capable of them all.

* * * * *

Rain pounded Tolaria, the first heavy fall of the year's stormy season. Special covers went up over the academy's tended grounds, protecting flower beds and in some cases the food gardens on which the students and staff relied upon for fresh produce. The deluge pounded against paving rock, clay shingles, and wooden slat roofing. Over fast-time areas the water was wicked away so quickly that the downpour simply appeared to lighten or even stop. The slow-time envelopes, as seen from without, appeared as strange bubbles, the water building on the surface until it began sheeting off the sides. It might be hours or even weeks before the first drop hit the ground as seen from real time.

Inside the island's protected harbor, rocking in the hard wind, the anchored *Weatherlight* sat with gangplank extended to the nearest dock. A few final supplies were carried onboard—the ship's schedule not to be interrupted by mere acts of nature. The crew loaded on provisions for the voyage, slow-time waters to be delivered to those few academy alumni allowed a return to the real world, and Legacy artifacts to be hidden away in other cities until needed again one day.

Gatha stomped his way up the gangway, working his fury out on the iron grillwork. He ignored the purser who was responsible for all stores loaded and passengers brought aboard. The man was currently debating the additional equipment being brought up the ramp by two of Gatha's assistants. Bypassing formalities, Gatha instead presented himself to the captain, who stood in a small sheltered overhang while supervising the last of the cargo being secured aboard his vessel.

"Help you, master?" she asked, using the title clearly out of habit than any awe for the academy insignia on Gatha's cloak.

She certainly did not move out into the rain so that Gatha could stand protected from the elements. Twenty years commanding a vessel might inure anyone to the regular formalities, Gatha supposed. Still, the tutor loathed her for his dry position, the buttons on her foul-weather coat done only halfway up while Gatha squirmed from the cold water leaking in at the neck of his cloak.

"I've been added to your passenger list," the tutor lied, presenting the forged papers stamped with Barrin's own seal—"borrowed" during one of the master mage's few classes he still taught.

Gatha could have more easily laid his hands on the seal of a chancellor but had decided against it for various reasons. Though Gatha despised Barrin for the other's weak stomach and lack of vision, there was no doubting the master mage's formidable powers. Since Gatha considered the other man a peer—even if he was a rival—

only Barrin's seal would be used. Shut down Gatha's primary labs would he?

"So I see," Captain Braven said after a cursory glance at the seal. "And that?" she asked, nodding toward the commotion at the head of the ramp.

"My equipment and some supplies. All papers are in order." Gatha tucked the documents back into the relative dryness of his dark cloak. "You are to transport me and my equipment. I will leave the ship at your first port of call." His tone left little room for arguing, and the captain seemed ill inclined to do so anyway.

"Erek, check the seals on that equipment and get it secured below," Captain Braven bellowed, ignoring Gatha's flinch at the volume of her order. "It's too wet to be arguing their timing."

Nodding an insincere thanks, Gatha backed away from the captain and returned to his assistants. The purser scrawled a brief description of each piece to his master inventory, estimating weight when necessary.

"Ether Mixer, what's that?" he asked, stopping a female student at the head of the gangway.

Gatha spoke up before the student could answer. "Lab equipment," he said. "For mixing ether, of course. Light, very durable. Store it wherever." It was his own private joke. How did one mix ether? By stirring around empty air. It was a reference to speaking without knowing of that which you spoke.

Naturally, the purser did not understand the reference. He nodded, grunted, and jotted a few notes. "Forward hold," he said.

Gatha fell in beside her for a few steps. "Remember, I count on you." The female student glanced over, rain plastered hair laying between her eyes and down over her face. Gatha nodded his support.

"You are my eyes and ears back here on Tolaria, in case I ever need to come home."

Not very likely, unless Barrin ever stepped down. Still, Gatha might eventually need access to slow-time waters if he were to run out of the supply he'd stolen and information on the latest academy breakthroughs when they happened. She nodded reluctantly.

"Master Gatha," the captain called out before he could bolster his student's confidence more. The rogue tutor stopped by the captain's alcove, bracing himself for discovery and the quick, violent action that would necessitate, but Isa Braven posed no true concerns of that nature. "You may take the first passenger cabin" she said simply. "You are our only guest."

The tutor nodded. "Where is you first port of call?" he asked.

"Argive."

Gatha smiled. "Argive," he said, repeating the name. "Well, well." After seventy-five years, Gatha would apparently be returning home.

*   *   *   *   *

The academy slept. Only a night watch roamed the real-time areas of the island. A few assistants monitored critical projects which required twenty-four hour surveillance, but for the most part, silence gripped Tolaria.

Karn never slept. His body did not require it. Though in times of decreased activity he could suspend his higher brain functions and enter a kind of hibernation—just to pass time until he was with purpose again. In years gone by he had done just that, but not tonight or any night in the past year since his alteration. He vowed he would never sleep again, though of course in time even that vow would be lost.

No bed ate up space in the golem's room. It simply was not required. There was a table and several reinforced chairs, but the most functional pieces were the shelves where Karn placed the memorabilia he had collected over the decades—the centuries—books and pictures, keepsakes and souvenirs. The aggregation of a lifetime. Nothing in this room was without meaning, without a memory attached, but there soon would be. All of it would become meaningless to Karn as his memory faded, except one thing.

A picture of Jhoira, sketched for him by a student of artifice also gifted in art.

It was all he had left of her, his best friend. Karn couldn't bear the thought of Jhoira returning to the island and him not remembering her. Karn stared at the picture and quietly spoke to himself. "Jhoira is my friend—my best friend. We met in the original academy, before the accident drove us from Tolaria. She named me. Karn, from an old Thran name. She said it meant strength." His voice sounded heavy in the confines of his small room of memories.

A wave of intense anguish rolled over the golem. All this for a person he had not seen in better than a century. There were events from as little as four days prior which he could no longer recall with exacting detail, fading for their lack of emotional significance as they would in a human mind. How did they stand it? Karn could not remember ever feeling frightened, and these days his lack of a memory no longer meant that it was true, but he felt frightened now.

Standing there, his memories arranged around him like trophies of the past, Karn started again. "Jhoira is my friend. My best friend . . ."

Chapter 7

Gatha leaned heavily on a staff of dark ebony, its headpiece a pair of ironwood crescent blades stained a deep crimson. Picking his way over the slide of rubble that obstructed the mountain trail, one of the larger rocks rolled underfoot and the mage earned a new cut against his lower shin. His quality calfskin boots—bought in the lowlands and assured of rugged wear—were nearly at an end to any useful life, scarred and scuffed against the sharp rock they'd clambered over these last several days. The thick wool coat, however, held up admirably, and it was a good thing. The sharp wind that whistled down from the snow-drifted peaks cut through anything lighter. As it was, the wind found its way past cuffs and collar to keep him always on the verge of freezing. The sweat from the climb stood out cold on his face. Gatha considered magicking himself warm again, but that was a draining use of power, and it never lasted long enough.

His guides, a Keldon trader and his son on their return from the lower port city of Agderisk, plodded on steadily and without complaint of the rugged terrain or cold climate. The shaggy colos hides they wore kept them warm. They did not bother to check on the young mage's progress. They showed the same disregard for the slaves who were leading a caravan of large colos—something between a war elephant and a shaggy mountain sheep, to Gatha's eye—loaded down with their wares and the mage's equipment. The slaves would follow because to disobey apparently meant a lingering death. Gatha would keep up or he would be left behind, likely to die.

The Keldons were apparently not big on alternatives.

They were, however, the largest men Gatha had ever seen. Drahl, nearly fourteen and still two years away from entering military service, stood nearly six feet with a build to match his fathers, heavily muscled, the two of them, with forearms and lower legs longer than upper arms and thighs. They had grayish skin, networked with scars, and thick, dark hair with the triple widow's peak that Gatha's tattoos simulated. They also tattooed themselves, filling in the skin around their eyes with a dark ink that lent a fearsome appearance. The elder trader sported a pike in the place of his lower right arm, the limb lost in battle at the age of eighteen he'd said.

Gatha understood so little about these people, even though his father had once served as the Argivian liaison to a Keldon warhost. He knew the basics of course, that the Keldons based their society almost completely on the waging of warfare. They existed as mercenaries, their mountainous lands effectively one large armed camp. Other nations paid for their services and paid well, since Keldon negotiation techniques were fairly straightforward and violent when opposed. Try to bargain down the price and the warhost was just as likely to claim the balance by force on their way home. Worse, they would simply claim the full price from your nation and then head home anyway. They carried back to Keld their blood price as well as pillage and slaves taken from the land invaded. Glancing back, Gatha counted at least three different nations among the human slaves. Benalish were easily placed by their cast markings and the Surrans by their ritual scarring of the face. He returned his gaze to the trail. Slaves were of little use to his efforts here except as potential subjects for experimentation if all went well.

Farther on, Gatha saw his first example of Keldon architecture, high enough into the mountains these hard people began to feel at home. The buildings sat on a small cliffside plateau half-buried into the mountain slope. Constructed of stone, several of the structures were three stories high, tiered as they rose to a steeply pitched roof of tan-colored wooden planks. They looked incredibly solid, as if called up from the ground on which they sat. The windows were dark.

"Stopping here?" Gatha asked in simple Argivian.

He had heard the trader speaking Keldon with a few others in the lowlands. A rough language that would be hard to learn. The Keldon people knew the basics of many languages, though, from their constant campaigning.

"Nah. At war," the trader said. He pointed toward the red banner spiked into an upper wall of one of the buildings then looked back. He made a gesture of butting his one fist into the sharp end of his pike. "Battle. Fighting." He bared his teeth enthusiastically.

Gatha nodded his understanding, wiping sweat from his forehead and pulling his greatcoat closed tighter at the neck. Soon, he hoped, they would rest.

The rogue tutor had discovered it more difficult than he'd thought, trying to set up a lab outside of Tolaria. His work was not looked upon favorably by most nations. Argive, in fact, had been merely the first of several nations to refuse him. His experimentation did not allow for a secret laboratory. The room required and indelicacies of the operations themselves were certain to attract attention sooner rather than later, twelve years of wandering, twelve *real* Dominarian years of work, lost, before his arrival in Agderisk and a talk with the local traders.

Everyone the world over knew something of Keld and its aggressive ways. Learning more of them now, in the shadow of their mountains, Gatha had been intrigued to hear of the rituals surrounding the creation of the Keldon warlords. The largest and most violent of the young, still several years out from entering military service, were sent on a pilgrimage through the deep mountains' frozen wastes. Those who survived were then enchanted to further their growth into larger, superior warriors. They became capable of extraordinary battlefield prowess that also worked to excite the troops being led into a frenzied state. To Gatha, this sounded very much like a eugenics program, if a bit crude in its methodology.

His trader guide, when Gatha first found him, had not been inclined to talk with the mage. Noticing Gatha's tattoos had changed his mind. Apparently they won him the courtesy of an interview, if that's what one might call

Gatha's simple speech and the trader's even simpler grunts. In the end, Gatha simply paid the man as a guide to the Keldon Necropolis, their capital where the *doyens* of the Warlord Council met.

The Keldons were a people very interested in anything that could improve the way they waged war and had already worked with the early stages of enhanced genetics. It had sounded too good to be true, Gatha remembered, then stubbed his foot against a sharp rock and nearly fell—too good to be true, until he had started this treacherous climb.

* * * * *

The Keldon Necropolis crowned a mountain peak, the fortress capital rising up out of the hard land. Frost and snow lightly dusted some surfaces but drifted deep in the several large crevices where sun never struck ground. Homes rose up from the dark gray stone—single dwellings lower on the slopes, and higher up, loose clusters were tied together by trails worn into the hard earth over centuries. Nearer the summit the buildings suddenly sprang up in thick numbers with little room for trails, most paths winding through caves carved into the mountainside. Above this mountainside city towered the great tombs themselves.

Here the Keldon warlords were finally laid to rest. This majestic vault defied gravity and earth as it challenged the sky. It was almost two hundred feet high with steeply sloped sides, and one entire mammoth wall was open to the thin mountain air. When he had seen it from a distance, it had reminded Gatha of the great Surran burial pyramids. Only these were steeper pitched and the top carried away to make room for the living witch kings' council chambers—the Necropolis, where Gatha now waited to address the Keldon ruling body.

The cold, thin air sat heavy in Gatha's lungs, as if reluctant to give up any oxygen. The mage had to work at breathing after his long climb. Waiting for his audience, Gatha's muscles burned in silent protest. He felt a poor excuse for an ambassador, especially one representing himself. He gave his wool greatcoat to the trader who had guided him up the mountain in exchange for a pair of tough coloshide boots and thick furs. He felt in need of a hot bath and smelled of the large animal that had given up this particular set of hides. At least he would appear more presentable, or so he thought. A footsoldier escorted him through a set of large bronze-plated doors and into the main council hall.

The same magical architecture that held up the great tombs below must certainly have been used for the hall. Like a giant cylinder it rose five stories straight up, with galleries set about each level for observers. Flags and banners from other nations had been crudely spiked into the walls. There were hundreds, thousands perhaps. Likely these were brought back from every war ever fought by Keld. The meeting area itself was actually an inverted amphitheater, a tiered pedestal carved out of the gray bedrock. The uppermost platform stood empty, possibly awaiting a speaker. On every ring after that sat the chairs of the council, each one different and again with some designs clearly belonging to nations represented on the walls. On those chairs sat the *doyens*—the warlord elders of Keld, half a hundred at least. The trader and his son, who had seemed so humongous to Gatha, could not begin to touch the smallest of these men, a great number of them easily topping seven feet. They wore thick leather clothing, ceremoniously studded and colored. No one wore furs or hides that might provide warmth. Many tunics bared chests and arms to the frigid air, scars standing out whitish on gray skin. The cold was a long-vanquished enemy of these people. Some carried weapons at their sides, those lower down the platforms. Those higher up carried short staves or rods of carved bone. A mist from warm breath haloed the great room, and from out of that mist fiercely tattooed eyes stared at the mage who suddenly felt very small and alone.

It was a state Gatha was not too familiar with and, secure in his own power, he quickly rallied from. He knew what he needed, and he would have it, somehow.

"Warlords of Keld," he began slowly, speaking Argivian. He had already been informed that Argivian was a language most knew, and that they would not speak with him unless he presented a subject suitable for their notice—or offered a direct challenge. He had decided to offer a little of both. "Into your lands I bring a gift, knowledge, which can help you and your nation grow mighty. Magics, which will make your sons stronger on the battlefield, your warlords more fierce and your victories more complete."

A few stirred at that, possibly taking Gatha's words as a slur against their own prowess. The mage waited for a challenge, but none rose immediately. He stepped farther into the council hall. Briefly he considered making his way up the platforms to the empty spot where all could easily see him, and then he decided against it. He possessed no way of knowing yet what the local rituals might demand. There was an obvious pecking order implied in the seating, and Gatha did not want to challenge anyone's pride, not yet. So he instead circled the tier slowly, explaining the basics of his studies and experimentation. No details, he doubted anyone here would understand. He couched the more unpleasant facts in vague references or dismissed them completely, concentrating instead on how his own work mirrored that which the Keldons already employed in the creation of a warlord.

"I only need a lab, support, and time," he finished. Always time, the devourer of his accomplishments that had stalked him for twelve years now.

A warlord on the lower tier near Gatha rubbed at his coarse beard. He growled a reply in broken Argivian, "Why *puny one* think we need his strength? Who is he?" There followed something more, this in the Keldon tongue that could only be derision from the laughter barked out by a few others.

Debate the mage would tolerate, but not even Barrin had ever insulted the tutor's genius. Gatha speared the large man with an angry gaze, eye contact being a challenging gesture in any culture.

"One who is strong enough to be able to think, *before* I speak," he answered with scathing disdain. Only in afterthought did Gatha wonder at his rash action.

The warlord sat forward abruptly. Muscles bunched and twitched, and one hand strayed toward the short stabbing sword he wore.

"You speak to me? Varagh? You, lowlander?" His dark eyes flashed dangerously.

There was nothing for it now but to establish himself in some form of ritual duel, a test of strength. Gatha walked slowly toward the warlord, carefully drawing mana from the lands he had touched in his recent travels. He remembered the river delta of Agderisk, its chaotic channels of muddied waters. Power swelled within his mind, begging for release. Eyes never flinching from the hostile warlord, the mage stepped up onto the first tier with calm and deliberate motion.

Varagh stood abruptly, one hand darting for his sword as the other clamped down hard on Gatha's shoulder, pinning the mage in place. Such deliberation in killing saved Gatha's life. The mage brought up one hand in a twisting motion. Energy danced from his fingertips and into the warlord's eyes. The giant man stumbled, sword falling from nerveless fingers, blinking away the sudden confusion. Gatha gathered himself up and physically forced the larger man from the platform so that he now stood at the same height, eye to eye, as if physically dwarfed.

The warlord rounded on Gatha, spinning in a fluid, catlike motion. Gatha thrust his left hand forward, sparks of blue energy dancing around his outstretched palm. Snarling, Varagh clawed his own face with his thick fingernails and then charged forward. It caught the mage, who had expected the Keldon to take more time to recover, off guard. He dodged to one side, releasing another blast of mind-numbing energy. This time the sparks danced outward . . .

. . . and glanced off the warlord's bared chest.

Gatha was picked up by his shoulder and hip then slammed down onto the tier. Darkness swam before his eyes. He felt detached, as if this could not possibly be happening. Battle magic! This is not how I die, he thought. Even so, he saw through the haze as Varagh reached one hand back and clench it into a hammer-like fist.

A dark blur landed heavily behind the Keldon, grabbed the raised fist and pulled it back. The pressure eased from Gatha's shoulder. He sat up and scrambled backward until he found the next tier. Another warlord had pulled Gatha's attacker away. Now the two circled each other, crouched low and barring teeth. Varagh shouted, attacked, and was dealt a cruel clawing across the face. The answering punch was weak, and the new warlord caught it up, snapping the arm at the elbow as easily as matchwood. Varagh never uttered a sound for the pain. He simply stood there with a snarl of anger on his face while the other warlord held onto the wrist of his broken arm. He glanced down then bowed his head at the neck.

The victor released the wounded arm, turned his back on Varagh, and stepped back onto the first tier, looking down on the mage. Gatha came to his feet slowly.

"I Kreyohl," the new warlord said in Argivian. He reached out slowly, placed a hand on Gatha's chest, and shoved him from the tier.

The mage stumbled and nearly fell to his knees. Anger welled inside Gatha, but he held it in check. This one might know battle magic as well, and there was no fighting them all at any rate. He broke eye contact and bowed his head as he'd seen the other warlord do. Both *doyen* retook their seats, Varagh below and Kreyohl on the next tier higher up.

Bloodlines

Kreyohl studied Gatha in silence for a moment. "You alive because I hear you more. Not want you dead."

Yet, Gatha finished for him. Still, he recognized now the procedure he had witnessed, the stronger male disciplining the inferior. They respected strength and little else.

"I *can* make you stronger," he said cautiously, not wanting to offend but not ready to give up. " I have special magics, and I need only time and a little help."

No one answered right away. Gatha saw Kreyohl glance from the side of his eyes, obviously reading the body language of his neighboring warlords.

"You make many promises," he said slowly. "Maybe keep, maybe don't." He paused. "What can you show us now?"

Now *there* was a sentiment Gatha could understand. Unfortunately, it was also one he had not decided a ready answer for. Few were those who thought of the present first and future later. It was that thought, of *the present*, that prompted a solution.

"I can scry the world of Dominaria." How to say that more simply? "Magic sight. See troubles and wars. Today and any day, where the Keld might find the best employment." No, not correct. "Take the best plunder."

That appealed to the assembly. Subtle nods were passed. A warlord on Kreyohl's tier spoke the group consensus. "Prove it, and your work supported."

Gatha smiled, breathing out between white teeth a cloud of frozen vapor. Proving himself was not a difficulty. It was, in fact, one of his favorite pastimes.

* * * * *

Two years and Gatha still could not stand the smell. The small room stank of the peat used for walls, corrupting the crisp scent of new snow which had fallen in the night. The tan wooden planking laid directly over earth shifted slightly beneath Gatha's feet as he crossed the temporary laboratory. He slapped his hands together for warmth and held them over a barrel of slowly burning animal fat. The sharp, final tock of a clockwork timer drew his attention to another table, but the sound of rock being quarried distracted him from checking results. He paused at a window cut into the southern exposure, looking downhill on the site of his permanent labs. *His* labs.

A winding trail cut down the snowy mountainside toward an area roughly leveled by natural erosion. The site was large, befitting the importance of the work Gatha intended to do there and the efforts he had already put forth on behalf of the Keldon people. A *doyenne*, one of the Keldon matriarchs, strutted imperiously around the site overseeing the project. The females oversaw everything which was not associated directly with warfare.

Slaves worked to burst away some remaining outcroppings. The dark gray rock was collected and then moved by colos to the building pile used by the Keldon builders. Among that small percentage of Keldons ill-suited to war—dishonored and sent to live as general laborers, traders or farmers—these outcasts would rate master builders in many nations Gatha could name. They worked slowly and methodically, building to Gatha's specifications but following their own designs when practical. In his fourteenth year of self-imposed exile from Tolaria, Gatha could finally hope to begin soon a serious continuation of his earlier work.

The Keldon armies were constantly on the move these days, preying on Dominaria wherever Gatha's scrying and a nation's coin brought them. The mage's commitments called for a great deal of his time and efforts, especially when the council preferred his presence at the Necropolis higher up the mountain. Those efforts were now being scaled back in favor of his experimentation. Permission had been granted to begin his work on slaves and second-class Keldon citizens.

He had already begun setting up his Matrix and the rest of his equipment in this shack the *doyenne* had built for his temporary use. The first trials on native Keldons showed incredible response. Slaves were not quite as easily altered, but they served as good subjects for initial experiments. The colos were even more so, their tough nature adapting to his changes and giving Gatha more ideas. He used the colos as testing boards for his more radical ideas, moved up from there to slaves, and then to the Keldons to observe an end result. No one complained of his few setbacks. Many of his Keldon subjects actually expressed appreciation that the mage had found a way they could serve their nation one final time. Gatha drank in the heady results as each day brought him closer to resuming a full work load. His work had certainly found a home here in the bloodlines of Keld.

Chapter 8

Urza was unprepared for the Phyrexian attack. One moment the planeswalker had been studying a cliff face for traces of Thran artifice, and in the next, a stream of hellish energy had slammed into him from behind and pinned him to the rock wall. It had required of the 'walker every ounce of his willpower to hold together his form in the face of the surprise attack. The second negator hit him from the side, a flurry of rending claws and razor-sharp fangs. Only by throwing the second Phyrexian into the energy attack of the first did Urza manage to break away and recapture a portion of his strength.

Now the three danced about wildly. Urza moved with preternatural speed. His attention divided between two negators, they came close to matching him. Lightning crackled at Urza's fingertips, striking out like some kind of whip, keeping the negators at bay. Where the energy touched the creatures it split the armor, exposing black, corrupted flesh beneath. He couldn't seem to reach anything vital in these robust creatures, and the energy cannon that replaced the arm of one Phyrexian continued to strike at him with dangerous effect.

Wherever the reddish stream touched him, the equivalence of mortal pain ate into his concentration. The more he devoted to keeping his form intact the less he had to deal with the his own offense. Urza settled into a defensive pattern, gambling that the Phyrexians could not come up with another surprise while he built up his own power.

The negator predisposed to physical assault uttered a long and piercing shriek that threw a disrupting ripple throughout the 'walker's entire form. A wisp of fiery energy from the cannon caught Urza in the arm, and for the briefest second he recalled the mortal pain of a burn as well as the disruption to his immortal form, a sensation he would have been happy to live without remembering.

Drawing power from his memory of the Hurloon Mountains, calling forth the powerful mana they offered, Urza cast lightning from both hands which began piling up in front of him. The collection pulsed and grew, spitting out arcs of snapping energy. No more time left to him, Urza cast the large ball of lightning forward. It sped toward the negator brandishing the cannon. It dodged the first pass but was caught up trying to shake the inexorable advance.

It gave Urza all the time he needed. Bringing his staff to bear, the planeswalker triggered one of its many functions: a sonic attack, one that he had devised decades before to deal with the Phyrexian infestation of Tolaria. The sound interfered with the composition of glistening oil—the lifeblood of Phyrexian living artifice. The high-pitched harmonics slammed into the second negator with incredible force, throwing it back and pinning it to the earth. Sprays of gray-black liquid gushed from the negator's open wounds, and it trembled and shook. Urza moved forward, the head of his staff pointed directly at the creature. With a final spasm the negator fell still, its fluids leaking into the ground and staining the soil black.

Only then did Urza notice that the second negator had ignored the attack of harmonic sound. It still dodged about nimbly, evading the pulsing collection of energies that trailed after it relentlessly. There would be no escaping the strike, only delay, but the 'walker couldn't be sure of it being enough to kill the negator. Tapping the mana as he had a moment before, Urza quickly built up another such electrical storm and flung it toward the cornered Phyrexian. Weak from the attacks against him and concerned that the remaining negator might have sent a summons to others, Urza cast his form into the chaos that existed between worlds and 'walked away.

While the pain of the burn had long faded, its memory continued to worry the back of his mind.

*   *   *   *   *

Flanked by four of the armored Phyrexian soldiers, their black armor gleaming dull orange in the fiery glow of the lava tubes, Davvol toured the main facility concerned with the production of flowstone. The massive, bladed dials spinning in their housing above generated most of the mechanical power required. Giant corkscrews pulled up the lava in black-crusted tubes from the geological furnaces of Rath far underground. They would be cooled by waters siphoned off a nearby lake and then fed farther up into the processing machinery. Yellow steam escaped the joints of nearby pistons, scalding and sulfurous. The machinery this far down had turned rust-red over time, standing exposed to the sulfurous steam.

Davvol filed away a mental note that the machinery should be overhauled as soon as the secondary additions were built and in full production. The megalithic proportions of two new attractors demanded an incredible investment of labor and time—another fifty years of work before the new facilities would be ready, this as the Vec and the Phyrexians measured time, both referring back to the old Dominarian calendar of their ancestors. The Coracin native measured years a bit longer. It didn't matter either way. Davvol never forgot a detail he had committed to memory. It was now one hundred thirty-three years since the Phyrexians brought him away from Coracin, and he could review notes made to himself over a century back that had still not come due.

So far beyond his normal lifespan, the Phyrexian collaborator still resented being trapped in the weak and diseased body for which Coracin physicians had once predicted an early demise. Now he had certainly outlived those physicians and any other Coracin living then. The Phyrexians kept him alive and offered a few improvements—when it suited their needs—but little else. They guaranteed him virtual immortality so long as he kept the machines running here on Rath, so long as he completed whatever task was set before him—so long as Croag decided that he was useful.

The Vec workers, a humanoid race with blunt features and knobby joints, stood nearby during the inspection. Their pale skin—from so long trapped away from any sun—flushed in the room's heat. They despised him. He knew that, but they would never do anything so long as the Phyrexian troops stood guard. Any one of the spindly limbed warriors could kill them all, easily, before Davvol was put in any mortal danger that the Phyrexians could not repair. That was the trick, to beat the Phyrexians' ability to remake and *improve*. Davvol was learning something of this in his attempts to kill the hated Urza Planeswalker.

"I want production increased," he said to the Vec supervisor in charge.

Nothing indicated a difference between her position and a common laborer, but Davvol still knew. It paid to single out those who should know that their lives would answer last if any trouble should arise. His policy was simple. If a supervisor failed to accomplish the tasks given to him, he would watch those who reported to him die. The policy was quite effective, and the Vec policed themselves to keep supervisors who would not throw away their lives needlessly.

"The borders must be pushed back faster with enough excess for my special use. See that it happens."

The Vec nodded, sullen but compliant. Sweat ran down her face. Her face a mask, only her brilliant blue eyes spoke her hatred.

Davvol departed, leaving behind two guards. The others came with him back down a long corridor lined with corroded metal pipes that ended in a large balcony open to the outside. He stepped up onto his flying disc.

Traveling around the Stronghold was no easy feat. From the caldera rim he had been unable to accurately judge its size. It was better than three kilometers in height as measured from the lower machinery to the top of Stronghold's cyclone funnel tower and twice that in width, its entirety filled with Phyrexian artifice or denizens over which he had authority.

His guards joined him, and Davvol mentally commanded the disc to rise and move through the open wall. The immense cavern, almost a second caldera beneath the first, knew a perpetual twilight. Some lights issued from the bottom side of the Stronghold, while the Vec city below offered slightly brighter areas where its thinly arrayed neighborhoods clustered together into shared warrens. The air was warm and very humid, with condensing steam eventually falling down onto the city as a caustic rain. The disc rose rapidly toward the sculpted ceiling and then through one of the holes that dilated open and allowed a vent to the upper caldera. Davvol noted that he must—in the next year or so—look into the sulfuric rain, not that he cared for the Vec's troubles. The escape of so much mineral content in the steam spoke of inefficiency in the machinery, which must translate into slower production of flowstone.

Flowstone, a wondrous substance. He had discovered its merits almost immediately upon assuming responsibility for Rath. Reaching into the wide sleeve that covered his right arm, he removed from a hidden pocket the sample of flowstone he carried with him always. Warmed by the trip into the bowels of the Stronghold's machinery, the fist-sized hunk of tan stone still seemed unremarkable, as plain as it had been when the steward had torn it from the barren landscape that stretched between horizons. It was so much more. Without much effort, Davvol mentally shaped it into a series of rough figures— a cylinder then a cube. The tan substance would soften under his command then melt like a candle in an oven, except, the stone would not run out of his hand but toward whatever new shape he desired—a ship, an egg, a short staff. It was much harder than any regular stone and apparently had no limits on what it might accomplish. He concentrated a bit more, and the short staff melded into a knife with a fine bone handle and a very sharp edge. A touch more thought and the handle softened as if wrapped in leather. Davvol had made such weapons with blades so fine as to be able to score the hardest Phyrexian metal.

Flowstone apparently obeyed those with power over the plane of Rath, both in small portions like he held or in massive plains of the material. An evincar, named by Phyrexia, would possesses full mastery. Now Davvol and Croag shared that power, the member of Phyrexia's Inner Circle a permanent *guest* of the Stronghold and constantly looking over Davvol's shoulder. Davvol did not doubt with whom Rath's final authority currently rested, but Croag showed little interest in manipulating the flowstone, and it was control of the flowstone that might end up being the deciding factor of who truly ruled Rath. The knife softened and changed shape in his hand.

The disc exited the upper vent and flew over the Stronghold's lower surfaces. Black metal gleamed as lightning cascaded in the sky high above and bathed the caldera in an unnatural and beautiful red wash. Davvol sent the disc on a long glide around the main tower to the throne room. In his hand he held an exquisite flowstone crown. Yes, flowstone was one of the two paths into full power here on Rath, power Davvol meant to have.

* * * * *

Urza Planeswalker guarded Rath's second path into power. The Phyrexians despised Urza as no single other entity in the known multiverse, and an unimaginable reward awaited the one clever enough to rid the dark race of him. Despite Davvol's best efforts through the six decades so far—planning traps and instructing negators on new tactics—the planeswalker kept right on existing.

Something had to be done—not just planned, but physically accomplished—not exactly one of Davvol's strengths.

He paced the floor where a seeker had brought the latest negator corpses after their discovery on another plane. Two this time, smaller than most but very deadly and extremely fast. Rath's steward had hoped that their augmented reflexes would offset Urza's defenses. Not so, obviously. Their armored carapaces had been melted open in a dozen places. The blackened flesh of the first corpse appeared thoroughly disrupted, and Davvol found it desiccated of glistening oil. The second negator arrived in three pieces, having been caught in a maelstrom of energies that Davvol could only begin to guess at. This one leaked oil in a spreading pool, the room's light flashing over it in a filmy rainbow. The area stunk of charred meat, scorched oil, and hot steel. He stood, watching the oil spread over the polished metal floor, and thought.

He heard the rasping of metal fibers sliding over each other—Croag.

"Urza Planeswalker lives," Croag said, not a question. The Phyrexian stopped beside Davvol, his cleft skull staring down at the ruined negators.

Davvol nodded. "Obviously."

The council member's voice still sounded to him like a series of chattering squeals and hisses, but the Phyrexian had found it convenient to compleat Davvol's inner ear, so those sounds actually made sense to him now. Removing the language barrier had also mellowed Davvol's fear of the Phyrexian, who was no longer *quite* so alien. Besides which, living in the shadow of death for better than a century would harden anyone to its presence.

Croag turned in Davvol's direction. "What do you do now?" it asked.

"I am thinking."

Davvol prodded at a severed arm with the toe of one armored boot. The arm was actually a cannon of sorts, capable of delivering a stream of hellish energy that could disrupt a planeswalker's energy patterns. It rolled over, leaving behind a trail of soot and oily sludge. They were fortunate to have the corpses to examine. Quite often they were never recovered.

"They did not perform as I'd hoped," Davvol admitted, not that predictions could be made easily.

Negators did not conform to any particular design. These Phyrexians ranged from short, bulky creations to large dragon engine war machines. Bigger did not always mean better, except at times a better target. For Davvol, who relied upon an ability to organize and categorize, such maverick functions made for difficult evaluations.

"Urza Planeswalker must be killed," Croag hissed. "He must not interfere again." A skeletal arm reached out toward Davvol, razor-sharp fingers raking slowly through the air before the steward's face. "You are failing."

Davvol's wide-set eyes stared at the talons hovering inches from his face. Swallowing against the knot in his throat, he kept any waver from his voice. "I am doing the best possible. Urza has lived for over three millennia. He will not go quietly into the void." That gave Croag a moment of pause, possibly reminded of the failure of so many others. The arm lowered a fraction.

Davvol sidestepped away, crouching down to closer inspect the desiccated negator. Croag expected some kind of action. The steward would find something. The easiest excuse would be to blame the negator's design. Obviously they were flawed, though perhaps Croag would not care to hear him maligning more perfect Phyrexians. Against any regular form of life the negators were fearsome assassins, but a planeswalker called for a new outlook—and innovation. There Davvol met an impasse. True innovation, the ability to make radical leaps forward, would be beyond him. He had a feeling that Croag understood that—that his immersion in the details and inability for radical thinking was an important reason he'd been selected for this position in Rath. It made him the perfect steward, able to be trusted so much as the Phyrexians trusted anyone not of their own race.

He did see areas in the Phyrexian negators that *might* be improved upon. The difficulty lay in his lack of understanding for the planeswalker's strengths and weaknesses.

"It will take time," he said after some thought. He reached out and traced a scar melted into the negator's armor. His pale fingers came away with just a smudge of black. "More time than I first thought," he said, stalling with careful words, "but I believe it is possible." He stood. "Urza Planeswalker can be killed."

Croag was not one for easy conversation. "How?" he screeched, and Davvol caught the hint of intensity behind that one word.

For the first time, Davvol wondered if Croag somehow had a personal interest in the death of Urza Planeswalker. Did the Inner Council member, too, live under the shadow of death? Punishment by the Ineffable—the Phyrexian Dark Lord? A chill trembled his pasty skin. It made sense, looking back on the last six decades of Croag's presence and constant interference. The data had been incomplete until now. Davvol had been unable to place a mental touch upon this Phyrexian, his mind too alien, and relying on speakers for so many of those years.

He answered Croag with his own question. "Can negators be compleated to my own specifications?"

Metal cloth writhed, wrapping itself up and about Croag's face for a second, leaving a glistening sheen over the Phyrexian's taught gray skin. "This can be done," he promised.

With such infrequent contact between negators and the planeswalker, it might take decades merely to enhance the negator's sensory abilities so that recovered corpses could provide better data on their observations of Urza as well as a negator's own ability to fight him. It could be centuries more before Davvol could hope to improve on their design. It was how he worked best, though, able to organize and manipulate an infinite array of details to find the most efficient path. His plan would show constant progress, purchasing an existence for him that would stretch out several times over the natural lifetime of a Coracin native. Also, this evolutionary process would allow him to create an army of negators the lethal ability of which Phyrexia had never known. With this presentation alone, Davvol might be brought to compleation himself and named evincar of Rath. Wasn't that the Phyrexian way, after all, to improve in the current generation that which failed in the previous?

Davvol felt the planeswalker's death was assured. The power of numbers was on his side. Eventually, Urza would be overwhelmed, but under a slow program of constant refinement to the creatures that hunted him that could stretch out perhaps another five centuries. Davvol would have his monsters and eventually the life of the 'walker as well.

With any luck, Urza would take a long time to die.

Chapter 9

Multani dug his toes down into Yavimaya's soil, enjoying its warm, moist touch. He felt young and energetic, revitalized. From halfway around the world he had felt Yavimaya's strength build, his body reflecting the sentient forest's state. As older trees fell to make room for newer growth, his own limbs grew more supple and strong. His size increased, and the mosslike growth from his head and shoulders that served for hair grew in thicker and more luxurious. Here, actually standing in the shadow of Yavimaya's coastal trees, his feet buried beneath the soil, Multani could almost forget Rofellos's greeting.

"Yavimaya welcomes you," he'd said as the *Weatherlight* had come aground.

To hear the words spoken even as Yavmaya's greeting was made known to his own mind felt strange to the nature spirit. It was unsurprising that Yavimaya had initiated contact with Rofellos. In the absence of Multani, what other way could the forest and the Llanowar elf directly communicate? Through the dual greeting the nature spirit felt the forest's casual use of the elf—its hold over him—and the elf's uncertain knowledge of his own place. Multani also sensed that Yavimaya had relied on Rofellos for some time now to also act as its voice, an ability the sentient forest had apparently grown to miss in the seventy-three years since Multani had last been called home.

In that time Yavimaya had also stepped up its accelerated mulch cycles. Even within the less dense coastal forests the creaking sway and final, limb-tearing crash of falling trees never quite ended these days. It would fade, as a distant tree toppled, and then rebound as a nearer growth bent to Yavimaya's will. One could actually see the trees growing, their limbs stretching upward and out as boles thickened and root systems swelled the ground around them. The grass continued to mulch itself too, new shoots growing up within the decaying green blades. Farther back in the forest's shadows the underbrush writhed, thinning itself and then growing back with slight changes to flowers and leaves in a never-ending process of forced evolution.

One student had exclaimed sharply, noticing that even the insects along the ground were growing and dying at an accelerated rate.

"Of course," Multani had answered. Rofellos took the opportunity of the distraction to slip away, back into the forest. "They are as much part of life's cycle as any plant. In so many cases, one can not exist without the other. Many of Gaea's creatures will follow the same pattern, though in some the changes will be brought about without actual rebirth." This had excited several of the student mages for some reason.

As natural as the process might be, however, Multani couldn't help now but wonder about his absence during the accelerated growth cycles, whether or not it could be another reason for Yavimaya's greater empathy with Rofellos. In the last seven decades how many generations had he missed in the forest? Sharing his thoughts with Yavimaya, Multani still had no good answer. The forest, for all its intelligence, had never undergone such a treatment either. It knew mistakes, trying to direct the evolution of its plants and creatures. It feared mistakes, worried at losing any life forever. That was the nature of the forest, to live in a ceaseless cycle where the living died but new life could always hope to be born from such loss. Multani wanted to stay this time, to remain with his parent forest, but he knew that Yavimaya had decided his work to be elsewhere. He was an ambassador and teacher, the forest's voice among other nations and peoples.

"Enjoying the day?" a voice behind him asked. Rofellos stepped from behind a large bush. His arrival had been silent. The Llanowar had truly made this his home.

There was no denying the undertone of challenge to his question. Multani opened his mind with that of Yavimaya, sharing the sentient forest's consciousness with Rofellos. As on the beach, he could feel the turmoil roiling within the elf—the relationship between he and Multani, between he and Yavimaya. Rofellos now saw the nature spirit as something of a rival. It cast Multani into an uncertain position with Rofellos, and the adversarial nature of the Llanowar was winning over memories of the awe he had once felt for the nature spirit. Multani recalled those times, and with the memory he realized something else about the elf—Rofellos was not aging!

Not as he should be—Yavimaya had obviously taken hold of the elf's lifeforce, binding Rofellos to itself.

While the sentient forest built its strength, Rofellos tapped into it in a way similar to Multani. The Llanowar looked to be only in the early stages of an elf's middle years, the long period that accounted for so much of their extended lifespan.

"You're happy to be back," the elf said.

It was not quite a question, that last. Multani could sense the elf merely reflecting many of the feelings Yavimaya already shared with him. The Llanowar simply put them into words, at times apparently unable to fully distinguish his own thoughts from the ambient feelings of the forest.

"I enjoy returning to Yavimaya," Multani answered in voice, sparing the elf any trouble in understanding "Yes."

The nature spirit moved closer toward Rofellos, stopping on his way to feel at the bud on the new grenade flower. He sensed the violent energies stored up within, energies that would eventually burst the pod open, raining seeds farther out so that the plant could spread. In later evolutions those seeds would grow larger and might be thrown so far as to cross rivers or rocky surfaces. The burst of strength now might also hope to discourage any of the larger herbivores from making a meal of the plant. That defense, too, would grow.

"A fascinating new growth," Multani said, testing the Llanowar.

"I have not had the chance to inspect it," Rofellos admitted.

An echo of his words, truer perhaps to his original thought, filtered through Yavimaya's consciousness to the nature spirit. Multani knew that Rofellos had plenty of opportunities these many years but failed to take full advantage of them. If the plant did not provide food, clothing, or any other practical use, the Llanowar could not be made to pay attention. How sad, Multani thought, to keep so limited a view of nature.

"You should try," he said to the elf, encouraging on his own behalf as well as Yavimaya's.

Rofellos stepped forward hesitatingly, his features so obviously clouded with doubts. Multani tried to feel for the Llanowar's spirit, but it eluded him. Rofellos was not a true part of Yavimaya, not yet, at least. The elf reached out, gripped the stem roughly. The pod burst with a light snapping sound, as if sensing an attack, and dozens of tiny, sharp-tipped seeds exploded outward. A few stuck into Rofellos's arm, enough to catch but not enough to even draw blood. Still the Llanowar jumped back as if attacked, hand darting to the sword at his side. More of Multani's gentle words of encouragement died unspoken as the nature spirit noticed Rofellos's wild-eyed expression of shock and confusion. The Llanowar was under more pressure here than the nature spirit had ever thought.

Then, swiftly, silently, Rofellos faded back into forest shadows and disappeared as easily as Multani himself could have done.

*   *   *   *   *

His feet hardly seemed to touch the forest floor, its soft bed of earth unblanketed by grass this far under the canopy. Thin branches whipped at his face as Rofellos allowed instinct to lead him, the roll of a hill pushing him toward easier paths, the warning creak of a nearby trunk as Yavimaya took hold and wrestled it toward the ground detoured him back toward the clearing but did not slow him. He clenched at the empty air.

Landing in a natural ditch formed between two gentle hills, Rofellos pulled up sharply and tested the air. He scented only the perfume of nearby flowers, grenades and poison mothers, their fragrance belying what would eventually be a dangerous effect. He heard no sound of pursuit, nothing but the distant echo of a felled tree and some birdsong overhead. He crouched to place one hand against the earth, feeling for vibrations of silent movement, and searched the nearby shadows for Yavimayan elves. Nothing. Even Yavimaya had retreated from his mind, for now, the forest's language forgotten in his mad dash. It would be back, slow and insidious, taking root again within his mind.

Rofellos had hoped that somehow Multani would help him—explain how the nature spirit coped with such a pervasive presence. The Llanowar should have known better than to place trust in anyone not of his home. If the forest spirit had tried, if there had been some hidden meaning in their discussion of the grenade, the elf did not understand it, so he had fled. It was the second rule of a potentially hostile situation, the first being immediate violence. Yavimaya had not allowed him that, so he ran and escaped Yavimaya. For a moment he was simply Rofellos, though already he felt the insinuating return of Yavimaya, felt it reaching into his mind, calling him. Soon it would simply *be* there, but for now the choice remained.

The Llanowar ran.

Chapter 10

A large fire blazed over the hearth in Gatha's main laboratory, holding at bay the freezing air outside. Snow drifted against the northern window, protected by stone and shadow far longer than the drifts that had begun to melt last week with the thaw. The labs smelled of smoke but were otherwise kept spotless by the slaves assigned to Gatha. The slaves were courtesy of the more influential warlords who were in the mage's debt. Keldons always paid a debt, whether for good or ill.

So far, in better than forty years of experimentation, Gatha had balanced out the good over the ill. It was not that he hadn't made mistakes, just none lethal to date. It was a simple matter of counterbalances. If he made an enemy of a warlord, he simply had to befriend a more powerful one. As he'd noticed early on, the pecking order was well established in Keld. Body language could tell you at a glance who was dominant between any two warlords or any two *doyenne*, except that those positions could change at any time through design or simple misfortune. Gatha knew that one of these days he might choose wrong, but that was something to worry

124

about later, when it happened, not now. *Now* was for his work.

The voices of his slaves rose in the hall, interrupting him as he placed a tray of colos muscle on the table and reached for his sampling tweezers. There was a heavy thud, no doubt the body of one of them hitting the wall, and then the door was thrust open. Trohg stomped into Gatha's lab kicking snow and mud from his thick leather boots. Seven feet plus, the Keldon dwarfed the mage by a good sixteen inches and over one hundred pounds. Immune to such size differences anymore, Gatha did not flinch from the hard stare. He scowled at the interruption to his work but nodded for a slave to remove the tray he had been about to sample from. There would be no work while Trohg remained inside.

The Keldon grabbed one of the chairs near the fire and pulled it farther back into the room, away from the warmth. He sat then nodded toward the hearth.

"You put it in a good place," he said, speaking in the *low Keld* tongue for Gatha's benefit.

It was a language relying more heavily on words, fit for ordering around slaves and non-warrior Keldons. He pointed to the ripped standard that hung down from the large iron spike driven in between the mortared stones. The other half hung in Trohg's manor near the Necropolis, and a second banner of the same kind also decorated the council hall. Trohg had shared the standard he'd brought back for himself from a victorious campaign. Such was a sign of rare admission that a warlord or witch king owed someone a debt for that victory.

Grandson of Kreyohl, the Keldon warlord who had saved Gatha's life, Trohg had been brought to the mage at the age of ten for augmentation. A runt birth—as the smaller Keldons were often called—Trohg had no chance of selection for the warlord trials. His father preferred to see his son dead in the frozen northland wastes or by the mage's unpredictable magic—and said as much to Gatha—than be bypassed for selection. For most Keldons this would not be so disastrous, but as the first son of a mating between a strong warlord and an influential *doyenne*, Trohg's failure would directly affect the position of both his progenitors. His son would not be passed over and indeed hadn't been. Trohg not only responded to the genetic alterations, but he was also one of the rare warlords now referred to as a witch king. In battle he excited his troops to a furious, fanatical pitch and could then draw off their combined strength to legendary effect. Young as he was, Trohg sat on the highest tier in council, a warlord with few peers.

Moving over toward the fire, Gatha took the more comfortable and therefore weaker position. Familiarity only went so far in Keld, and he never forgot the delicate niche in which he lived here. His mastery of their language and the Keldon cut of his clothes would never make up completely for his lack of a warrior's background. A warlord could take his life at any time, provided Gatha could not first maneuver a stronger one into his path.

"I am honored to share in your victory," he finally said, staring at the torn standard rather than be tempted to make eye contact with Trohg. Argivian—his birth nation.

The witch king grunted in agreement. "I take strength from the warhost," he said, voice strong and deep.

"Nothing hurts me. I stomp out the lives of my enemy as if they were snowbound, slow and weak." His dark eyes sought out Gatha. "You did this for me, and I remember." He paused. "You will do same for my son."

Gatha glanced back to the warlord, courtesy forgotten in the shock. What he had thought would be a social visit, such as they passed for in Keld, had turned suddenly to business. The magical ability of the witch kings created incredible demand for Gatha's work, no matter that fewer than one in ten survived the process in any shape to fight. He had even begun cutting Phyrexian genetic material back into the Matrix, using it as he used colos genes—the adaptable material working to fill in the "gaps" his own work left behind. Still, a stable process had yet to emerge. Gatha did not want to make an enemy of this man.

He averted his eyes, swallowing against the dryness that had suddenly parched his mouth. "I did not know you had a son," he said, stroking the rough goatee he maintained in nervous habit. "Congratulations on your new warrior." Even as he answered with the standard salute for a son, Gatha was estimating the boy's chances: not good.

Trohg shook his massive head. "I have no son, yet. You will help me make him a witch king too."

Preconception? Gatha had done very little of that in his four decades in Keld except with captured slaves. Keldons wanted things done now. They worked for the day, never next year or into their children's lifetime. The future took care of itself. Trohg must have a strong dose of his grandfather's genes to look so far ahead for himself. Gatha had given up trying to convince a warlord or witch king to allow preconception adjustments years ago. Why should they suffer his unpredictable magic before they see the result of their labor?

"You will do this," Trohg repeated, hard voice on edge now.

The mage nodded. "It is possible," he said, the Keldon language thick in his mouth, "but not easy, and there is no way to predict if magical ability will be passed on to your son." Basing the new life off Trohg's genetic make-up, a successful subject, would dramatically increase the chances. It would take additional resources in equipment, the development of some new procedures, and time of course. He cursed silently. There was always a cost in time. "You have *doyenne* who will agree with this?" No small concern there. Trohg had two mates that Gatha was aware of, and he couldn't see either of them trusting the mage enough to allow preconception magics.

Trohg nodded. "I have a new manor and a new *doyenne*. She is eager."

Meaning *ambitious*. "It may take a few tries," Gatha warned him, "but I believe I can do this."

Standing abruptly, Trohg saluted with a clenched fist held in up in front of his face, the hand blocking part of his vision. Gatha was sure to return the salute but not hold it nearly so long. The inferior could never afford to impair his vision for as long as a superior. It implied insult to the stronger warrior.

"You will make my son a witch king," Trohg said, "and his son. For as long as you do this, Gatha, you will need nothing. If you ask, you will receive. If you need, we will supply it." He paused, then in *high Keld* continued. "You will sit on the Warlords' Council. This I pledge to you."

This was the highest praise, both the switch of tongues as well as the message. Gatha took a chance and replied in similar fashion, with a grunt of thanks and slight bow at the neck to signify his unworthiness before a superior warrior. Trohg grinned, baring his teeth, and the mage bowed again as the witch king took leave of the labs. The strength fled his legs and Gatha stumbled for a chair. An impressive pledge Trogh had made him, though Gatha knew it to be a false promise. No one sat in the presence of the Warlords' Council atop the Necropolis.

However, with a witch king and Keldon warhost at his back, Gatha would never fear for his life again and would never want for anything again. That was power the mage knew how to spend. Labs to rival Tolaria? Done. The Tolarian academy itself? Done. Barrin's head on a Keldon pike? Done. The future was opening up before him. Gatha only had to seize upon the course he favored, and if it did not quite suit his liking, then the mage would remake it to his desire.

* * * * *

"I don't like it, Urza." Barrin threw the pages of material down onto his desk. They spread across the marble slab top, a few sheets drifting to the floor with a whispered flutter. "We—I—curtailed Gatha's work because it represented a danger to morality as well as the lives of his subjects. His defection proved that he was never to be trusted, though you later defended his right to leave. Now he has set up his own labs? With one of our minor Eugenics Matrices?" Barrin rocked back in his chair, shaking his head, voice plaintive. "Urza, I wanted him stopped, not set loose on Dominaria."

The planeswalker stood on the other side of Barrin's large desk. He appeared the Urza of his youth again, years numbered in the teens instead of the thousands. His seamless face was too serious and intense for his apparent age.

"It's not as if the Keldons are suffering him involuntarily," the 'walker said. "They gave him a home and labs because they *want* what he is offering. They've practiced selective breeding and magically enhanced evolvement for far longer than you or I, Barrin. Why debate their choice, especially when it gives us the chance to observe such useful events?"

Barrin rubbed at eyes red and scratchy from late nights at work. He stood, fingers sifting among the loose pages that had spread over the desk until finding one of the rough sketches Urza had provided.

"There," Barrin said, drawing the page out from the others. "Have their breeding cycles ever turned out something like that before?"

Roughly man sized, the creature was a misshapen excuse for a Keldon—monstrous in size with an exaggerated bone structure that hunched it over and built an almost domelike carapace across its broad back. Sexless. It had malformed hands and feet with webbing between what few fingers and toes had formed. Bony barbs protruded from its heels and elbows.

Urza shook his head, his appearance aging a few years as Barrin cut into his excitement. "We've had similar catastrophic failures here on Tolaria," he said. "I think that one was from Gatha's cutting colos genes into the Eugenics Matrix."

"That thing was not borne from a faulty experiment," Barrin said, exasperated that Urza would compare the two programs. "That was created out of a living being in retroactive manipulation, something we have never done except when Gatha broke the guidelines."

Urza slammed an open palm down against Barrin's desktop. "It *is* possible. He has created from under-strength subjects viable warriors worthy of the high criteria Keldons hold for warlord selection." He sat back into a chair, calming himself obviously by force of will.

"Barrin, I'm not saying we should adopt Gatha's methods, but they might be used to temper our own. What if they would allow us a higher success rate? No radical mutations but simply to nudge and guide a subject into the pattern we tried to establish prior to conception. Preventative therapy, Barrin."

As much as he wanted to resist the idea, Barrin could not help considering it. Though deformities were rare after a century and a half of relative real-time work, they still occurred. Many of those born normal still exhibited signs of personal maladjustment later. Those were nightmares the mage could do without. He gripped the edge of his desk.

"In that light, I am forced to agree that there might be *some* benefit to review of this matter, but why should we allow Gatha to continue his work?"

"You've seen the latest reports. Most bloodlines have entered cascading failure because of earlier fast-time growth. We can treat them, but they will never be viable generations leading to the heir. Of the Tolarian generations, only the ones raised strictly outside of fast-time environments are looking strong enough, and Tolaria's ambient blue mana is beginning to influence their heritage too strongly. We are facing a serious setback. I'll need the kind of data Gatha is generating to start again and make up for lost time."

Barrin slowly stood, an eerie chill shaking the mage. *Tolarian* generations? Urza was not one to qualify a statement unless necessary. He swallowed dryly through a blocked throat. When he spoke, his voice was little better than a hoarse whisper.

"How many?" he asked. "How many bloodlines exist off this island?"

"A few," Urza admitted as if the subject bore little consequence. "Nothing different from what we have done here on Tolaria. Dominarian, raised in heavy white mana-rich areas, most influenced by Thran genetics." The planeswalker frowned. "My first generations were much more stable as well, though later generations did not degrade nearly so badly as the ones here on Tolaria because they stayed in contact with the white mana lands most likely."

A second program carried out by Urza alone. Barrin sat back into his chair, numb. "Why didn't you tell me?"

Urza shrugged. "They were not part of Tolaria's program, and you already had so much to worry about. If you recall, I worried from the start about using Tolaria's mana to make adjustments to plains-dwelling subjects, and then with Timein's work—"

"Stop, Urza." Barrin held up his hand in a gesture of submission. "Just stop."

He massaged the bridge of his nose, feeling a throbbing headache building. He remembered once, so many decades ago relative time, when all he had hoped for was a simple life. He did not want virtual immortality or to be in control of so many lives other than his own. He did not want to be caught up so intricately in the insanity that was Urza's program against the Phyrexians.

Even threatening to walk away now, though, would accomplish little. Urza Planeswalker could not be argued with and certainly couldn't be controlled. All Barrin could do was attempt to mitigate the collateral damage. Like it or not, Barrin was responsible for those lives, not the least of which were his wife's and—eventually he hoped—his children.

"Do you have data on your outside experiments?" he asked, hating himself for the question.

Urza visibly paused then nodded slowly. "Of course, with arrangements that all data would be delivered to you in case anything ever happened to me."

"I want it now," Barrin said. "I'll put Timein on it. Tutor or no, he is still one of the best—most *reasonable*—minds we have." Even to his own ears, the mage's voice sounded tired—defeated. "I'll put the academy on it, Urza. We'll see what might be done to correlate all the data—yours, mine and," he couldn't keep the disgust from his voice, "Gatha's. I'll do what I can."

"I never doubted that for a moment, Barrin." Urza stood. "You are the best I could have ever hoped to find for this work." He started to say more, hedged, then continued on anyway. "Go home and rest," he suggested. "Visit with your wife." He was gone, with a step between worlds.

Barrin sat alone, his work prior to Urza's arrival forgotten and absolutely no enthusiasm for the new work laid before him, but he would do it, he knew. Not today, not until he had completely assimilated it into his brain, but he would do it because it needed to be done, and because there was no one else who could.

$$* \quad * \quad * \quad * \quad *$$

Timein met Barrin on the hill overlooking the Colony—the small hamlet of bloodlines subjects who had moved to this far corner of the island to distance themselves from the academy and the project into which they had unwillingly been born. A few people were in evidence, a couple still bearing evidence of the bloodlines legacy. A man with a withered left arm worked a sparse field of vegetables. One large woman, her upper body swollen out of proportion to her lower, lifted a large rock out of the way of a plow.

"Don't they know that we can fix most of the gross deformities?" Barrin asked, the light wind pushing the front hem of his cloak back against his legs.

Timein nodded. "They know." He reached up and tucked back a stray lock of hair. "I'm not sure why they don't come in." He spread his hands expansively. "Look what magic has done for them so far."

Barrin glanced over sharply at the sarcasm. The student met his gaze easily, secure in his own ability though he still refused anything resembling promotion.

"You brought me out here for a reason, Timein. What is it?" He looked down on the Colony again. "I know you don't pick your meeting places casually."

"I'm leaving the academy."

Barrin's face hardened into a mask at the declaration. "I don't have to allow that you know. Only scholars are allowed access back into the world, and you are not yet a tutor."

The sorcerer smiled thinly, sensing Barrin's bluff. They both knew how much was owed to Timein.

"I didn't say I was leaving the island."

The master mage caught on immediately. He glanced downhill. "Here? Will they let you in?"

"I'm hoping so. I'll need help to build any kind of home before the storms arrive."

Barrin shook his head, in frustration more than denial. "Timein, you could be reassigned. Other projects . . ." he trailed off.

"Not so long as the academy supports Urza's Bloodlines project," the sorcerer promised, folding thin and spindly arms over his chest. "I've gone as far as I can. Now I need some distance. The Colony is about as far as I can get and remain on Tolaria." He paused, uncertain. "Maybe I can do something here to help these people. Master Barrin, I'm tired of fighting an enemy I've never even seen and with questionable tactics at that. It's over."

The look of despair that flashed briefly on Barrin's strong face nearly bent Timein from his purpose. He knew that in a way he was running out on the academy, on Barrin and Rayne and especially Urza, but the truth was in his words. He had gone as far as he was able, and by Barrin's slow nod, Timein knew the other man understood that. He watched as Tolaria's master mage braced himself up, shouldering that much more of the burden himself.

"When you are ready to come back, Timein, the academy will be there."

Timein watched as Barrin turned away from the Colony and headed back along the path. With the decision made and accepted, there was no longer any hesitation to the mage's step. He would go forward because there was no one else, and Timein respected him for it. As the sorcerer marched downhill in the opposite direction, he only hoped the feeling was returned. Entering the Colony, he put such debate from his mind.

There was work to be done.

*　*　*　*　*

Urza's lab holding the Thran Eugenics Matrix was one of the most secure sites on Tolaria. Two chancellors were required in attendance for any work. No one adjusted the complex machinery except Urza or Barrin. Rayne stood near the device cradling a massive leather-bound volume in her arms, her husband next to her. Marking her place in the Thran Tome, she studied the intricate artifact. A complex design built from delicate-looking components of Thran metal, it had lasted underground over many millennia awaiting Urza's discovery. The Matrix also had a touch of magic to it, very rare to find in Thran artifice, and in Urza's belief, an inadvertent addition.

"In all probability," the 'walker had once said to an assemblage of the scholars, "the Thran never realized the significance of magic, and so even they did not know exactly how their Eugenics Matrix worked."

If that was supposed to make them feel better for their tampering in a science they only half understood, it failed to do so. Rayne was one for the more straightforward work of artifice—clear established relationships and predictable results, yet the order of accomplishments of the Thran empire suggested greater understanding than Urza suggested. Rayne couldn't be sure that the planeswalker was correct in his theory.

"Can it be done?" Barrin asked, impatient and unable to help the question.

Rayne glanced up, sighed a frustrated breath. She gathered up her long, dark hair with a quick twist around her hand and tossed it over her shoulder then bent back to her task.

"Thirty generations," the mage whispered, shaking his head and pacing off to one side.

Rayne sensed her husband's weariness and wanted to console him, but she also needed to concentrate on the work at hand. She hadn't seen Barrin so despondent since the day Karn's memory had been capped.

She certainly understood his concerns. Newly promoted to chancellor herself, one of the administrative leaders of the academy now as well as a head scholar of artifice, she had reviewed the final results from Timein's research. It would take approximately thirty generations to approach the empathic mixture Urza required of the heir to his Legacy. Better than six hundred years and it all had to be in real time. No more shortcuts could be taken, not in the actual rearing of bloodlines subjects, and all needed to be raised off of Tolaria in virtually uncontrolled experiments. In the end, who could be sure that the empathic mixture would produce an heir with the exact qualities Urza desired? The person he wanted was strong and willful with as much empathy for the enemy as for the world of Dominaria itself—the ability to understand and so defeat the Phyrexians, without turning to their dark purposes.

Rayne set the large tome on a nearby table and allowed it to fall closed with a quick, dry ruffle of pages and a heavy slap from the binding. She breathed a heavy sigh, rubbing at her temples as if trying to massage into place within her mind all the information she'd just absorbed.

Barrin was back at her side in three quick strides. "Can it be done?" he asked.

She smiled wearily at his impatience. "Never bet against Thran artifice," she said. "There wasn't much they apparently couldn't accomplish." She placed one hand on the tome. "I even found some references to the idea of binding artifice with flesh on the most basic cellular level. I wonder if that remained theory?"

Her husband shook at that thought. "Having seen the monstrosities of artifice bonded to flesh, I can only imagine the horror of artifice *blended* with flesh."

Frightening shadows stirred at the back of Rayne's mind. Still, the thought would not let go. There was potential there.

"We only want to be able to make subtle alterations to a living being," Barrin said, as if reminding his wife of their current goal, "but they will have to be applied throughout the entire biological system to prevent genetic rejection from causing rapid breakdown."

This was a vague way of saying that a change must seem to be naturally present from birth to prevent what could be a terrible death. Rayne nodded, her eyes dark with the strain of reading into the late hours. She glanced around, suddenly uncomfortable to be in one of Urza's workshops.

"I think we can do this," she said, "and with greater effect than Gatha's crude experiments since we'll rely more on the precision of artifice over his unpredictable magics." She looked to Barrin with a frank openness. "The question is, should we?"

"A question I ask myself every day, my love," Barrin answered after a moment's pause, "but after learning from Multani and others about Yavimaya's forced evolution, Urza believes more firmly than ever that we are on the right track, as if our work here reflects nature's own course. Urza will proceed with or without the academy's assistance."

Rayne glanced over at the Thran Matrix, the ancient artifact so compact and precise and utterly devoid of malice or empathy. *That* would come from its user. "I believe it would be better *with*," she said.

To that Barrin simply nodded.

BOOK II

The Spark of Life

(3655–3856 A.R.)

There is a point—some might say a moment—in scientific experimentation known as the *complexity cusp*. Whether artifice or magical in nature, this is a dangerous area where the procedure or process reaches such a complex stage that it can no longer be controlled by scientific method. We, the progenitors, begin to react to the experiment rather than the reverse. The larger or wider the scope of the experiment, the easier for the cusp to be reached and surpassed without immediate notice.

—Barrin, Master Mage of Tolaria

Chapter 11

The sun rode low in the west. Lyanii doffed her helm as she approached the caravan's merchant leader, holding the visored headgear in her right hand in a display of neutrality—not quite peace. A few long strands of her chestnut-brown hair drifted next to the high cheekbones of her face, the majority of her long tresses caught up in the tie she used to keep it out of the way while in armor. Merchant swordsmen took ready positions at the sides of the caravan wagons. She carried no weapons herself, but the phalanx of archers backing her by one hundred paces argued her strength. The merchants would only be able to guess at what forces remained behind the gates of the newly-built village of Devas. It left her in the superior position, where she would remain. As a former marshal of Serra's Realm, the artificial plane fallen in the war between Phyrexians and Urza Planeswalker, it was what she knew best.

Still several paces out, she began to gauge the merchant's measure. He looked to be sharp of mind but soft of body, commanding through his purse. The merchant displayed the tan of a traveler. His clothes were fine silks threaded with spun silver. He had an earring in each ear, large rubies both, and a gold tooth, which flashed in the sun when he smiled. He returned her interest, finding no help in her unsmiling face but obviously impressed with the quality of her armor. The opalescent finish to the light steel promised well-guarded wealth. The Serrans' ability to blend in was one of the reasons Lyanii had chosen Benalia for her people, second only to its affinity for the ambient white mana of sun and plains and open sky.

Lyanii spared barely a second for the merchant's personal guard of four pikemen, unconcerned with their presence. "I am Marshal of this village," she said in greeting, neither challenging nor welcoming.

The merchant would have to make the first effort. The Serran people were too new to make assumptions. Assumptions had hurt them before as well.

"Trader Russo," he said, smiling wide. His Benalish accent rode his voice in softened vowels, though the heavy-scented oil he wore spoke of trade with foreign lands. "I travel through here once a year, usually stopping at the river bend where your village is being built. It is beautiful work and erected with impressive speed."

White stone was favored in Benalia. Their village used it in abundance, polishing each wall until it shone like alabaster. Fluted columns rose to impressive heights to either side of the gates, ending in platforms far above like those which might carry statues but currently remained empty—the lookouts having winged back down into cover. Inside the gates, rising over the few finished clay-tiled roofs, were the beginning walls of what would be their cathedral fortress.

"This is our land now," Lyanii said, speaking for her followers as well as herself, "but Devas welcomes trade. You may camp nearby."

The trader allowed the touch of a frown. "Capashen or Ortovi?" He spread his hands in a gesture of ignorance. "You sit between their ancestral lands, but I can't place you by the architecture."

Lyanii had hoped to brush over the heritage of her people and the method of their arrival, but clearly some explanation would be warranted. "We are refugees," she said, and that was true. "We hold no allegiance to the Benalish clans." His frown deepened. "Surely they would not object to the presence of a new village?"

"One that raises solid walls and employs its own guard in the same custom and fashion as a proper clan manor?" The merchant ran fingers back through his curly black locks. "They just might." He glanced back to the line of archers, and again at her crest, as if trying to place them. "Refugees from where?"

"A land devoted to Serra," Lyanii said, measuring out truth with a careful hand. This trader was obviously well-traveled, so he might have heard of those Dominarian sects that knew of Serra and worshiped her as a goddess. "On the continent of Jamuraa," she said, pretending to relent. "We were attacked. The invaders drove us away, despoiling our lands . . ." Her explanation didn't even begin to touch upon the whole story. The destruction of their homeland and how the Phyrexians had found the Serrans was left out. Now the surviving refugees from Serra's Realm were scattered in small groups, hiding. "Armies of the dark lord with no name."

Russo tried a tight grin. "Ah. Another Lord of the

Wastes," he said with false solemnly, trying to recapture a lighter mood. When Lyanii did not respond he flushed in embarrassment and explained. "I hear a lot of old tales in my travels. There is one about a dark figure and his armies of evil minions who will one day sweep whole nations from Dominaria. I've heard everything from the Ice Age to the small wars in Efuan Pincar blamed on him." He laughed, hollowly. "Of course, who actually believes that?"

Lyanii found no humor in the idea. "Who indeed," she said simply, voice tight with her loss and upset with herself for the momentary loss of control.

The merchant stumbled through an apology for his bad humor.

"No matter," she said finally. "I will have to contact the local clans then to make them aware of our presence and our preference for solitude."

"Yes," Russo agreed, "but do you know which to approach? Such procedures can make all the difference in Benalia."

She didn't see why, but then ignorance was not to be ashamed of—only corrected if possible. Russo might have suggestions, but then he could not appreciate the Serran refugees' position. As marshal she must choose. "Where are you bound for next?" she asked.

"I've just come from Ortovi and am on my way to Capashen Manor and the Capashen villages west of there. That doesn't matter. You need Clan Blaylock. They're the ones overseeing foreign diplomacy, until the next moon of course."

Lyanii nodded her agreement, but frowned at that last. "Next moon?"

"You did fall from the sky," he said, trying to recapture some of the mood lost earlier. "How did you travel so deep into Benalia and not hear of the Clans' lunar rotation?" Lyanii only shrugged. "On the glimmer moon's lunar year, two months from now, the ruling clans all rotate their duties. After that it'll be Clan Capashen's turn at diplomacy for a year, while Blaylock moves to the ruling clan." He grew thoughtful. "You could, I suppose, hold on until the moon's change. Then you are dealing with a local Clan. The Blaylocks would want to enforce the caste system on you sure enough. The Capashens are more tolerant of outside ways." A glance to the ranks of archers. "Your warriors will be a sticky point, regardless. It might be better if you formally adopted their system to begin with."

"That will not happen," Lyanii said, head swimming with all the new information.

She was marshal because Serra had decided it so, just as others were archers or guards. They were suited for their positions because they had been created as such. Why should they let an outside force determine their roles? Still, the trader had been more helpful than she'd at first thought.

"Thank you for the advice, Trader Russo."

Russo shrugged, neatly separating himself from the matter. "Advice is free. Here's hoping you do well, Marshal Lyanii. In the meantime, shall we see what my caravan can offer you and yours?"

Lyanii nodded for him to lead then turned and signaled for administrators from Devas. They would better know what was needed and what could be traded away. She would accompany the administrators and later perhaps invite Russo into the village for a discussion on Benalish customs. This land was their home now, and Lyanii would need to know everything possible if they were to survive.

* * * * *

The formal reception took place in Capashen Manor's ballroom. Gold flake had been mixed into a sealant and brushed over the white stone walls, leaving a smooth golden-glitter finish. Stained glass windows along two walls offered multi-colored views onto the impressive grounds in the back of the estate. A cathedral ceiling arced majestically overhead, rising up to the stained glass dome heavily trimmed in gold. The open space muted the soft music that rained down from an overhead musician's balcony, the perfect volume to enjoy while also engaged in discussion.

Karn walked into the room at the side of Nathan Capashen, leader of his Benalish Clan. Around them the Capashen nobles mingled cautiously with those of Clan Ortovi—their guests. Karn noticed that a strained cordiality had settled over the assembly as everyone carefully skirted the purpose of the state visit. By custom, it wasn't until the second day of a visit that business could be discussed. Of course, everyone already knew from the guests in residence what that business would be. Now they merely awaited the final member of the convocation—the third party that tradition demanded put the question forward, though certainly it would be rejected—again.

"This race of lizardmen, the Viashino, they actually live over a live volcano? Amazing, Karn." Nathan

Capashen looked sideways at the silver man. "*Almost incredulous.*"

He shook his head, obviously trying to compare such a life with the open plains of Benalia. Nathan was an avid audience for news of the larger world.

It was Karn's turn for a question about Benalia, trading his knowledge of Dominaria for more intimate information on this land. He found it interesting, as his journals were mostly filled with memories of Tolaria until only thirty years back. He began to accompany Urza in frequent travels about Dominaria. The golem knew some pain for those he saw so little of these days—Barrin, Rayne, and Timein. Delving into the details of new lands helped to ease that sense of loss. His question was interrupted by the sudden heightened pitch of conversation in the room as people passed along a single name and then fell into an expectant hush. Malzra.

Urza Planeswalker strolled with intent across the large floor, bearing down on Karn and Leader Nathan Capashen. He wore a closed-collared garment of royal purple and a blue leather vest. Urza stopped, glanced about as if just now noticing the silence and smiled at the surrounding people. Conversations picked back up but at a much more subdued level, and many crowds edged in closer to Nathan and Karn's location. Three others broke from their own groups and moved in for the official matter, one taking up position behind Nathan and two joining Urza.

Nathan nodded a friendly greeting. "Master Malzra, you honor us with your presence here. Am I to understand you wish to put forth a formal proposal?"

"I do," Urza said. The 'walker's blue eyes were sharp

and bright, and Karn followed his gaze past Nathan to the clan leader's young cousin Jaffry.

The young clansman was nervous, acutely aware of the attention focused on him. He was also just as obviously smitten with the woman who trailed Leader Trevar Ortovi, his eyes always coming back to her.

Urza nodded to the young noble lady, Myrr Ortovi. "I am honored to invite both clan leaders present today to consider accepting Myrr Ortovi as wife to Jaffry Capashen."

Benalish law stipulated that leaders of each clan had to consent publicly and in the same forum before a marriage could take place between clans. In this match, Clan Ortovi gained most of the advantages. Though she would live among the Capashen, Myrr would forever be Ortovi—clan affiliation was determined by birthdate and nothing else. Her loyalty to Clan Capashen would always be secondary. So on those years when the Capashen ranked higher than the Ortovi in Benalish government, she might hope to use her influence in favor of her clan.

Nathan Capashen didn't even look to his cousin. The feelings of the couple came second. "This match was denied last year, Master Malzra. Why should I reconsider now? Your sterling recommendation notwithstanding, of course."

"Leader Trevar offers as dowry control of the lands and both villages bordering the river Larus. Also, in his position as head of taxation this year, a reduction to only one part in ten of all crops." Urza turned to look at the young girl.

Myrr nodded, showing that she was a willing participant in this ritual and stepped forward, offering Urza her hand.

Nathan shook his head sadly. "I cannot agree." Several gasps of disbelief erupted across the room. "In two months the Capashens take over foreign policy while the Ortovis handle trade. After that, the Capashens shall rule Benalia, and the Ortovis will be in place for diplomacy. I would be a fool to ignore the serious advantage given Clan Ortovi by placing Myrr within our manor." He paused. "I might consider such a marriage in the year after, of course."

Of course, then the Capashens would be back at the lowest position while Ortovi ruled. Karn looked to Urza, as did all others, knowing that the matchmaker would not have brought forth the invitation without something new to offer. Urza did not disappoint.

The 'walker had not released Myrr's hand, pulling her forward gently to stand next to him. "It saddens me to see two people kept apart over a trivial matter of dowry. I'm certain Trevar Ortovi would offer more to see Myrr's happiness if it would not be a detriment to his own clan. So in his place, I would like to add to Myrr's dowry."

An allowable custom, though Karn doubted anyone could remember the last time a *neutral* third party had done such.

Urza nodded to his golem. "I offer Karn as part of Myrr's dowry, his services devoted to their family in specific and Clan Capashen in general for no less than fifty years."

All eyes speared the silver golem. Karn dwarfed all present, but at the moment he felt very small under those piercing gazes. Fifty years! Better than twice his memory span. Forgotten would be Tolaria and his friends there. He was shocked that Urza would simply make such a decision without first warning the golem, but then something also spoke up inside of him that warned that this was not the first time.

Urza's offer had struck the right target in Nathan. The clan leader couldn't help the smile that followed his initial surprise, but then he sobered, looking at the silver man carefully.

"Karn, is this what you want as well?" he asked his friend.

Did it matter what the golem might want or decide? If Urza was to be believed, nothing else mattered but the threat of Phyrexian invasion. The golem had seen one battle already, a negator catching the 'walker and golem as the two traveled to inspect the mana rig under the Viashino's care. He could only imagine the horror of an army of such creatures. If Urza believed Karn's service to the Capashen was warranted, could he gainsay the planeswalker?

"I will stay," Karn said slowly, feeling out the words.

Nathan nodded once, abruptly, then turned back to Urza and Trevar. "It is a good match," he said. Nathan motioned Jaffry forward, and Urza joined his hand with Myrr's, then said loudly, "We welcome Myrr Ortovi into our manor."

It was a signal for the others in attendance to flock in and congratulate the newly engaged as well as each other for a fine bargain struck.

Urza found the golem quickly. "I will be off, Karn. I will bring the balance of your personal effects on my next visit." He paused a long moment, giving the golem an evaluating stare. "I had hoped your travels about Dominaria would give you an appreciation for its lands and people. It's good to see that I was right."

Karn read into that a reluctant admission that Urza might actually consider the golem a being of his own, not that it mattered in the larger picture of course. Still, it helped to reinforce Karn's resolve that his choice had been the right one. So long as he—and Urza—believed that the golem could make a difference in the preparations against Phyrexia, Karn felt compelled to answer that higher calling. What else was there in any life— human or artifact, mortal or immortal—beside a useful existence?

Chapter 12

Gatha's colos pens were heavily reinforced. Extra thick walls were tipped with spears of valuable iron pointing inward and down to keep the beasts from getting too aggressive. Now a head reared up, the colos butting aside one spear. It had learned to use its protective scale already.

From his viewing platform, Gatha studied the single incredible beast for the results of his latest experiments. The massive colos—larger than most by five hands at least—clawed at the ground with razor-sharp split hooves. Its rank breath frosted in the crisp morning air. Gatha found no physical deformities except the one he had given it—the same hard bone armoring its horns now grew in plate-sized scale over half of its hide. It was patchwork still, spaced in between large areas still shaggy with the usual coat, but no longer suffering degradation problems. His attempts at developing a superior war beast were hitting closer to the mark. Another three trials and he might try cutting the armored scale into the Matrix and use it on some Keldons crippled by earlier testing and now good only for experimentation, perhaps after one more trial.

Though occupied with studying the beast, Gatha still kept a wary eye on the party being led carefully down the trail toward his labs. In Keld, it never paid to be unobservant. Gatha knew his visitor would be no descendant of the long-dead Trohg. All warriors with a pedigree from the witch king had been given the safe routes and passes to his lab. Even now, a pair of Trohg's descendents, six times removed, stood guard at the laboratory's main door with wickedly barbed halberds. Twelve years old, the both of them were already standing above six feet and taking early warlord trials the following year. Gatha considered them mild successes.

The approaching party passed beneath the crude arch erected over the path. He recognized Varden, a minor witch king and—lately—a troublemaker in council. His escort was none other than Kreig, another of Trohg's descendents and Gatha's best subject ever. This would demand his personal attention, and he scaled back down the short ladder to the frost-bitten ground below.

He doffed his fur-lined cap and gloves and tucked them beneath his armored breastplate. The armor of Keldon design was made of thinly beaten, overlapping steel plates trimmed in red leather and gold. It was one of many rich gifts presented him by Kreig's two *doyenne*. He ran a hand over his oiled hair, slicking it back so that his tri-widow's peak tattoos stood out prominently. On the back of his right hand the personal sigil of Trohg had been tattooed. It bound Gatha to Trohg and the witch king's lineage and signified his acceptance in Keld with all rights and privileges. More, it shielded him from any immediate danger—by tradition any dispute with a protected person must be taken to the senior warrior of that line. Kreig, with Gatha's latest help, that would forever and *always* be Kreig.

"My friend," Kreig greeted, a *high Keld* salutation rarely offered inside the Keldon nation and never to an outsider. Gatha steeled himself to prevent a wince as Kreig squeezed down on his shoulders. "Varden demands an audience with you," he said dropping back into the lower tongue. He shot a glare back toward Varden who averted his eyes from the more powerful witch king. "I took his manor and mate hostage to insure his good behavior."

This meant that Varden came with an argument and possible challenge. Kreig may have overstepped himself slightly—certainly Varden thought so, his nostrils flaring with pent rage—usurping what was traditionally the censuring power of the council. Gatha doubted many would argue with *his* witch king.

"I will hear him."

Varden wasted no time. Though several inches shy of Kreig, the smaller warrior showed no fear of the other's presence. "You," he thrust a thick finger toward Gatha, a fighting offense between any regular Keldon males, "you refused my request for The Gift." *The Gift* was how Keldons referred to the preconception process Gatha had started with Trohg and applied judiciously depending on his own needs and whims. Usually, the effort was not worth potential returns—not with the strong line already backing him. "I desire another son, one who deserves warlord trials."

Varden's first son had been born lame, guaranteeing him a position in Keldon society barely more than slave labor. At least with a battlefield injury, one might expect to live out life as a craftsman.

Gatha had expected something like this. "No," he said.

Hands balling into sledgelike fists, Varden barely controlled his fury. "No? What do you mean, no?" he yelled.

"No," Gatha replied with quiet strength, his *low Keld* tongue perfect these days. "I refuse your request. I thought it was clear from the message I sent. If you need to hear it from my lips, then so be it." He shrugged. "No."

"Lowland fodder," Varden stormed, spittle flying from his lips. "You will change your mind," he said, more a command than a threat.

Carving his place within Keld had taken Gatha better than four decades. He still remembered those early years, always self-effacing and at times cowering because it was expected. Trohg had changed that, first ever to name the mage a friend after the successful advancement of his own son to warlord and then witch king status. Gatha had over a century since to grow into his new power, and he knew how to wield it. Varden neither frightened nor even worried him, and the warlord's lack of understanding of that only proved the legitimacy of Gatha's refusal. He was genetically damaged in body and mind—in the mage's opinion.

"I will not change my mind." Gatha folded his arms across his chest, resolute. "Your son is not fit for enhancement." He dug the barb in deeper. "Though perhaps I will request him for," and he had to drop back into Argivian for the word, "experiments. I will never use *your* blood in my work again. I expect your diseased line to die out." Gatha turned to Kreig. "This interview is over," he said. The message was apparent—Varden no longer mattered.

Varden shook with rage. One hand fastened onto the hilt of his broadsword. His darkly tattooed eyes glared fiercely down on the smaller man. "You do this to us," he yelled, "To me. Your work over the years, deciding who travels on and who falls. It will stop soon, little one. I vow it."

Varden stomped away, his terrifying exit made comical when he realized that he would require Kreig or another escort to pass him safely through the snares that warded Gatha's labs. Gatha waited for him to bluff it through alone, but in the end Varden waited just past the arch, fuming.

"You have made an enemy for us," Kreig said, careful to keep their conversation from Varden's ears. "Varden will summon his warhost. Other warlords might stand against me now. I had hoped this wouldn't happen for another year."

Left unspoken but implied with his last statement was the fact that Kreig *had* anticipated such a day. Gatha had merely accelerated the timetable. It left the mage feeling confident in his greatest subject, who would grow greater yet with the slow-time waters being given him the last several years. His initial supply kept preserved in a stasis field, the both of them could easily live another century, then, if necessary, Kreig's warhost could visit Tolaria and *request* more.

Gatha was not about to see his work ruined now by something so easily overcome as chance. "Give me the names of those who might stand against us. I will entice them to stay away from Varden." The easy offer of withholding of his magics could influence most warlords. Kreig cocked his head to one side, considering, then grunted a simple acknowledgment. The mage smiled. "You then only have to crush Varden."

* * * * *

Even as breath came in frosted clouds, the battle cries of the Keldons warmed the air and stirred bloodlust. There were screams of challenge, personal conquest, and the bellowing of orders as commands of the opposing warlords were routed. Only a few shouts of pain were heard, except perhaps in the most tragic of cases where limbs were lost or backbones cleaved, allowing those final seconds of painful clarity before oblivion. No fearful shouts were called—not so much as a whimper—not from these men. They would bleed their flesh white, staining the frostbitten earth and stone dark with the red of their life before admitting to cowardice in any fashion or guise. It was a clashing of titans, marauders who would fight and die to the last man if so ordered here on this lonely plateau, no ordinary contest. Mist wreathed the land farther down, piling into a dense fog that cascaded down the mountainside to fill the lower valleys. It was as if the gods themselves had elevated the battleground above the ken of mortal man.

A broken ridgeline split the plateau unevenly, the scarp of sharp rocks pushed up during a recent movement of the earth. The battle raged only on the larger side—a thousand warriors joined in ferocious combat. A few had claimed the higher ground for their fighting, loosing hand-pitched rocks and the occasional axe down on those below. Boulders large and small littered the battlefield, minor obstacles Keldon warriors dodged to get at their enemy.

Leather-armored footsoldiers carried hooked longswords or wickedly spiked maces. Nearly all tied smokesticks of colos horn into their hair. The smoke drove many Keldons into a battle frenzy and was known for the nervous anxiety it bred in other races. They fought in single combat only where a blood feud was acknowledged between two warriors. Mostly they clumped together and dashed madly into enemy groups, bristling juggernauts of steel and sinew. Against any other foe, a Keldon warrior would have trusted the tough coloshide leather and his own strength to stand up to a blow, setting up a killing stroke of his own. Those who relied on such tactics lay among the fallen here. This was not a battle to be won on ferocious strength alone. Here strength and skill carried the battle only so far. It would be won by the warhost commanders, the Keldon warlords, the witch kings.

Kreig held the inside flank of his warhost, turning his broad back to the sharp ridge as he slashed his way through the thickest fighting, well armored with metal gauntlets and greaves, interlocking plates covering chest, shoulders and hips. His helm allowed a narrow slit for vision, the opening guarded from a lucky sword thrust by twin crescent-shaped blades. A ridge of curving spikes stood out from his shoulders, each one vented to a cavity built into the neckline where smoldering embers had been placed to wreath his headgear and shoulders in fearsome smoke. The leather joints in his armor were made with the shaggy colos hair still in place to bring about the illusion that the armor concealed beast rather than man.

Gatha's greatest witch king wielded his Keldon greatsword with both hands, the silvery finish of the blade now marred with gore and running droplets of blood. The bloodlust of several hundred warriors coursed through his veins, exploded in his heart, pounded at his temples. He drew upon the warhost's strength, their courage. His eighth opponent lay in two at his feet, cleaved from right shoulder to left hip. The warrior's stabbing sword had pierced the witch king's right thigh. The Keldon simply drew it out as if it was a mere annoyance and tossed it aside with a howl of derision for Varden's warriors.

"Varden!" he called out, challenging the other witch king to stand against him.

His own warriors, those close enough to hear the challenge, called out his own name in a chant. "Kreig! Kreig! Kreig!" It left little question from where the great witch king commanded. Sporadic calls of "Varden" were little more than half-hearted answers to the general chant, not a reply to his challenge. None could stand against this witch king. No being of Dominaria could hope to match him.

Another warrior came at him, this one slashing with a halberd. With a spinning cut, Kreig took the head of the polearm off just behind the blade. He continued his spin, coming back around in a straight-armed attack that took the warrior's head easily from his shoulders. Kreig picked up the head and tossed it into a knot of Varden's men who were trying to protect the lower slopes of the scarp. A sickle-axe sunk into the ground near his foot. Kreig picked that up as well. His return throw found an enemy warrior halfway up the slope of sharp rocks. Even throwing upward, his strength punched the point of the weapon through armor and chest to stick out the other's back. No one would be protected from him.

Where Kreig walked the battle turned in his favor. His closest warriors fought and died to keep abreast of him, which pushed the witch king forward all the harder. They were lucky to simply trail back from his lead in a deep arrow, leaving behind a field littered with dead or dying men and a few scattered fights. Kreig could see Varden now, leading his men from behind—ordering them forward while he and his private guards advanced much slower. A thick line of Varden's supporters separated Kreig from his enemy—but not for long.

His greatsword flicking like a dragon's tongue, Kreig forced his way into a knot of mace-wielding soldiers. He left amputated limbs, shattered bone and cleft armor in his wake. Two heavy-spiked clubs stuck into him, abdomen and elbow. A downward slice took the arms off one man. The other he dispatched with an easy thrust through the chest. The weapons still sticking in him, he felt no pain and never slowed from wounds which would have killed a mortal man. He was more than mortal at this moment, the energy at the core of his being multiplied several hundred-fold. He was Kreig. He was *Keld*.

Kreig looked over the field at two Keldon warhosts joined in battle. Each one, by himself was a superior warrior. Together they were a proud and fierce nation. Where each warrior fell to a brother the nation diminished. *His* nation diminished.

He chopped the head off a war sickle aimed for his

neck, his sword edge slicing through the wooden shaft with ease. Instead of a return stroke, taking another life, Kreig fastened one gauntleted hand onto the other's long hair and pulled the warrior to arm's length to stare into the witch king's dark gaze.

"Keld!" he bellowed a new war cry, taking the nation's name for his own.

He shouted it into the warrior's face, turned him with an easy roll of the wrist, and set him facing against his former comrades. He could feel the man's loyalties swaying on the field, caught between the powers of two witch kings. Kreig took up a stabbing sword from a fallen warrior of his own host and thrust its hilt into the warrior's hands.

"Keld!" he yelled again, a cry the warrior took up for his own.

Kreig swept forward—invincible in his power. Any warrior brave enough to meet him was converted with the call of home and nation and set back on the side of Kreig. With each convert Varden's power waned. More rallied to Kreig, in singles, then pairs and then trios. Finally the remaining enemy forces fell back, regrouping around a solid center. Varden pushed his way to the fore, broadsword in one hand and his personal crest in the other. Kreig summoned his own colors, taking the greatsword one-handed despite the awkward grip.

"Varden," the smaller force called out, summoning the last of their strength in a mad rush at the opposing center.

"Keld," the warhost of Kreig answered.

Led by their mightiest, the army swarmed forward and over Varden's group. The witch kings came against each other. Kreig's greatsword punched through metal plating to slice into Varden's left leg. Varden's own stroke slipped into an unprotected space and stabbed deeply into Kreig's side. Powered by their greater strength, each witch king felt the pain of near-mortal wounds. Kreig rebounded faster. He swept his blade down and then around in a grand overhead sweep while Varden barely had time to bring his own sword up in an attempt to parry. Varden's broadsword shattered under the vicious stroke, and Kreig followed through to split open the witch king's head. His blade turned slightly by Varden's spine, Kreig's stroke finally died when it stuck into the other man's left hip.

Kreig stood over the fallen witch king, the battle over. He wrenched his weapon free, held it aloft with blood dripping down in a christening shower. No more challenges were called forth, only the victory bellows of his followers. Keld was his now. He would lead its greatest armies into the field, and here in the mountains he would rule. He saw a tiered throne in his vision, decorated with bodies of his fallen enemies. He looked his nation in the eye, challenging it, and it glanced away, subdued.

* * * * *

Gatha remembered a time when he had stood in Council, ready to address the assembled *doyen*, and had deliberated taken the uppermost tier in order for all to look on him as he spoke. He had demurred then, unsure of protocol. This day, standing with Kreig as the witch king set forth to claim that empty spot, the mage could only think back on that moment and count himself fortunate to be alive for even considering the idea.

Kreig carried the tattered and blood-stained colors of Varden. The other witch king's warhost no longer existed, all survivors having pledged their loyalty unto death to Kreig. He had come to the council as the greatest warrior—the greatest witch king—ever known. Dressed simply in ceremonial leathers, his chest and arms bared to the cold, he walked over to the wall, withdrew a spike from his belt, and used it to stab through the heavy cloth and into the wall. Never before had a warlord's crest been displayed here among the spiked standards of every nation the Keldons had ever fought against. It was both proof of victory and threat to those who would stand against him. Kreig nodded to Gatha, and the two walked straight over to the lowermost tier. Kreig mounted it first, staring down those nearby, and then turned to offer Gatha a hand in aide.

Where the mage may have come into his own power here in Keld—able six months ago to stand up before a furious Varden and believe himself sacrosanct—here his nerves sang tightly for the role Kreig expected him to play. The witch king did not need to include him but did so for an old promise made by Trohg himself. Shrugging aside the offer of assistance, Gatha mounted the tier and stared directly at the warlord to his immediate side. The Keldon stood, his massive frame towering over Gatha, but after a quick glance to Kreig he averted his gaze and stepped back, leaving room for Gatha to stand as an equal—as *doyen*, one of the leaders of Keld.

Gatha swallowed a tight knot in his throat, his mouth dry and scratchy for lack of spit. For the first time ever the council hall did not seem cold, a full-body flush warming him.

Kreig, however, was not finished. He stepped upon the next tier, then the next, again meeting no challenge.

On this third tier a crippled warlord rose, his age impressive and showing in the weathered face and slightly stooped shoulders. One arm had been replaced by a stabbing sword, his left leg a sharpened stump of metal.

"I do not speak against you, Kreig," He thrust the bladed hand toward Gatha, "but he does not belong there."

Gatha knew that those warlords crippled in battle still retained their place. The council of the aged was given weight in all deliberations, but in the end the strong ruled. Kreig locked gazes with his elder.

"He is here because my great sire, Trohg, promised that one day Gatha would sit on the council. I am keeping that promise. Gatha has proven himself as the greatest ally of the Keldon nation. My victories are his victories."

Kreig's death would likely be Gatha's own as well. The mage was again thankful for his hoard of slow-time water. Now he was merely gambling on Kreig's martial prowess. His entire life in Keld had been a gamble. At least here he had loaded the dice.

The elder glanced away first. For his challenge, he decided to step down a tier rather than be thrown down later. The warlord next to his abandoned seat, though, rose and drew a dagger. No words passed nor needed to. Kreig leapt for him at once, taking a savage slash to his side but fastening his hands about the other man's neck. Muscles bunched on his shoulders. A sideways twist and the other man's neck snapped with a bone-crunching sound. It echoed in the chamber. Kreig threw him from the tier.

A warlord *doyen*—no witch king this one—rose beyond him. Kreig moved forward, and the other dropped back into a defensive stance. The witch king paused, then walked forward slowly and with great deliberation to each step. He stopped barely a foot from the other warrior, hands at his sides and eyes boring into the other man's face as if daring him to strike first. Brutal seconds passed, and then the warlord broke away his gaze and bowed his head in surrender unable to bring himself to follow through on the challenge. He also demoted himself to the second tier. Kreig continued to stare down at him. Still there were no words spoken but some subtle body posturing that Gatha could not quite follow. The warlord stepped back down to the first tier, and Kreig turned his attention back to the final level.

Behind Kreig, the *doyen* shook themselves into a new structure of power. With three vacancies now on the third tier, a witch king from the second tier stood and moved up next to Kreig. Toward the dominant witch king he kept eyes averted and head slightly bowed. To his right he stared his neighbor in the eye and then sat. No one challenged. Another rose from the first tier and took a seat in the second. A few of the younger but stronger witch kings replaced older warlords higher up as well. To Gatha's eye, it became apparent who supported Kreig and who was simply bowing to his greater strength.

Kreig ignored it all. With deliberation he stepped up to the fourth tier, holding only six chairs—one of them his usual seat on the council. One witch king stood in challenge. At this level none carried weapons, considering it beneath their martial prowess. The fighting was brutal and silent. Kreig held up under a stiff-hand blow to the throat and a rib cracked by a knee body blow, giving as good as he received. Finally he managed to catch his opponent on the jaw with his elbow. Kreig picked the stunned man up by shoulder and crotch and threw him from the tier, his skull caving in when it dashed against the hard floor below. The witch king then picked up his own chair and threw it down after the body, leaving him no actual seat. He stepped up into the open space where no chair had ever been placed and where, by his action, none ever would. This place of power was his by right if no one challenged.

No one did. The four remaining *doyen* who sat on the high tier averted their gaze, and Kreig's power was assured. Again the *doyen* maneuvered around to fill vacancies. No fights marred the quiet. The others did not presume to compare their ability with Kreig's glorious rise. They recognized and honored Kreig's strength—and Gatha's, the mage realized, remembering how Kreig had shared all victories past and future.

It was a feat never before managed, an event out of legend. Kreig had taken the uppermost level. From before recorded time the promise had come down: When the Necropolis below the council hall filled with the warlord dead, they would all rise in an invincible army and sweep Dominaria. The warlord who sat the final tier would lead that army. Gatha had never understood if that warlord would be one of the dead, the greatest of them all through history, or whichever warlord had seized the position for the great event. Here, with the mage's help, it seemed that Kreig might be able to await that rapturous time.

Chapter 13

Davvol stood on a small rise that he'd shaped up from the mountainside's easy slope of dull tan flowstone. His flying disc rested upon the ground behind him—a black altar guarded by two Phyrexian soldiers standing a silent guard. On the horizon the great volcano that held the Stronghold thrust its imperial presence into that chaotic sky. It dwarfed the mountain on which he currently stood and reminded Davvol of that which he ruled.

A cutting wind sliced through the gaps in his armor, breathing chills against his grayish flesh and billowing his cloak out behind him like the leathery wings of a giant bat out of nightmare. The cold also gripped at his head, squeezing it in an invisible vise, except where the black Phyrexian skullcap armored and protected it even from the elements. A Coracin physical characteristic—in his mind, a defect—was that the bone plates in their wide skulls never quite closed and so left a vulnerable spot over the brain, a vulnerability that Croag had agreed to remedy, as Davvol's mind was of importance to both Davvol and the Phyrexians. Only one feature to the skullcap bothered him: The small circular indentation high over his forehead. Phyrexians did not adorn their work with art or meaningless design. That indentation had a purpose, which Croag had not seen fit to pass on and Davvol preferred not to draw attention to by asking.

"You intend to attempt a transfer." Croag's voice squealed and cracked behind him. This was not a question. Croag obviously knew.

Davvol looked over his shoulder, his black eyes guarded against his surprise at being interrupted here. The member of Phyrexia's Inner Circle stood next to the steward's disc, a portal still opened behind him and flashing as Davvol's soldiers passed through and away—back to the Stronghold, no doubt. Now Davvol frowned. The soldiers were a precaution since the Vec had been known to roam far from their underground city searching the landscape. Of course, Croag could easily handle anything a common soldier could, but those guards were *his*, to be dismissed only by Davvol himself.

"I am considering it," he finally admitted.

"It would be better if your troops did not see a failure." Croag glided forward slowly, the metal bands that formed his semblance of clothing rasping against each other. Croag carried his staff today, a twisted metal creation with no apparent purpose. Davvol knew better than to assume such was true. "Failure is too often the genesis of recycling. You might weaken their loyalty to you."

Croag had done him a favor? Perhaps. Davvol did not blind himself to the possibility that Croag might be concerned that the guard witness his *success*. The centuries were stacking up behind the steward of Rath, and with each passing year he accumulated more data through which he better understood his position and that of those around him. Davvol smiled, thinking that none of his race could ever have hoped for such a long life holding the power he did. He would gain more so long as he maintained appearances and worked carefully.

"My appreciation, Croag. I hadn't considered that." Because he truthfully hadn't considered failure as an option, "What would happen to the subjects if a failure occurred in mid-transference?" Would the Phyrexian even know?

"They would be gone," Croag said simply. "Lost between worlds. It has happened before, yes. During the first steward's reign."

That told Davvol quite a lot that he hadn't known before, the most important, of course, being that Rath's rulers had changed in the past, and by extension could easily be changed again in the future. The thought bred hope and concern both. He turned to the task at hand, staring down the slope at the smooth wash of flowstone.

Davvol mentally reached back to the Stronghold. There the great control machinery for transference currently lay dormant, though it, like the flowstone, was attuned to the mental commands of both Davvol and Croag. The machinery sparked to life with his mental touch. When Rath was complete, ready to provide access to Dominaria for the armies of Phyrexia, this great machinery would overlay one to the other, the mutable quality of flowstone bridging the gap between planes in one final expenditure. Until then, the ease of a transference was limited by many factors, the closer to Rath's final form, the better. The size of the attempted transference and physical distance from the Stronghold's control machinery made a difference as well. The only variable was apparently the strength of mind of the steward or evincar. As always, Davvol trusted his mental abilities.

First in the valley, he sensed the machinery powering to life, softening the flowstone over an area measuring in square miles. Pressure built within his mind, an avalanche of malleable stone poised overhead, threatening to engulf him. Just beyond the promontory the land sank as if undermined by some great cavern beneath. Edges to the valley appeared as flowstone sloughed downhill.

As the flowstone continued to evacuate, the machinery built up the lower sides and generally shaped the valley into the picture Davvol held for it—slightly crescent shaped with weathered southern slopes and a steep cliff face to the north. His consciousness plunged into the land, following the forces at work. The pressure eased, the incredible raw weight of the flowstone falling away as the valley took its basic form. The machinery then began to pull details from Davvol's thoughts—from the memory of his trip to Dominaria. The seeker opening the portal for him had promised the perfect site, enclosed and isolated, and such had been delivered. Davvol spent days memorizing the finer detail, from the spicy pine scent to the cool touch of dew-laden fern. Now he transferred that detail to the Stronghold's control machinery, and again his mind strained under the weight of his undertaking. Flowstone leapt up in columns and spikes, filling out to become trees and bushes and grass. They stood in frozen relief, a true-to-life forest valley apparently sculpted from simple sandstone.

Only it was not so simple. It was an incredible display of power, both from Davvol and from the flowstone itself.

The process continued, memory becoming reality in this artificial valley. Now buildings rose up, adding to a renewed mental weight. Never before had Davvol felt his mind so completely at work, the machinery simply taking all he allowed. He saw animals in the forest and people on the streets and walks between buildings. They moved— were alive—and many stared up into a sky turned suddenly dark. Voices cried, shouted, and screamed. Davvol stood on the threshold of worlds and planes, looking between the chaos of the multiverse as the great machinery folded one into the other. The people were aware of Rath, of *him*, and many fell to the ground out of abject fear for what they could not understand.

Several hundred lives, the town residents, were but tiny sparks within his consciousness. The true life carried across the hole he had opened in the void, their sobs and screams of terror piercing the background roll of Rath's eternal thunderstorm. Their tormented cries distracted Davvol, forcing the machinery to pull stronger at his mind. Slowly Rath's steward sank to the ground, his hands splayed down against the flowstone promontory as he came to his knees under the stress. Still he did not take his eyes off the valley, then the pressure receded, and the forces raised by the machinery brought Davvol back from the threshold. The tortured wailing faded. He felt a few small sparks of life evade his final grasp. Some were lost in the chaos between Rath and Dominaria.

It was done.

A deer sprang nearby, jumping from verdant valley to the lip of Rath's unnatural flowstone landscape. It froze in fright then scrambled back to the safety of trees and undergrowth. Far in the distance, carried to Davvol by the final vestiges of his connection with the Stronghold's control machinery, came the terrified cries of people now gazing into an unfamiliar and hostile sky of dark clouds and vivid lightning. These were the newest residents of Rath.

Davvol smiled fully. These people would be taken as slaves. Davvol planned to accelerate the schedule and bring Rath closer to the point of final convergence, then Rath itself would cross the threshold and merge with Dominaria, bringing with it the armies of Phyrexia. Davvol would rule Rath and open the way for Phyrexia. He saw no other future. Even Croag would admit this now.

When he turned back Croag and the portal were gone. Davvol stood alone over his valley, left with his creation. The steward laughed, his harsh voice carried away on the sharp wind. That was fine by him. He felt no desire to share the moment, preferring the solitude of his success—his first success, but certainly not his last.

* * * * *

Storm clouds over Benalia hid stars and the blurry reflection of the Glimmer Moon. The Null Moon, a hard point of light often mistaken for a bright star, had recently cleared the overcast horizon. Only one being in the Capashen village of DeLatt knew the Null Moon's exact position, no need of direct sight to sense the satellite. Its lips curled back revealing a feral smile of sharp, gnashing teeth. Thunder crashed, shaking clay tiles and rattling window panes.

The blackness that formed inside the small courtyard had little to do with the dark Dominarian night. Pale gray flagstones reflected a cascade of lightning into the most remote corners. The bright wash bathed everything in a preternatural glow for one split second, except the round portal of pitch dark that sat tucked behind a wall of hanging plants. The home of the village magistrate framed three sides of the courtyard, the fourth opening up onto a wrought-iron fence with a gate offset on the right-hand side. An engraved metal shield over the gate offered a welcome to those who passed within. Though the gate remained locked, three figures moved among the shadows of the courtyard. Lightning flashed again, the scar standing out in the dark sky for a long second as violent thunder assailed the earth.

Croag already felt at home here. The electrically charged air felt invigorating, reminding the Inner Circle member of Rath and certain portions of Phyrexia—and something more, a sense pulling at Croag's mind in a way that more closely spoke of home and *kindred*. He could detect the barest scent of glistening oil—the scent exuded by meat once bathed in the vats. Croag chattered a brief acknowledgement to the seeker who had found this place. The minor Phyrexian stepped back with a groveling bow, taking a subordinate position to Croag and Davvol.

Davvol studied the surroundings, no doubt committing every last detail to his extraordinary memory. Croag did not mind—encouraged it, in fact. Davvol proved ever more useful as the centuries played out. Though he had yet to kill Urza Planeswalker, his improvements to negators could not be gainsaid, and his management of Rath was adequate, if uninspired. He had surprised Croag those months ago, able to guide a transference between Rath and Dominaria. That was not to say that the Inner Circle member considered the other dangerous. Davvol displayed no real aggression or ambition, not in any way the Phyrexian could gauge at least. Perhaps in another century or two he could be trouble, but who could plan so far ahead when today there was so much to accomplish?

A twinge, more direct this time, centered Croag's attention toward a pair of glass-paned doors. "There," he said, a simple screech of sound. It pointed one skeletal finger.

Rath's steward squinted in the direction, unable to pierce the gloom so deeply as Croag with his uncompleated eyes. "Where?" he asked as more lightning streaked across the sky. "The doors?" He moved off, his armored boots scraping against flagstone.

Croag moved quietly, making only his usual metallic rasp and the occasional scrape of metal bands against stone. With the booming thunder and a damp wind rattling the metal gate, the sounds of their passage should go unnoticed. If not, there would be one less Dominarian. Davvol tried the door latches, and they opened easily on well-oiled hinges. Croag was the first through, shredding the diaphanous white curtains as he passed. He moved directly to the side of a bed on which an old man slept. Weak and frail looking, as were most Dominarians, Croag found it difficult to reconcile the dark call that pulled him toward the human. He was not a sleeper but something very similar.

Reports from Dominarian agents—the sleepers, negators and seekers who came into contact with many of the weaker races—had spoken of such humans. Meat creatures with a dark affinity and a special strength build-ing within that drew the Phyrexians toward them. Croag had considered such reports in error, confusing the nature of humans born in black mana environments with true Phyrexian purity. The Vec and others now living in Rath knew such empathy.

Croag had changed his opinion when he had walked Davvol's new settlement. Most of the people there had fled in terror, but one did not. Donning chain mail and mounted on a similarly armored horse, he came at the Phyrexian, intent on destroying Croag—no fear or hesi-tation showing in his steel-blue eyes. Croag had felt that connection then, as if both beings recognized in the other that which was black—that which was *Phyrexian*. It brought the human strength enough to resist and to fight. Spurring his mount, he thundered in at the alien creature with furious hatred. The Inner Circle member destroyed the human with very little conscious effort. He plunged his talons deep into the lesser creature's brain to draw out what final information he could. Delicious in its intensity, Croag reveled in the sensations that only meat could know.

In light of this attack Croag had come here, to the home of a Benalish nobleman serving as village magis-trate. Here a seeker had recently sensed that spark of dark matter in the soul of a human. Again Croag knew the pull toward one not of his kind—but similar.

With a gesture from the Phyrexian, Davvol placed the artifact Croag had ordered him to carry near the human's head. A braided metal cable uncoiled and slithered across the pillow to set itself into the old man's ear, whis-pering a series of tones and noises. At normal volume, issuing forth from one of the larger Phyrexian war engines, the sound would frighten and confuse. At sufficiently high levels it might even be enough to interfere with the nerve processes. Here, at such a muted volume, it would merely induce a deep slumber. The human would not awaken, though he might remain aware of the nightmares that Croag would subject him to. The Phyrexian rested his left hand over the man's face, first and fifth talons rotating inward to burrow through flesh and bone above the temples and into the soft brain matter beneath. It was not enough for permanent damage, not yet, but meant to draw upon memories of the sleeping man. Croag was searching for answers.

The old man's eyes opened. Alarm and then terror flashing through them, quickly replaced by a furious hatred. This was not supposed to happen. His hands came out from the covers to fasten around Croag's wrist. Blood ran down his arms and splashed against his face as the skin on his hands split against the razor-sharpness of Croag's construction. Still he did not let go and actually budged Croag's hand, forcing the talons to cut laterally through sensitive brain tissue. His hands locked as the seizures took him, and he thrashed in the bed. Croag dug deeper, pulling out what information he could.

His name was Jaffry Capashen, son of Steffan and distant cousin of his current clan leader Thomas. The concepts and context of family and clan and caste all flooded the Phyrexian's mind. There was no time to enjoy the sensations, the knowledge pulled deeper to be reexamined later as the frail body faded into death.

Croag drove inward, cracking bone and squeezing the gray meat for more. He sensed the other's affinity for

Phyrexian methods and manners, the reason no doubt he had resisted the artifact. Dim images of years spent in a large clan manor swam at the Phyrexian. He saw brief memories of a battle fought in service to Benalia, an arranged marriage and the birth of two children, the death of his wife Myrr, and the taking of this assignment to the local village where he dispensed justice and collected taxes for his clan.

Croag withdrew his razored talons, leaving behind a pulped mess of bone fragments, brain and blood. He turned to find Davvol waiting patiently, but the seeker was no longer in the room.

Davvol did not wait for the question. "I sent the seeker away," he said calmly. "The old man was certainly never supposed to wake up and defy you. I thought it better for the seeker to not see a failure here. It might cause," he paused, "problems."

Immune to the embarrassment of feelings, Croag still knew of the respect due his status and that in Davvol's eyes he was now being subject to very careful ridicule. The Phyrexian hunched down, not to diminish himself but in preparation of attack, though Croag restrained himself. Davvol remained too useful a tool to dispose of at this time.

"Yes," he said in a metallic screech. "At this time." It was not an answer to Davvol's comment but a reinforcing of his own thoughts.

Davvol apparently sensed some of the danger he stood in, turning back toward the ruined mess of a man who slowly soaked the white linen dark red. "Anything useful?"

Use would be determined later, but certainly Croag had been given a measure to pause and consider. "There are two offspring," he said slowly.

A plan formed, reflecting Davvol's efforts with the Phyrexian negators. Perhaps Croag could guide the development of a few Dominarian natives who showed affinity for the Phyrexians similar to Jaffry. Such an empathy was rare enough to justify further investigation at the least. If such affinity could be manipulated . . . this he would not speak of to Davvol. It was not truly the steward's concern. This was a matter which demanded Phyrexian attention, and hope as the steward might, Davvol would never be of Phyrexia, never compleat.

"Urza," Croag said, remembering one other image. "Urza Planeswalker was known to this human. He has been here." Croag could not afford to take chances wherever Urza might be involved. "I want an account of everywhere Urza Planeswalker has been tracked on Dominaria, everywhere humans with a dark affinity have been noticed. Seekers must be sent to investigate those areas." If there was a relationship between the two he would find it. A taloned hand slashed at the air between them. "You will kill Urza Planeswalker, soon."

Davvol nodded slowly, obviously unable to help a look of resignation. "This can be done," he said, echoing Croag's words of so many years before.

The Phyrexian did not wait for further conversation. With one final glare, eyes burning like hot coals within his cavernous sockets, he stalked from the room and back toward his portal. He had had enough of Dominaria, but he would return soon.

Chapter 14

Fire rained down in a burning cascade, washing over Urza's arm and scorching the golden finish on his staff as the planeswalker failed to move in time. A flaming, gelatinous substance which stuck even to his form of energy seared into him at a dozen places now. Each wound drew off that much more of his strength, leaving him more vulnerable to the negator's next attack. Urza's options were rapidly decreasing in direct proportion with the waning power left at his command.

The planeswalker had come back to Efuan Pincar to see after the bloodlines in this small nation. He hoped to mix the best results from here into a weak Femeref line, rejuvenating it. Though marriage and preconception treatment of the parents with the Eugenics Matrix was preferred, the 'walker was prepared for more drastic methods as necessary. With a few genetic samples from the local subjects, he could *cut in* appropriate traits and qualities—*post*conception. As a rule, he tried to avoid such procedures, but with the strange loss of the bloodlines in Femeref, Urza lost one of his best. The people simply vanished, by all accounts just over

181

ten years ago, and only a few insane tales of a night of storms were left to offer any explanation. This was a matter of needs versus means. Dominaria's safety required it.

Urza still couldn't be sure what had drawn him back to his old home in Efuan Pincar—the remote cottage he once shared with Xantcha now falling into ruin. In this place the two of them worked on ways to defeat Phyrexian incursions into Dominaria and later, with the help of a local boy Ratepe, had finally won the battle against Gix. Nostalgia? Not likely. Maybe he came to remember Xantcha whom he'd traveled with for so long. She would've understood the necessity of the bloodlines, he felt certain. The Phyrexian couldn't have simply been waiting for him. Either this location was checked often, and Urza had simply chosen the wrong time, or the negators were getting better at tracking him without giving away their own presence. The planeswalker preferred to believe the former, so he did.

Now the cabin burned, having caught a spray from the negator's fire-throwing weapon. Small trees sprouting up in the clearing were also afire. A sooty smoke trailed the area, the gritty clouds having trouble escaping into the sky and beginning to wear on Urza's visibility. The large creature-construct appeared to have little trouble tracking the planeswalker. A long arm snaked past a blazing pine tree, the crackling flames of little bother to it, swiping at Urza's side and scoring bloody furrows from ribs to hip. Such an attack would rarely have shown blood, the manifestation of energy bleeding away from Urza's consciousness, but on top of the burning wounds the 'walker was simply unable to regenerate the illusion after clawing.

A large dark shape loomed through a hazy black cloud, standing twice as tall as Urza. Its incredibly bloated body expanded and contracted with an over-exaggerated breathing motion. One arm nearly dragging the ground ended with razored claws. The other looked stunted, but in actuality it had been replaced by a type of slender cannon that spewed the dangerous substance. Urza swept back, avoiding a new stream of fiery gel and focusing mana into a lightning strike. A blue-white arc leapt from his fingers and smashed into the negator's carapace of hard, glossy black skin. The energy danced over the outer form, all of it drawn over to the Phyrexian's left hip where it entered. The glossy carapace split down the outside of the left leg. Corrupted flesh sizzled and burned as the lightning was somehow channeled down into the ground and away from anything vital.

This negator was immune to natural fire and resistant to lightning. The two creatures Urza had found time to summon early on had met with fiery deaths, and now the 'walker was losing too much mental strength to tap more mana. It was a hard realization for Urza Planeswalker to admit. He was losing this fight.

When one understands the nature of a thing, one knows what it is capable of—a saying once passed to him and his brother both from Tocasia, the old Argivian archaeologist who first taught the brothers about the recovery and restoration of artifacts. His attention was divided between an attempt to build his powers up and searching for the Phyrexian he had lost again among the thick gritty smoke. It took Urza a moment to understand why he had dredged up that old memory, then transposed it. Once a person understands the capabilities of a thing he might also know its nature! The creature was disgorging an incredible amount of burning fluid, but even the Phyrexians could not violate the laws of conservation. That substance had to be stored or somehow produced by the negator. The bloated body and its bellowlike breathing suggested a combination of both.

As a planeswalker, Urza was capable of casting all colors of magic, but his first love, his initial rise to power, had been with artifice. He thumbed a stud on his staff's contoured grip. One of the crescent-shaped tines on the staff's head reversed itself on a clockwork gear, bringing a special edge to bear. Another switch triggered the harmonics that attacked glistening oil. The 'walker had made adjustments to the sonic device after its failure with the one negator decades before, hoping for an improvement. This he received, but not much.

The Phyrexian screeched in pain and anger, wading forward through fire and smoke to reach the hated device. The fire cannon tracked in, but a slight tremor in its musculature gave Urza all the edge he needed. The planeswalker swung his staff around, slicing the blades into the creature's shoulder joint—the one that held the slender cannon to the negator. The blade, magically sharpened, cut through reinforced skin and metal supports. The cannon fell to one side, a gush of glistening oil and burning gel vomiting forth before the negator's body clamped down on the wound. Still, the escaped gel burned into the Phyrexian's outer flesh, distracting it even more.

Urza was already moving, circling about the negator and trying nothing fancier than slicing at its bloated body. Now the Phyrexian suffered the same problem as Urza, deciding between the strength and attention necessary to deal with its physical wounds and how much to spend on the 'walker. It became a race to see who could strike a fatal blow first—a race the Phyrexian lost. Urza sliced long and deep across its wide back and then quickly swept back to avoid the unstoppable gush of gelatinous fluid.

There was no stanching this wound, and once the substance was exposed to air the negator apparently lost the immunity it possessed that allowed it to store the material. It screeched in agony, high pitched and actually painful to Urza's hearing as the gel continued to eat away at it. The planeswalker picked up the severed arm carefully and moved back from the conflagration. The scent of scorched oil and burnt meat followed him.

He stood back and watched his old cottage burn.

* * * * *

Rayne slipped out of her usual work habit, donning instead the special garment she had designed for increased protection. A long jacket of blue cotton, thin pads had been sewn into its entirety and specially woven steel threads reinforced the chest and abdomen area. It was a bit heavier than she preferred, but when dealing with Phyrexian artifice it seemed better to be safe than comfortable.

Ehlanni assisted, an academy tutor who had proven herself very adept in disassembly and evaluation. An added benefit, Ehlanni was of a human tribe that shared the Hurloon Mountains with the minotaurs. Powerfully built, she could be counted on to help move the large objects and test equipment. Also, in terms Rayne had once heard Gatha employ, Ehlanni knew how to take a hit. A Phyrexian device had blown up in her face a year ago, and she had walked away from it, though Barrin's best healer-mages spent a good week restoring her to full health. Again, this was just another precaution for dealing with Phyrexian machinery.

"Only not quite machinery, this," Rayne said softly, bending down to examine the cannonlike device, a weapon which, according to Urza, had once sprayed a fiery, gelatinous substance that clung even to Urza's pure-energy form and burned ceaselessly.

What the 'walker had not mentioned was its origin. Rayne first assumed that it had either been taken from an artifact creature like the dragon engines or was more of a handheld device. She swung her wrist-mounted lens over to peer at the destroyed mounting hardware. What could only be artificial fibers exuded from a steel coil and burrowed into a small blackened lump. She had wondered at this earlier, until cutting into it and discovering it to be a slice of tissue similar to human muscle. This close, she also smelled the charred scent of the flesh. The fibers were bonded to the meat by a process she had never seen before. It was at once hideous and wondrous.

Ehlanni did not share Rayne's latter sentiment. "What is it, then?" she asked.

Rayne squinted and readjusted her looking piece. "I would guess that it was once part of a Phyrexian negator." She felt at one of the fibers with a bared finger, cool and smooth to the touch. Flexible. "Some kind of special metal alloy, maybe a metal enhanced form of cloth." Who could tell? "Urza must have removed it after a recent fight. These fibers are actually fixed to the muscle as if they were large nerve endings. I've found three other cables with similar function, including the thick metal-braid tube that had residue of the fire-gel." She looked up at her assistant. "Do you think this creature could be biologically producing the burning gel?"

"I think I'd rather not find out," Ehlanni said with a look of disgust for the artifact. "You're saying this was actually part of a living being? An artifice graft?"

The chancellor nodded. "Far beyond anything we are capable of here at the academy." Rayne had serious doubts saying so about Urza. Master artificer that he was, Urza almost certainly knew how it was done, but would he ever attempt to duplicate it? Would she herself if she understood how it was accomplished? Her initial reaction said no, but then immediately her mind seized upon circumstances where such grafting might be desirable. It could be useful for replacement of an arm lost to misfortune or war or as a treatment for a birth defect. It was such a small step from there to improving on the natural order. Improved eyesight? Stronger heart? Faster reflexes?

"Where would it end?" she asked no one in particular, bending back to work.

The magnifying glass brought her a level of detail she could only have guessed at without it, and even so, the intricacy hinted that buried even deeper than she could see might be found a third level of complexity.

"It violates the law of simplicity. At some point the construction of this device should begin to get simpler as we deconstruct it, not more complex, unless the

Phyrexians are able to work on a scale we can't even observe much less touch." In the back of her mind she recalled the Thran Tome and its suggestion of artifice and flesh blended on the cellular level. Excitement touched her voice, warmed her skin as she considered artifice on such a level of mastery. "Urza never mentioned anything about this. I wonder if the Phyrexians are improving or just sending their better designs after him these days?" Or both?

"Are you feeling well?" Ehlanni frowned her confusion and not a little shock. "The closer I study these creatures and their work the more I see that Urza was right in his pursuit of *anything* which might destroy them. What I can't believe is that others haven't noticed this as well." She shook her head. "I swear you seem to be admiring them."

Lost in her observations, Rayne barely acknowledged the comment. "There is something to be said for the *theory* behind such accomplishments."

Ehlanni reached out and tapped the device, her finger thick and blurry under Rayne's glass. "Would you like to see one of these grafted to your husband?"

Rayne recoiled at the question, the horror of such an idea hitting her like a slap. She realized then that earlier she had considered exactly that. Shivering for a deathly cold touch caressing her back and scalp, Rayne pressed such thoughts from her mind. Ehlanni was right, this was nothing to be admired. No matter the *potential* for good, such artifice was only in the hands of those who used it in the birth of abominations and the support of evil desires. Improved eyesight and reflexes were nothing. Where would it end, she had wondered?

The scent of the charred meat now suddenly stung at her sinuses and burned acrid in her throat. She swallowed dryly and removed the wrist-mounted magnifying glass as if it represented the same principle of augmentation. This type of procedure would create a never-ending process of replacement and refinement until . . . what? The word came to her at once, both appropriate and obscene in the same instant: until compleat.

* * * * *

Timein had scheduled no meetings. He had, in fact, dismissed for the day those few students who had left the academy to join him at the Colony. He felt exhausted in that pleasant way which reminded someone of a full day's valuable effort. From the new well he helped dig to the students he—hopefully—enlightened on a few of the finer points in thaumaturgic studies. He needed a warm bath and perhaps some time for private reflection. He was looking forward to an early retirement for the day.

Why, then, was there a light on in his home?

The sorcerer did not think to be worried. Nothing dangerous happened on Tolaria—not counting Urza's catastrophes of course. He paused a moment upon discovering the door to his home still locked. His mind still puzzled on this as he turned the key in the lock and swung the door open. Someone waited within. The man's back was to the door and he studied a shelf of books all written by Timein. Timein saw only blond hair trimmed at shoulder length and a coat of finely tailored leather.

"Can I help you?" Timein asked, noticing the golden staff leaning nearby—its headpiece of joints, wires and gears—just as the figure turned. It was Tolaria's one recurring catastrophe—Urza Planeswalker.

"Timein, it is good to see you again." The 'walker looked about the single-room home. He nodded approvingly. "You've done well here."

Timein steeled himself against the false flattery, doubting Urza ever lived in such fashion. "It's simple," he said of his surroundings and the Colony both, "but it suits." He crossed his arms over a narrow chest. "It pales next to the academy, of course, but then we've had far less to work with in the way of material and resources."

If Urza caught the reference to the island's slowly deteriorating state, the 'walker either did not care or was more concerned with other subjects. The two stared at each other for a silent moment before Timein reminded himself that Urza was not of true flesh and so would win any staring contest.

"What is it you need, Urza?"

The 'walker looked nonplussed. "You act as if I've done something against you, Timein. I can read it in your posture as well as your voice. Have I given you cause for anger or grief?"

Timein unfolded his thin arms, relenting only a little. Pulling off his hat, the sorcerer tossed it over to his bed. "If you haven't you are likely about to," he said, loosening the drawstrings on his cuffs for comfort.

This apparently amused the planeswalker. "Sorcerer *and* soothsayer?" He smiled, his face lined and careworn as a middle-aged man. "Do you think you know why I am here?"

Nodding, Timein moved over to his desk and leaned back against its edge. Urza, he noticed, had a way of wearing people down very quickly. He wondered how Barrin stood up to it for all those centuries.

"You're here to bring me and the others back into your program," he predicted. "Come to bring the strays home?"

"I want your help, yes," Urza said, shaking his head. He picked up his staff and laid it in the crook of one arm. "But I've never forced anyone to do work he hasn't wanted or at least agreed to do, ever, Timein. Remember, you never complained about serving under Gatha's instruction. And so long as you didn't I needed you there."

In Timein's view, Gatha had kept control of the younger man's life those early years. The sorcerer had never had the chance to complain. "You're saying I have the choice to refuse you or not?"

Urza shrugged. "Of course."

Timein almost said it then—refused without hearing the proposal to be rid of Urza Planeswalker. The Colony was Timein's home now. It was a place where occasionally Tolarian students sought refuge when they could no longer reconcile conscience with the work being done at the academy. Some returned to the school, eventually, but others were often ready to take their place here. So long as Timein hosted this refuge, he wanted it kept clean of Urza's influence.

"What do you want of me?" the sorcerer asked.

Urza accepted the invitation to speak with a simple nod. "I need more detailed processes for judging empathies—a person's connection to the lands of Dominaria and any predisposition toward . . . *other* . . . lands as well."

Toward Phyrexia, Timein translated. He had no doubt that Urza could talk straight out about it but was hedging for the sorcerer's benefit. "Why not do it yourself?"

Urza spread his hands. "No one is as adept at these magics as you are, Timein. You are a mage of the natural body, the near-physical spirit. By inclination and more than three millennia of work, I am still primarily an artificer. Not even walking the planes changes you so much that you deny your basic nature." He lowered his arms. "Nothing you develop will be—can be—used to change someone's nature, if that helps, but the Bloodlines project will continue, and the better my tools the fewer my mistakes."

Now *that* admission rattled Timein's belief, if slightly. Urza Planeswalker admitting to mistakes had to be a rare sight indeed. His cynical side argued that the 'walker could afford to save such momentary admissions for just such occasions. Dealing with Urza reinforced Timein's admiration for Barrin.

"Directly or indirectly, I would still rather not," Timein said, surprised that he did not say no at once. It felt more as if he was slowly talking himself out of it. Obviously, Urza's appeal on behalf of the bloodlines subjects had hit him hard. "I've worked hard to help this colony survive on its own and to make a small refuge here away from the madness of the academy."

"I have no wish to disrupt the colony," Urza said. "I wouldn't think to spoil your exemplary work here. I'm simply asking *you*. Indirectly you help all the time, Timein. This refuge you've created gives students something we never thought to include—a place to escape for a time and so come back with minds fresh and unburdened by too many years of pressured work. Also, there's your silence. Barrin and I would trust you to leave Tolaria, but once away you could ruin the Bloodlines project by making it public. What local nations did not find out and interfere in, the Phyrexian sleepers would." He looked at Timein with frank interest. "If you are so opposed, why haven't you done this?"

Timein couldn't help but wince at Urza's detailed evaluation of the sorcerer's work and life. He felt as if Urza had laid bare his mind and knew better the sorcerer's reasons and motivations than Timein did himself. Truth be told, Timein knew that so long as he remained on Tolaria he wasn't truly free of the academy and its work. He was still a part of the pattern and likely forever would be. Had he been waiting all these years for someone to arrive and offer him a reason to come back?

"I'll do it," he said softly. "On my own time and without anyone else's involvement, but I'll do it." He shuddered, knowing the nightmares he would open himself to because of this. "I've often wondered, Urza, what my research would show me of your nature. Have you ever wanted to look into it?"

"All the time, Timein." Urza nodded, slow and slightly sorrowful. "All the time." Then, with a final tight smile, the 'walker was gone.

Timein cursed both Urza and himself for the necessity that had drawn him back into the 'walker's plans. If his work could prevent the suffering of people in Dominaria, didn't he owe it to them to try? He sat behind his desk, leaning his lanky frame back in the padded chair as he stared up at the ceiling. Urza just might be right. That was the problem Timein faced anytime the 'walker came for assistance.

If Urza was right, would Timein's years of inaction necessarily be proven wrong?

Chapter 15

Summoned to the Stronghold's throne room, Davvol smothered his anger over Croag's blatant ploy to show the steward as subservient. His armored boots struck heavily against the floor, grinding his rage against the flowstone surface. Before entering the room he settled a neutral mask over his face.

"You requested my presence, Croag?" The words were drained of any emotion, spoken between thin, humorless lips.

The member of Phyrexia's Inner Circle seemed melded into the huge metal monstrosity that was the Stronghold's throne. Sharp edges gleamed dully in the cold lights of the room, and the ridged back shone with a light sheen of oil. Even as uncomfortable as it looked, Davvol craved it for his own—to be shared with no one.

"You were inspecting the machinery?" Croag asked, voice full of rasps and squeals. "Down in the secondary attractors?"

Not that Davvol needed the reminder because the summons had come while he was doing an inspection only added fuel to his ire. Flowstone production was up to levels never before known to Rath, pushing back the energy curtain that surrounded the artificial plane.

"Yes," he finally answered. "Some structural supports gave way last week from poor calibration of the bladed dials."

The screws turned easier now with Vec blood to grease the equipment, the responsible workers having been made a proper example of. Davvol wondered briefly how well the Inner Circle member would act as a lubricant. Very well, he thought—glistening oil being so much a part of his body.

"You have a *request?*" he asked, stressing the word. The summoning message from Croag had used "demand."

Some bands wrapped up over Croag's face, trailing oil over the taught gray skin that surrounded his mouth. His voice did not sound muffled when he spoke, as if the sounds were not made by his throat or mouth but simply reverberated from his entire being.

"I would like you to conduct a new transfer," the Phyrexian said.

Davvol waited, but nothing more followed. He crossed his arms defiantly, deciding to risk a touch of Croag's displeasure by pressing for more information. "Why?" he asked. When Croag volunteered less, it usually meant the Phyrexian trod uncertain ground—like the night they both visited Benalia.

The Inner Circle member waited a moment, as if deciding what or how much to say. "Our sleepers in Askaranton reported a skirmish with a large number of warriors. Some possessed heavy affinities for Phyrexia. These warriors were not acting on their own interests but for Askaranton's rival. Dominarians call such warriors mercenaries. Phyrexia might call them negators. I wish to assess their level of threat."

Croag was admitting that the Coracin was needed for more than the simple stewardship of Rath—even needed for something other than killing Urza Planeswalker. That concession alone was worth quite a bit. It was a simple enough request, Davvol decided.

"Where and when?" he asked.

"The armies are traveling back to their own lands now. We will meet them once they arrive."

"You want me to bring them here, to Rath," Davvol said, predicting the request.

"No," Croag replied, the red embers burning dully in the dark recesses of his eye sockets. "I wish you to send an army there. To Dominaria. To Keld."

* * * * *

War cries echoed off the steep passes that lead deeper into the Keldons' mountain nation. The grinding internal noises of immense mechanical engines roared, and massive treads chewed at these softer, lowland grounds. Fire spewed out of heads forged into the shape of dragons and demons, raining a burning substance over rock and earth and Keldon warriors. For a very few, it was all they could do to stay on their feet while the fire ate down to bone. Others, too caught up in their own bloodlust, ignored the pain and fought on until they finally dropped lifeless. Blades and armor were splashed with dark ooze and glistening oil which sprayed from engines. One massive engine rocked and then toppled, its treads ripped from heavy iron wheels and internal mechanisms so ruined that balance could no longer be maintained. It fell onto a knot of heavy fighting, crushing the black-armored warriors and Keldon footsoldiers alike.

At the head of three warhosts, the battle fury gripping Kreig elevated the witch king to new heights. Filled with the strength of his followers, he stood a titan over the battlefield. The sun's corona licked at his temples, its fiery arms wrapped over his eyes coloring the field red as blood. He stood shoulders brushing mountaintops, raking down avalanches of white snow and gray rock. The cold touch of Keld anchored his feet firmly, and no creatures of Dominaria could shake them loose. He was the witch king, undisputed heir to the supreme army of the Necropolis. He was *Kreig the Immortal*—and in the histories of the Keldon people, nothing more need ever be written.

Laden with plunder taken from the former kingdom of Askaranton, the army had shipped back to their own continent to begin the trek up into the mountains. An enemy encampment had held the main pass. Massive engines of warfare backed a legion of spindly limbed, black-armored troops. At their center stood such beings of grotesque shape and nature that Kreig had been reminded of Gatha's failed subjects. They had leathery black skin, some parts scaled with a natural armor. Some were carrying or melded with strange devices. One immediately leveled an arm at the combined warhost, a stream of hellish energies whipping into several Keldon warriors and burning them alive. Kreig did not know of this enemy or how they might have brought a small army into his lands, but such an act he understood perfectly.

Yelling the war cry handed down his line from Trohg and Kreyohl before him, Kreig charged forward leading his host to battle.

Three witch kings fought at his side, each in nominal command of a separate warhost. They held the center of the field. Their courage and savage nature excited the warriors around them to greater acts of ferocity, even as those same warriors lent back a portion of their strength to encourage their leaders beyond bounds. No witch king inspired Kreig. He drew from each directly, just as he tapped every warrior brought to the field, filling his mortal shell with their strength and lifeforce. In return he offered them the pinnacle of Keldon achievement to which they might aspire but never reach.

Now even *he* was brought to a standstill against the black abominations that fought with a savagery most Keldons would be hard pressed to match. They shrugged aside lethal blows. Hooked claws, bladed fingers, and artifice weapons struck back with incredible force, enough to rend a regular warrior in one swipe. The enemy warriors in regular black armor were more easily dispatched, arms and legs cut or ripped from the body with ease. He learned after splitting one open that those limbs were merely mechanical extensions, and the true warrior was a stunted growth of a creature hidden away in the main armored shell. It took several sword thrusts through the armored body to finally kill one of the strange knights.

In the fifty years since his ascension, none had stood against the witch king Kreig, not his own people and certainly no outside force. Unlike some *doyen*, Kreig took to the field nearly every year, constantly challenging the world to match him. That these creatures even dared step into his domain offered an insult that demanded punishment, and here they presented a challenge that so far matched the best fight three warhosts offered. In a lesser race this would certainly have raised fear—in a lesser witch king, perhaps doubts or concerns.

In Kreig it engendered a near-blinding rage, lending new strength and stamina to his already terrifying nature.

The caustic scent of his own charred flesh overpowering the smoldering colos horn, Kreig shouldered his way past a stream of burning energy and closed with the largest of the demon-spawn. Nine feet high where its curved back finally hunched forward, head and shoulders actually at a lower level, the creature might once have been humanoid. Its evacuated abdomen was ringed with bands of blackened metal. Several steel tubes sprouted from its upper back, wrapping down to connect where the base of the spine might be on a normal being. Its feral grin of steel teeth was stained with the green-glowing slime. Large crystals set into its upper body threw out searing waves of focused heat which shimmered in the air and burned through armor and flesh. Kreig leapt into an embrace with it, his greatsword held high and angled back down in front of him like a rock scorpion's striking tail.

It moved impossibly fast. Serrated talons fastened onto the witch king's armor, points piercing through to flesh beneath. Its teeth clamped onto the hollow beneath his left arm, and the chest-mounted crystals flared with renewed assaults of scalding heat which seemed to strain at the very bones of his body. The viscous slime on its teeth burned through the wounds and into his blood, lighting his entire body afire. Kreig brought the point of his greatsword down into the muscled joint that held the creature's shoulder and thick, scaled neck. Reveling in his own pain, a sense he had not known for decades, Kreig drew hard upon the battle frenzy of his warriors and continued to place his full strength behind his sword. It drove through, spearing the creature along the length of its body. It shuddered, claws now removed from the witch king's body and flailing the air, but its teeth set in harder, crunching bone and rending flesh.

It was as if a giant hand had reached down to swat at the Keldon who had thought to place himself on par with the gods. An eruption of flame picked him up and lifted him into the air. The roaring thunderclap deafened his ears to the shouts of his followers and the metal grinding of the war engines they fought. Acrid smoke clogged his nose, ran acidic down his throat and into his lungs, and then he was falling back to earth and into the charred ruin that had once been his opponent. The ground rushed up with bone-jarring speed, embracing him with crushing force.

The witch king rose shakily to his feet. His armor gone, bare skin braced with blisters and angry burns, he barely felt the chill touch of the air. Blood trickled and then clotted as his wounds responded to the powers the combined warhost still engendered within him. Where the green spittle clung to him, those wounds did not close immediately and continued to pain him with agony like molten iron dripped into his veins.

He could not remember coming so close to the threshold of death, ever, yet here he stood, in defiance of the

Keldon Necropolis for eighty-six years of life and enough mortal wounds to slay a full warhost. Kreig pulled his greatsword from the foul remains of the creature, its length deformed from the explosion but still deadly in its weight and edge. Laughing his rage at the sky, the witch king stood bare-skinned against the battle continuing around him.

Whatever these things were, they could be killed, and he was still Kreig. He could not know defeat by mortal hands.

*   *   *   *   *

Snow-chilled lands fell away to blankets of hoarfrost. An overcast sky of gray cotton, touched darker with pockets of rain, promised a storm. A light rumble voiced the heavens' discontent—answered only by the dull echoing of footfalls and shouted commands from within the mountain pass that led to the lower lands surrounding Keld.

Warriors in full armor led the way from the pass, their red leathers and bright metal weapons standing out against the dark ground. They moved with military precision, anxious for battle but still wary of ambush. The lead elements finally trumpeted back an all clear with small instruments made from hollowed-out colos horn. Another band moved from the mountain pass. This was Gatha's personal guard, their armor bearing his adopted crest—the ancient Keldon sigil for life, from the times before Keld developed a true script for writing. The military procession was followed by a baggage train of three colos pack animals, slaves tending them or laden under packs of their own.

Gatha walked at the center of his guard, nods of respect following his every movement. At times when he passed close to a warrior he received an awkward bow as the Keldon stepped aside. Despite his smaller size, Gatha felt the tallest among them, resplendent in finely designed armor of the best Keldon craftsmanship. He wore metal greaves, chestplate and shoulder mantle, trimmed in red leather and a black, heavy cloth cape with everything tooled in gold. He carried a riding crop—a leather-wrapped handle on a sharp, hooked piece of steel that might have been called a footman's pick back in Argive. The crop served more as a badge of rank. Gatha never attempted to ride the large colos beasts.

The traipse down from his mountain labs caused a regrettable delay in many experiments, but it was necessary after reading the reports and then spending long hours with Kreig in honest conversation. The witch king's detailed description of the invaders sent chills through Gatha's spine, and then had come Kreig's reluctant admission of what had followed the battle—the enemy's method of retreat. Such an event Gatha would prefer to consider a bloodlust-spawned illusion.

Bodies of the Keldon fallen, those that had not been *taken*, Kreig had ordered carried deeper into the mountains for burial beneath rocky cairns. One minor witch king had been interred in the Necropolis. One never returned. The Keldons were most distressed about *that*, one of their chosen denied the Necropolis and so eventual resurrection. In the Keldons' long history, not one warlord had ever failed to be brought home to rest.

Signs of the battle were still obvious in the scorched rock and the scraps of blood-stained leather. All metal had been scavenged, including that of a fallen war engine—pieced down so Gatha never did get a fair look at its original design. The warming air, moist with spring's coming, held a touch of carrion in it. Gatha paused and knelt over one large patch of ground stained black. He pinched up some dirt between his fingers, rubbing it and then bringing it closer to his nose. It felt gritty but not as true soil should. It was a fine dirt ruined with the saturation of some foul substance. The scent gave it away. Oil. Glistening oil.

"Phyrexia," Gatha whispered, naming the foe.

He placed a sample of the soil in a metal container and moved on, his dark eyes sharply deconstructing the battlefield and missing no scrap, trail of blood, or splash of gore. He found some globs of dark flesh that no scavenging bird had touched set about an area of scorched, pockmarked rock. It was the remnants of the thing Kreig had destroyed. A negator? He gathered every last piece of the ruined meat. Genetic comparisons back inside his labs would confirm it as Phyrexian, and the rogue tutor actually considered this procurement of fresh genetic material a small boon to his work. Who could tell what advantages the Phyrexians had bred into their minions since the samples he had stolen from Tolaria, advantages Gatha would attempt to duplicate for the Keldon people, breeding them into the bloodlines he controlled?

It was thought among most Keldons that there was little Gatha could not accomplish, but one must prove himself worthy of any requests and then more so if the magic was to take hold. Of course there would never be any recriminations, no resentment or rancor held, if the request was denied or the process failed. Not since Varden *the foolish* had anyone challenged Gatha's decisions. Never since Kreig's rise to power and the preternaturally long life that followed had another thought to criticize Gatha's presence in Keld. Such were the conveniences of deification, except that now the game had changed with the arrival of Phyrexians.

Gatha did not actually require tests to tell him that his theory was correct. He knew, just as he felt sure that the force Kreig had fought was little more than a scouting party sent to investigate. How had they learned of his work? What more did they know now? He stood from gathering another sample and looked up into the blanket of gray clouds, expecting to see the "face of the sky" staring back down on him. Gatha would like to believe that Kreig's explanation had been more of the religious trappings that layered their lives these days, except that the witch king had always seemed to know the truth behind it all even if he did enjoy the benefits as Gatha did.

That left the method of enemy withdrawal as a fact. That the sky had suddenly roiled with steel clouds broken only by cascades of lightning—red, green, and glaring white. Eyes of gray metal within black orbs stared down out of the chaotic sky like twin cold suns. A face of pale skin, sagging and without animation like the flesh of a corpse, appeared over the battlefield. It was cut only by a thin, cruel mouth that issued orders to the invading army in booming thunder. Kreig and others all reported feeling a pull tugging at them as enemy troops stepped away and simply faded from plain sight. Several Keldons surrendered to the arcane forces, vanishing under the gaze of those cold eyes and the call of its thunderous voice. Gatha did not want to believe it, but he did. Kreig had said something to him had made him believe.

Kreig the warrior, the mightiest the nation of Keld had ever seen, had felt afraid.

Dwarfed in power, the witch king had known his first moment of fear, but rather than be cowed, he railed against the forces tugging at him—challenged them. His warriors borrowed from his great strength, rallying. Fewer Keldons slipped away, as with a final scowl of displeasure the creature faded, and the sky cleared. Kreig's combined warhost had stood alone on the battlefield.

With the Phyrexians defeated at the hands of the Keldons—*his* Keldons—Gatha hoped for a reprieve. Perhaps they would not return, seeking easier prey elsewhere. Defeat couldn't sit well with them. Defeat never sat well with anyone.

* * * * *

Croag threw the lifeless body to the ground, skull shattered, gray matter mingling with yellowish fluids, white splinters of bone, and red blood. Two weeks he had spent in interrogation of the prisoners Davvol returned with. One every day, no matter how tempting it was to rush through them. He savored the moments—the memories—but also took the time after each to consider the information imparted. Davvol had taught him something of patience, with the other's slow process of improving negators in the steady and relentless hunt of Urza Planeswalker.

He chattered an order to a nearby guard who removed

the corpse. The guard would add it to the others, Keldon and Phyrexian alike, for a seeker to later take the entire store of meat to Phyrexia for the vats. Resources were never to be wasted. Perhaps the Keldon matter would serve to make newts stronger and improve the compleated Phyrexians they would eventually become. In that way, the defeat today would only lead to a greater victory in the next generation.

In a few of the Keldons there had been large deposits of the same essence that the member of the Inner Circle detected in the old man on Dominaria, recognizing in them that which was familiar to his own nature—that dark perfection of the Ineffable from which all else should and would be derived. Only in the old man—a white-mana creature—that dark core repelled Phyrexian influence. In the Keldons, it made them stronger and therefore a threat.

So this was Urza Planeswalker's plan! An army of Dominarians with the physical resistance to meet the invasion on an equal footing. How broad the vision and yet so juvenile in the attempt. Of course Phyrexian substance made Dominarians stronger, bringing them closer to perfection. If the planeswalker had a thousand generations he might hope to spread such resistance over enough of Dominaria to make a difference. Here and now, with the scope Croag sensed, that influence would barely be felt, except, of course, in the Dark One's displeasure.

Organized resistance to Phyrexia's plans for conquest could never be tolerated. The Dark God would see it as Croag's failure. *His* anger would consume the Inner Circle member and deny him continued existence.

Croag must destroy such efforts—subvert them. Davvol would be encouraged to continue testing forces against Keld, so that Croag might receive a better idea of the effectiveness of Urza's current plans. Croag would then destroy the system perpetuating the danger, including the capture and consumption of this Gatha—surely a scion of Urza and possibly with knowledge of the 'walker's private retreats. Other large programs of such a nature must also be located and destroyed.

Chapter 16

Passing through the gatehouse, its gleaming white spires thrusting upward into a blue sky, Ellyn entered the flagstone-paved courtyard of Capashen Manor. She carried a collection of scrolls bundled loosely under one arm, occasionally dropping one and having to stoop for it. They were taxation estimates for local villages. No matter how important they might be, especially this year, she couldn't bring herself to invest much enthusiasm. Why should she care how well the crops came in, so long as the farmer caste supplied the manor with plenty? Instead of the scrolls, her hand itched for the comfortable feel of a sword hilt, for the chance to prove herself.

Strange creatures stalked Capashen lands these days. Monsters, some called them, of black flesh and metal with a taste for devastation. Farms had been left in ruins, and the people were frightened. Some of the clan's best warriors had already taken to the field, leading bands of Benalish soldiers as they tried to protect harvests and clear Capashen territory of these things. Only "some" of the best, though, because *she* hadn't been considered.

Even in the noble Benalish clans, one's position was so often determined beforehand.

Since the marriage of Jaffry Capashen and Myrr Ortovi, her great-grandparents, Ellyn's family line had been relegated to minor status in an attempt to contain any attempts by Clan Ortovi to abuse the relationship. Ellyn's parents followed a similar course, as taxation officials and village magistrates and minor diplomats depending on the year and needs of the clan. Ellyn had been born . . . *different*. She challenged the rules whenever possible, stubbornly pushing forward. Whenever a person of higher stature made a mistake, they turned around to find her ready to assume the greater position. She learned the ways of the sword, drawn to weapons like a piece of metal to lodestone. Sometimes she felt that the metal called to her, a feeling she could not shake, as if a piece of her were missing.

Ellyn heard a whisper at the back of her mind, felt a dark presence seconds before her sharp ears picked up the sound of booted feet hammering against the bleached flagstone courtyard. Shouts of alarm echoed through the manor followed by a screeching snarl. Ellyn turned away from the manor front, walking swiftly at first and then running for the corner, a trail of scrolls bouncing on the flagstones behind her. She slid around to the east side of the great building, where the manor's shadow fell, just as three guards raced up from the other direction to catch the creature between them and her.

The semblance of a young dragon, it was like nothing Ellyn had ever heard described. Five feet at the shoulder, the creature's leathery wings stretched up another three feet over its mutilated back. Its head and neck were devoid of flesh or muscle, cleaned down to bone. Thin metal cables connected the eye socket to the base of the skull, and long, coarse hair sprouted from the thick scale armoring its shoulders. Its four legs and a long barbed tail were spot-covered with muscle and some skin, but in several areas ran uncovered down to bone or steel replacement. It screamed again, the chilling screech of metal knives scored against slate.

Two nobles lay on the bleached flagstone, throats and chests clawed open, staining the ground with Capashen blood. A third figure was pinned up against the manor wall by the creature's bulk, robes tattered and bloody but obviously still alive as he tried to crawl past. The soldiers attempted to drive the monstrous form back. It struck out with its metal-tipped claws, shredding the arm of one soldier who dropped his sword and staggered away, screaming shrilly for the pain. Ellyn's gaze flickered to the abandoned weapon, part of her eager to seize it and join the battle while another part stood immobile, unwilling. This creature was from one of her recurring nightmares from as far back as she could recall—turned from imagined image to deadly reality in front of her.

Ellyn might not have broken from her trance, torn between loyalty and a strange, unholy sense of fear and familiarity for the creature, but then the beast reared back, one massive back leg coming down on the fallen noble and pinning his leg against the ground. He cried out in pain, hands grasping at his leg to pull it free. Ellyn recognized him, even past the smears of blood masking his face.

So did one of the guards. "Leader Purceon!" he yelled. It was the leader of their clan. The warrior didn't hesitate. "Capashen!" he yelled out in battle cry, rushing forward. The dragon beast's tail whipped around and impaled him, the tail's bladed tip driving through his midsection and thrusting out of his back.

The danger to her clan leader and the sacrifice of the guard broke Ellyn's catatonic state. She dove forward, snatched up the fallen sword and rolled to her feet as the creature cast away the broken body. The leather grip felt strange, too soft, but the balance was familiar. She moved shoulder to shoulder with the remaining guard, adding her swordplay to his. Checking one slash, Ellyn almost lost her sword as it vibrated madly in her hand. It felt as if she had slashed her sword into a steel post.

As one they advanced, forcing the beast back from their fallen clansman. So close to the creature, Ellyn could smell the reek of oil—at once foul and enticing.

With a last swipe at the two sword-bearing humans, the dragon beast turned and held them at bay with violent slashes of its bladed tail. Its scream resounded with pure fury and hatred as it reared over Purceon. It slashed down once, twice. The creature's head bobbed in time to its clawing, always keeping its attention divided between the fallen noble and the two wielding swords.

Th guard standing next to Ellyn moved toward the beast, and she followed. The creature turned with incredible agility. Its claws struck out, rending long mortal furrows down the guard's face and chest even as its tail sliced deeply across both legs. Its attention diverted for a crucial second, Ellyn slipped past and ran her sword through the dangling loops of metal cable running from the creature's eye sockets to the base of its skull. She thrust downward with all her strength, pressing her full weight behind the stroke. The cables parted, and the metallic screech of the dragon beast's pain half-deafened her. She stumbled forward, fell and rolled out of the way.

A slashing breeze brushed at her hair. The creature's long tail, barbed with a dagger-sized blades, whipsawed the air over her. Ellyn tried to bury herself down into the flagstones, thankful the beast could no longer see her. The furious beat of wings buffeted her, digging grit out from between the flagstones and dusting it into the air. With a screech of rage the blinded beast took to the air as new guards ran around the corner, weapons drawn.

Ellyn rolled over to Purceon's side, her breath coming in short, gasping fits. She felt as if she had passed a test of sorts, though to pick at the thought any more brought only confusion. Instead she checked her clan leader for life and found him staring at her with guarded eyes. One side of his face bore a parallel set of deep scars ripped through his cheek. He nodded a cautious greeting to her.

"My thanks, Ellyn Capashen."

She nodded back, not trusting her voice just yet. Ellyn stood up and walked over to a fallen guard. She stripped him of his swordbelt and buckled it on over her tunic. Ramming the sword home, the weight of its steel comfortable on her hip, she moved back to where soldiers were applying pressure to Purceon's open wounds.

"More of those creatures are out there," she said simply, knowing it to be true. "I will take charge of a band and hunt them." Ellyn knew that further tests awaited her.

Purceon paused, winced as a new bandage was applied over his leg, and then looked skyward for the retreating creature that had taken the lives of five other Capashen. He nodded to himself.

"Yes," he finally said. "You will."

* * * * *

The village of Devas spread along the river, the normally white stone bathed pink in the late afternoon sunlight. Stubbled fields lead away from the settlement as far as the eye could see. The harvesting season in Benalia had just ended. A few missed stalks of grain wafted in the warm breeze that drifted in off the western plains. The high fluted columns flanking Devas's gates cast long shadows east over the parade grounds established just outside the walls. Those shadows ended in winged silhouettes, the platforms up high occupied by a pair of sentries who watched the surrounding lands with a hawk's gaze.

The bulk of Devas's martial force gathered outside the white oak gates for a training session. Archers tacked paper targets over bales of straw. They practiced long flights in which arrows fell from the sky in a thick, steel-tipped rain. The House Guard worked with sword and halberd, their dance as graceful as it would be deadly. By counterpoint, lancemen thundered by on the plains-bred *eponaes*. It was an impressive sight, and one the Serran refugees allowed few to witness.

Lyanii gauged the sky, judging another thirty minutes of good light left. Raising fingers to her lips she blew a shrill whistle then circled one arm overhead and pointed toward the archers who would need more time to gather their equipment together. They set about picking arrows out of the bales and the ground. Lyanii looked back to her soldier *under instruction* and frowned lightly at the sword he rested, point first, into the ground.

"That was not meant for you, Isarrk. Again. Another pass."

The young Isarrk did not bother coming back to attention, but he rubbed the blunt point against his leggings to clean it. "Apologies, Marshal. It won't happen again."

He grimaced his false contrition toward Karn. Lyanii hid a deeper frown at the youth's somber spirit. As he came back *en guarde* she focused her attention on his every movement, watching for a mistake. His body suddenly taught with lean but well-toned muscle, the youth nodded a reluctant readiness to his two sparring partners.

As the two young Home Guard attacked with fluid sword strokes, Isarrk turned one blade into the other, fouling both. He checked his own answer cut short, leaping back to avoid the swift response of one assailant. All three paced an uneven circle, the two guards never allowing the young man a respite and Isarrk always wary of allowing them to split apart and trap him.

"How is he doing?" Karn asked, the golem's deep voice reminding Lyanii of the rumble of distant thunder drifting across the plains. "Well, it would appear."

Lyanii pulled a cloth from the belt of her training leathers and dabbed away sweat built up from her own exertions in practice. Her lips were salty with the residue.

"Adequate," she said.

Rarely did she take on a Dominarian. Isarrk's training came at Karn's behest, the marshal remembering the time when Urza Planeswalker had rescued so many of her people—herself included—from the decaying plane that had been Serra's Realm. Karn had been there, and Lyanii understood the debt owed all who risked their lives to bring them away from the Phyrexian infestation.

Once she had tried explaining this to the silver golem, only to find that he knew nothing of the episode except from brief historical notes Urza left for him at ten year intervals. In fact, Karn's return to Devas every few decades always came in the same manner, as if he had never been to the settlement before. He would simply arrive with a new student, asking the Serrans to please instruct him or her in combat—until now always a young noble. Lyanii remembered her sorrow, learning that Karn's memory had been capped. In a land of mortal humans, the Serrans were incredibly alone in that they outlived all around them. The first generation aged, but slowly—a human life but a splash of time to them.

Here was Karn, as near immortal as the Serrans except that he simply relived a life of twenty years—endlessly. For a while he would become a bridge between Clan Capashen and the village of Devas. Karn could be counted on during these times to help allay suspicions, at least in regard to the Capashens, then the golem's other duties called him away, and when next Lyanii saw him they began again. It didn't matter that he couldn't remember the debt the Serrans owed him. She did.

"No," she yelled when Isarrk overextended to score against one guard but left himself open to the striking sword of the second. "No, Isarrk, not a parry. A riposte. *Riposte*! You turn the one blade back against itself, and that leaves you still ready to defend against the second. Again. Do it again." She glared at the young man, daring him to make a remark. Isarrk blew out a long sigh of frustration and set himself back on his guard.

"Is there a way to accelerate his training?" the golem asked after a moment's silent observation. "To make him," here the golem paused, trying to capture the words for what he meant, "better?"

Lyanii had noticed that this time Karn's preoccupation with a student had taken an edge to it. "This boy is different, somehow, isn't he?" she asked. "More than just being a commoner's son?" She wondered if it had something to do with Urza Planeswalker's last visit to Benalia, or the unsettling tales of dark creatures preying upon the Benalish people.

The silver man nodded. "He is different, yes, but not *quite* a commoner. One parent was a Capashen noble, though he died before it could be proven. That leaves Isarrk a farmer for the rest of his life, trapped by the caste system. Purceon Capashen asked me to look after his training this year."

"He has the ability," she admitted, "but he must have the drive as well. You can't force a person's basic nature."

"Don't be sure," Karn said softly.

Lyanii glanced over, Karn studied Isarrk with a gesture of fondness. "Is it the Capashen Clan or is it Urza?" She felt certain now that the planeswalker might have more to say on this than Purceon Capashen.

Karn stiffened, wary, but then whispered for her ears alone, "Urza."

That was enough for Lyanii. Any debt she owed Karn was far outweighed by that owed to Urza. "He can be pushed to excel, Karn, but I'm not sure if it will help. A just cause isn't enough. He has to have the heart to defend it. If he cannot rise to my challenge, I may do more harm than good."

On the field Isarrk skipped back, arm clutched to his side against the pain of a solid hit. He tossed his sword down in disgust, not for his opponent but at himself.

"I can't do it, Marshal. It's not that either one is stronger than I am, but they aren't committing to probing attacks I can turn easily. When a sword comes in driven behind their full weight, how am I supposed to match that with the strength of my arms alone?"

Lyanii looked over at the silver golem. She knew Karn liked the young man, and that he must be weighing that fondness against his orders from the Capashen noble and Urza. It surprised her how long he stood there, immobile, the sky's riot of sunset colors washing his silver sheen with a touch of red.

Karn nodded. "Push him."

Lyanii drew her longsword and stepped into the practice circle. She threw it to Isarrk, who caught it properly by the hilt. An easy flick of her foot and his abandoned weapon flipped into the air. She struck an *en guarde* position with it, anchoring her feet flat against the ground.

"Come at me."

Isarrk studied her with wide-eyed amazement. "This sword will break that one in two, Marshal."

"If I let you do that, I deserve to bleed," she said, voice steel. "You'll come at me," and she quoted him, "driving with your full weight." She gestured with her weapon, and when he hesitated she slashed at the air and screamed in her best commanding voice, "Do it now!"

Isarrk leapt forward, almost as if not by his own volition, the gleaming sword whistling a quick feint and then driving in with a slashing attack that would hope to overpower any defense the marshal could offer. Lyanii brought the smaller weapon up at an angle to the flat of Isarrk's blade, catching it in a spinning parry that she held into a full arc, until turning the blade back toward Isarrk's right shoulder. She kept her feet planted. Not wanting to drive the sharp instrument back into the young man. She released it and extended her arms to rap the side of Isarrk's head with the back of her closed hand. The youth crumpled to the ground, dazed.

Lyanii stood on her guard, ready for another attack. Tossing the small sword down onto his chest, she stalked back to her place of instruction. Isarrk came reluctantly to his feet, one hand pressed to his new bruise.

"Do it again," she ordered him. "Do it right."

Chapter 17

Rayne stood in the shadow of the captain's raised quarterdeck near enough to the gunwale that she could stare out past the peaked bow and watch Yavimaya's appearance. The tall forest grew slowly out of the horizon, like an immense wave suddenly frozen in permanent relief. As it spread across the horizon, color tipped the lower edge, a long pale strip promising fair beaches. It was a false promise, Rayne knew.

Captain Pheylad brought the vessel in under topsails only. This was Pheylad's first and likely only visit to the sentient forest, and this without Multani to forewarn Yavimaya or direct their course. Multani was in the elven lands of Shannodin inspecting some forest sites where entire villages had supposedly gone missing. Rayne was here—needing a break from Tolaria and her study of Phyrexian methods in creating negators.

Why she had thought a visit to the sentient forest might allow her the chance to reclaim some peace of mind, she could not now say. Yavimaya bothered her with its unnatural cycles and strange growths. There was a process at work here she could not understand. There were no set laws and relationships like she dealt with in artifice. Allowing for the forest's sentience, Rayne sometimes wondered if the feelings of unease were mutual. Yavimaya might be as uncomfortable with their presence—with her presence—as Rayne was with it.

Rayne grasped the polished railing and stared down, watching as the first slender root tentacles reach out to brush against the *Weatherlight's* hull of living wood. The impaling points pulled back, and on the shore the root network writhed and split open, allowing a path of firm ground from beachhead to the magnificent coastal forest. Rayne breathed a short sigh of relief. At least Yavimaya still recognized the *Weatherlight*.

It was a comfort which lasted only long enough to bring the longboat ashore. No elf met them. No sound of birds or even insects cascaded through the trees. Silence reigned except for a light breeze wandering the trees and rustling brush. Leaving the strange root network behind had helped to ease nerves, the students and crew present spreading out in the relaxed setting of calf-high grasses and flowering underbrush. Now they each shifted uneasily, suddenly nervous in their unannounced arrival with no welcoming party.

"Too quiet," Rayne said, uncertain of what else she expected. Suddenly she put a name to it. "No falling trees."

Rayne's previous visits had been during the advanced mulching cycle of the forest as it built up stores of raw matter. Now the sound of falling trees was absent, replaced with a simple whisper of the wind through treetops and interlocked branches rubbing lightly together. The tall sparse grasses rippled only with natural movement, their own fast-growth cycle apparently complete. It was as if Yavimaya slept.

"The forest must know we are here," she said. She nodded to Pheylad but wondered who she was trying to convince. "The elves will be along soon enough."

The captain glanced uneasily at the dark shadows beneath the trees, his shipboard confidence lost on dry land. "They might already be here," he said. "Can't see 'em unless they want to be seen."

One of Rayne's senior students pointed farther into the forest. "There, isn't that new?"

Rayne didn't bother to point out that after fifty years, everything was likely to be new. The normal rules didn't apply to Yavimaya. "Yes, looks like a tropical flower of some kind."

The new plant was extremely large, its finlike growth reaching ten meters high. Colorful winged bugs flew around it, some of them occasionally flitting out to fall into the grass. A caustic stench welled up over the meadow as several bugs were stepped on by advancing students and ship's crew. The offending crushers exclaimed sharply, trying to wipe the residue off against the ground.

Rayne stood off to one side, indecisive as she waited for some form of contact. Rofellos, would he still be alive? The academy chancellor did not like the silence that continued to greet them even after these long first minutes. Rayne noticed beside another of the strange tropical plants some thorny vines and another plant with spikes standing out three inches like small daggers. Something off to her left rustled as with hidden movement, though she did not believe it to be the elves. Their passage tended to be silent and hidden.

She had just decided that they would all return to the ship—to await the arrival of Yavimaya's emissaries—when she noticed the color shift in the nearby trees. It was subtle yet fast enough to be tracked by the eye as light green darkened and shifted to various blue hues. The trees closer to them were in advanced stages of the color change, while deeper into the forest the change was just beginning. From her previous journeys in the *Weatherlight*, Rayne immediately grasped what it would look like from an aerial view and how Yavimaya would no doubt sense it—an expanding circle of disturbance at the center of which was the *Weatherlight* and her people.

"Back to the ship," she said, voice low with carefully concealed concern. Only a few turned to look. "Back to the ship!"

Everything seemed to happen at once. A trio of wolves, so heavily muscled their shoulders blended in with their neck, sprang from concealment to suddenly encircle one of those crewmen who had protested the stench of a squashed bug earlier. Another offender found herself encircled by a cloud of stinging creatures. With a shrill scream she tried to plunge into a thick wall of brush, hoping to lose the winged insects in the heavier growth, and was caught in a tangle of vines covered in sharp thorns. Blood welled in cuts and streamed down her face from the crown of vines wrapped about her brow. Another creature, a sledge-headed beast, shouldered its way past the thorny brush to snarl a challenge.

The chancellor took a step in the direction of the trapped crewman, whose thrashing drove thorns deeper into her skin, and the forest suddenly closed up in front of her. She saw a pair of vines leap up to opposing trees for support, animated like a pair of striking snakes and forming an immediate barrier. They suddenly sprouted enough thorny vegetation to create an impassable wall. The wall then sprouted jade-green blooms which Rayne recoiled from as if struck. The innocent looking blooms touched at her core and drew strength away.

Acting from instinct, Rayne reached into a pocket for globe-bombs, an invention of Barrin's for those traveling away from Tolaria in case they should meet with Phyrexians. She tossed one into the wall. The globe shattered, its force automatically channeled away from the thrower, shredding the thinner plant life and scoring deep scars into nearby trees. A Tolarian student was not far behind Rayne's action, tossing one of his own globes at the wolves and careful not to throw too near the beset crewman. The wolf yelped as splinters of glass impaled its hind quarter. The wounded beast and one other companion streaked back for the safety of the forest. Rayne tossed another of her globe-bombs at a suddenly active bush covered in globular blossoms. The plant disintegrated under the force. Behind it, previously screened from view, an elf riding a great moa raced toward her, cradling a war bow in one hand and reaching back for an arrow. Rayne drew back for another throw.

"Stop!"

The voice sounded off trees and quivered in the branches and leaves surrounding them. It seemed to shake the very ground and was reflected back from the upper boughs of the great trees. The reflections echoed among the plantlife, which shook under the order. It was as if the forest itself spoke, except Rayne remembered that voice. Rofellos.

The Llanowar elf stood nearby, just inside the forest and at the top of a grassy knoll. He carried what appeared to be a halberd, a long smooth pole of silver wood topped with a wide, green leaf that seemed to possess the rigid sharpness of a blade. He had changed little in the relative centuries since Rayne's last visit, except now he boasted a trimmed mustache.

Rayne suddenly realized that her intended target was an elf—not the animate vegetation or even one of the creatures that had assailed them—but a sentient resident of Yavimaya. The elf's own wild-eyed glare of anger faded, his face going slack with a sudden lack of animation. He lowered his bow as Rayne brought down her own hand, returning her globe-bomb to a pocket. She noticed that the creatures had all retreated, and the vines released their grip on her student.

"Everyone calm down," she said as easily as she could, heart pounding in her chest with the adrenaline rush. "Just stand where you are until Rofellos tells you otherwise. Don't worry. We are among—" friends? Not exactly— "*allies* here."

Watching Rofellos's slow approach, his weapon still held tightly at the ready, Rayne could only wonder if that were still true.

*　*　*　*　*

"The forest is," a pause, "distracted," Rofellos said. Standing on the beach as evening fell over the island, his polearm resting in the crook of one arm. The Llanowar focused on Rayne alone as he spoke. The coastal roots had closed up, allowing only a narrow path from the water's edge back into the forest. "Yavimaya is working to tailor its defenses before the Phyrexian threat finds its way here."

Rayne had watched Rofellos treat the wounded with herbs and a jellylike salve taken directly from the folds of a large violet-colored plant. He moved with purpose, efficient in his every act but lacking the energy and enthusiasm with which he had once assailed life. Certainly this was not the same elf Rayne remembered from before. Now, listening to him explain the initial lack of contact, she couldn't be sure that his reference to Yavimaya came from an individual's view of the situation. It reminded her too much of the imperial *we*.

"Are *you* saying Yavimaya is dormant?"

Rofellos shook his head lightly. "Not dormant. The accelerated mulch cycle is complete, and Yavimaya is spending intense resources in the evolution of the forest and its servants."

"And you, Rofellos, how have you been?"

Obviously the elf had not aged much, but without slow-time waters even a long-lived elf should be showing signs of time's passage by now. She performed a quick review of the years, checking her dates. Rofellos should actually be dead, though here he was, looking still to be in the middle part of an elf's long twilight of middle age.

Frowning, the Llanowar concentrated on the question. "Ro—," he began, then corrected himself, "*I* have been well." He blinked hard, his brown eyes momentarily clearing of their indifferent gaze. By the mage-lit stones some students had set out on poles, burning with their own cool fire, those eyes seemed to broadcast a private pain. He blinked again and it was gone. "Yavimaya takes care of my needs."

He then walked over to a net bag of glowing stones set up on a pole, inspecting it at close quarters while Rayne continued to observe him. Technically their business was complete, having gained a new supply of special woods for use in developing artifacts. Rofellos, though, appeared to be in no hurry. Rayne couldn't decide if the delay was on Yavimaya's part or his. She waited, uneasy with the heavy forest scents pressing in from the dimming lands. Captain Pheylad waited near the longboat with a few crewmen. He shook his head in confusion.

As before, during their approach, Rayne sensed her own unease with the sentient forest. There were no set relationships she could take apart and understand—no gears or cogs. The mechanisms that drove most people were so complex as to be unfathomable.

"Excuse me?" she asked as Rofellos muttered a question. Something to do with Multani?

The elf started, then turned back. "Yavimaya would like to have one of these glowing stones. The light is a good match for one of the forest's needs."

To Rayne the light was too soft for proper illumination, a subtle white-blue inappropriate for working under, but then, she didn't have the superior eyesight of an elf either. "Take it," she said, certain that the request was not his original question. Rayne walked over and unhooked the net bag from the pole then handed the small bundle of glowing stones to Rofellos.

Again there was a flash of pain in Rofellos's brown eyes. He glanced about carefully, searching the shadows as if for dangers. "Have you seen Multani?" he asked, voice quiet and trembling.

Rayne could only shake her head. "No, not for many years."

"I should like to see Multani?" The words came out as part question, part uncertain statement. His face tightened, a hard look of determination dominating his features. "You should not come back, Rayne. Yavimaya has become dangerous."

"Tolaria may need further supplies," she said. "Without the *Weatherlight*—"

"Not the *Weatherlight*," Rofellos interrupted. "You, Rayne. *You* should not come back. The troubles in Keld make Yavimaya too uneasy."

To wonder what possible connection she had with Keld was Rayne's first reaction. Other than her previous acquaintance with Gatha there was nothing else. Rayne dismissed the thought as the outright affront of the recommendation hit her. True that she'd wondered about the forest's own unease, but to have that confirmed struck her with a cold slap of reality. She would've asked after such a dismissal, except that Rofellos now hurried to the path left for him and disappeared into the rootwork. Only the glow of the magicked stones marked his trail, and those too finally vanished as the coastal roots closed after him.

Rayne stood on the beach, hugging her arms to keep back the sudden chill that had swept her, lost in her confused thoughts of Tolaria and Yavimaya, and not of Keld.

* * * * *

The *Weatherlight*'s departure was marked with a more rapid speed than its arrival. It danced over the rough swells, gaining headway until it hit the gentle roll of deeper water. Soon it was a pale smudge beneath the gray light reflected down from the Glimmer Moon.

Where dark promontory jutted out into the ocean, the weathered rock able to grow no heavy plantlife despite Yavimaya's relentless attempts, a black oval spread open. It grew in size. When viewed side-on it disappeared, the portal so impossibly thin because it did not actually exist but was more a hole in the chaotic energies that separated the planes. A leg thrust through, black armor gleaming as it reflected the Glimmer Moon. Arms and a body followed, the thin form stepping through and rising to its not-so-impressive height. Its compleation did not demand size but a compact, tough form that could visit countless planes and bring back detailed news to its masters. It required neither breath nor food, not anymore. The rush of glistening oil through its artificial veins was sustenance enough.

It turned non-augmented eyes toward the ocean, but the Weatherlight was gone. The seeker's gaze fell back to the forest-island. No dangers here, it seemed, but orders were to be followed. It would explore and observe. Others would evaluate. First it needed to return and provide a report on this location for Davvol and the Master, Croag. After a last scan of seemingly defenseless coastline, the Phyrexian left Yavimaya.

Chapter 18

Smoke from the burning granaries trailed up dark against Benalia's clear-blue sky. To one side of the flaming structures, the hamlet's soldiers had driven back nearly twice their number during the furious first moments of their counterattack. Other men worked beneath them, dumping grain into barrows and wheeling it quickly away, never concerned for their own safety. The flames, fueled by the incendiary mixture the strange enemy was using, could not be extinguished. Any moment the fire might lick through to one of the grain-dust filled voids which would then go up in a great explosion. Every barrow of grain removed fed a family for that much longer.

Sweating from exertion, Isarrk pushed his barrow under an overfull load of grain. It had been twenty-three years, he figured, since he had last held a weapon in his hand—since Karn and Marshal Lyanii gave up forcing on him a life he didn't desire. The memories hounded him as the now elderly man strained to lift the full barrow, choking on grain dust. He didn't want to remember. He was afraid to.

His arthritis bit into the joints of his hands, but it wasn't enough to distract him from the shift in the fighting. By sheer numbers alone the spindly-armed warriors in their black armor were regaining the edge. More than from their impossibly-thin arms and legs, Isarrk knew these things were not human. A gut sense told him they were fighting drones—better trained than the local soldiery though perhaps not so good at working together as a unit. However, the Benalish soldiers weren't taking advantage of that, allowing themselves to be drawn away from each other—broken into several small fights where the enemy's two-to-one advantage would spell immediate ruin. Isarrk knew the soldiers should be sticking to a tight line of battle, even a three-sided box, where the attackers would foul themselves if they pressed in with greater numbers. He also knew he should be keeping his mind on his own responsibilities.

What good would saving the grain do if the battle was lost? The black enemy would only set upon it again.

If they did, *when* they did, then he would defend it. They *all* would, but what would happen if all the farmers, now busy moving grain, placed aside their duty and ran to battle now? The enemy would be defeated and the grain lost to fire. That was the advantage of caste. Everyone knew his place and responsibilities. Almost everyone.

One person broke away from the granaries. Grabbing a wide-bladed, curved hoe used to push the grain around, he set one foot against the head and another on the shaft and bent the blade out straight. With his improvised polearm, he ran to the side of the Benalish warriors yelling, "Capashen!"

Isarrk stumbled, spilling his barrow over onto the ground, as he recognized the other by build and voice— Patrick. His son.

"No!"

Isarrk made it five paces before slowing to a confused halt, glancing between the fight and the workers who continued to rescue the grain. His instincts pulled him onward while his basic beliefs warned him to go back. Both sides needed him. He remembered Lyanii's comment about having the heart to defend a just cause. He stepped in the direction of battle then quickly worked back up into a run. Right now, the warriors needed him more.

Patrick was already in trouble, never having been trained for such action. He had also split the Benalish line with his presence, forming a weak link that two enemy warriors were pressing against. The young man, barely out of his teens, slashed about wildly with his device while yelling his defiance. One wild swing smashed the strange longsword from the grip of a black-clad soldier. It cost him, though, as the force spun him halfway around. The second enemy dealt Patrick a vicious slash across his ribs, parting the thin sleeveless shirt he wore and flaying back skin and muscle. The youth screamed in a mixture of his pain and the anguish for failing. He fell back as another swing aimed for his head missed by mere inches. Stumbling, he dropped against the ground as the enemy shoved aside its disarmed companion and came at him.

Isarrk had one chance. Ignoring the fallen sword that lay next to Patrick, no time to snatch it up, Isarrk lashed out with his foot, aiming for the other's wrist. He connected solidly, knocking the other's stroke awry and falling to the ground next to his son as he lost his own footing. Pain flared in his hip for the rough landing. Still, not the worst move to make, he decided, grabbing up the sword that now lay between the two farmers.

Its long, metal handle felt strange in his hands, and his arthritis protested the angular grip, but the lethal weight seemed to suddenly add strength to Isarrk's arms. He brought up the slightly curved, black-metal blade, parrying a quick backhand slash which would have opened up his own chest. The sword had an impressive reach, so he brought it around and bit deeply into the standing creature's ankle. It screeched as it stumbled back, giving Isarrk the time he needed to climb back to his feet.

"Pull in!" he ordered. "Don't split apart. Form a solid line!"

For the Benalish warrior to his immediate left, the advice came too late. A sword thrust snaked past his defense, skewering him through the heart. The withdrawn blade dripped crimson, and the man crumpled without a scream. Isarrk immediately bought a measure of revenge for his comrade. He lunged forward against the warrior Patrick had disarmed. He expected the blade to turn against the armored head, but he was surprised when it pierced metal and sliced through the faceplate. There was a stuttering screech, and the creature toppled. A jet of warm, black blood gushed out as Isarrk removed the sword, staining his lower arm and the front of his own sleeveless cotton shirt. The fluid was tepid, reinforcing his assumption that he fought something not quite human.

The remaining guards were pulling back into line, but now Isarrk faced a pair of the dark-armored soldiers—his own remaining and the opponent of the luckless fellow who had dropped on his left. They hammered at him with their own weapons, pressing forward in staggered attacks trying to drive him back, except on the ground just behind him lay his son, hands pressed over his wounds in an attempt to preserve his life.

Isarrk refused to give up one inch, turning back each stroke. He planted his feet solidly against the ground, waiting for the next disconcerted rush. It came, one of the enemy warriors leading the other by a long second. Isarrk parried with the circling maneuver Lyanii had demonstrated to him so long ago, using the attacker's strength against itself as he twisted the blade's tip around and led the cutting edge of his opponent's sword right back into the creature's own shoulder. It severed its own arm, the mechanical limb dropping off with a spray of foul-smelling oil. Isarrk spun around quickly, catching the second attacker's stroke and again turning it, this time into its companion. The edge bit into the lame creature's side, wedging the black metal blade. A quick backslash by Isarrk took the armored head off the second warrior. Dark slime and oil spewed out, drenching his sword arm and staining a dark swath across his body.

At the far right, the last Benalish warrior in line traded a deadly embrace with one of the enemy. Both swords buried themselves in the other's body, and they fell together in death. Still, the odds didn't look quite so uneven now as five men faced off against seven attackers. There was no apparent communication, but the enemy warriors began to withdraw. The one Isarrk had crippled pulled the sword from its side and limped away on its own strength. They were heading out into the low hills surrounding the hamlet, wary but moving with purpose now.

"What should we do?" one Benalish guard asked, nodding toward the retreating figures.

He glanced around to his companions and obviously included Isarrk. The respect they showed the farmer as each looked to him for guidance spoke volumes.

Isarrk avoided their gaze. His muscles screamed protest for the abuse he had put them to, and his joints felt as if on fire themselves. Panting heavily, he buried the sword he carried point first into the earth and then knelt at his son's side. Patrick didn't look well, but he might pull through yet. The first explosion sounded as a granary burst, raining splintered wood over the area. Men ran, those who could, knowing their time was up. The other two went in close order; brief gouts of fire swam through the sealed chambers, and then a ground-shaking explosion rang everyone's ears as more wood fell from the sky. One burning chunk of wood landed near Isarrk, and he ignored it. It looked as if most of the grain had been saved, but he noticed at least three bodies lying near the granaries. Fire caught on the clothes of one. Isarrk looked down at his own hands, blackened by oil and foul blood.

Silent tears fell against his hand and arms but did not wash away the stains.

Chapter 19

Kreig roared a defiant laugh, his deep voice echoing within the wide-open vaults of the Necropolis—his Necropolis. The bellows challenged the sleeping corpses of better than one thousand years of Keldon rulers. None answered. He growled a sharp oath, enjoying this moment among his ancestors.

Three exterior walls banked inward as they rose majestically overhead to a ceiling of polished, dark-gray stone. The entire fourth side was open to the thin mountain air—as no mortal walls could hope to contain the warlords and witch kings of Keld. The scent of new snow carried in on cutting winds, the frigid grip tugging at Kreig's long, dark braids and brushing an icy touch against his bare chest and arms. Thousands of tombs lined the walls, each no larger than the slab of marble on which a warlord would some day rest. Many of these were already bricked up, sealing fallen warlords into place until the final battle.

A faded mural painted over the ceiling's wide expanse depicted that promised legend. The Call to Return—the moment that marks the end of the world—that would sound of a thousand battle cries after the Necropolis filled. The warlords would rise again to be led by the greatest of their number. An army unto themselves, they would lead the rest of the Keldon nation to war. The mural depicted the great army sweeping down from the Necropolis to conquer all of Dominaria, a bright sunrise over the Necropolis bathing the land red as with blood.

Kreig walked among the several hundred sarcophagi that rested upon the vault's floor, each trimmed in a varied measure of silver or gold depending on the fame and prowess of the warrior within. The greatest of the Keldon leaders were these, placed lower down in the Necropolis and so ready to lead the way out once the dead rose. Only here did Kreig walk among peers. Even the greatest war lords eventually came to rest here, all warlords. Except Kreig?

It was not a question he felt able to answer with any degree of certainty. Not anymore.

In a century and a half of life and warfare, Kreig had never felt the mortal coils settle about him as in the last decade. Since the dark invaders began pushing at the edges of his nation he felt it. Gatha knew something of them as the mage knew about nearly everything. They were beings of another world. *Phyrexians*, he had called them—born of nature and made over again with machine. Such ideas confused Kreig's sense of the natural order where the strongest led and others followed. These Phyrexians bled and died the same as other races. They were innumerable, perhaps, but not invincible.

In twenty-three battles against them, Kreig had yet to personally know defeat. Four other witch kings with their warhosts had, though. The Keldon warhosts no longer traveled out into Dominaria except on the very rare and highly paid expedition. It was only enough to support the nation, if barely, as the majority remained home and continued to fight the dark ones. Kreig tracked the battles over fifty years, at first beginning only with minor raids and probing maneuvers. Those attacks gradually stepped up in strength until no other nation on Dominaria could have matched such an enemy. The Keldons remained battle-ready, even in their own homes, their lands having always served as a large armed camp. The mountains were known to them, comfortable to them. No one could hope to fight as well in this territory.

And they were losing.

The Keldons were not in danger of being completely overrun, though Kreig believed that the invader could do so if they wished. He understood warfare like nothing else, and he recognized a purpose in the enemy attacks. They had spent decades learning the Keldon strengths and weaknesses, as if a thousand dead—even ten thousand—meant nothing while probing at those depths. They turned heavier strength against the foundations of Keld, destroying the best of the witch kings—those on which Kreig relied and whom Gatha had named as his superior bloodlines. This was a purposeful campaign to isolate the two, slowly dismantling the work of a century and a half. One by one the witch kings finally succumbed until only he was left to hold the nation together: Kreig the witch king. Kreig the Immortal, Kreig, who had come to the Necropolis to visit his own crypt.

Made of obsidian, it was glassy and mirrorlike in its thousands of facets. The small building was trimmed in heavy gold with weapons adorning outside and inside walls both. A gate of wrought iron barred entry but allowed for viewing within. A hanging rack for his armor occupied one corner, and the sarcophagus waited with lid half-drawn as it had for one hundred years. No similar structure decorated the vaults, just as there had never been a warlord such as he. It had been built a century before, on his order, right at the very lip of the vaults, built where Kreig knew he could hurl a spear out over the edge and have it not smash into ground for a good half mile drop or more, depending on the winds. The warlord had never thought to occupy that crypt, knowing within himself that no Dominarian could ever hope to kill him. He had been right—the Phyrexians weren't Dominarian.

Fingers wrapped into the iron bars of the crypt door, the cold metal sticking to his warm skin, Kreig ground his teeth in fury. One hundred fifty years of experience promised him that the enemy would come for him soon—for Gatha and he both. His warrior instinct drove him to fight, and he would, at the head of the largest combined warhost the Keldon nation had ever known. An event which would survive centuries of retelling, it would be known in the oral histories until the day when The Call to Return finally sounded.

His muscles bunched and strained, his mortal limits set against metal and stone. Coarse-threaded screws set into a mortared jamb wrenched free. He yelled his anger and defiance in a guttural shout. The iron gate twisted and came away in his hands. He held it overhead and with another savage cry pitched it from the lip of the Necropolis out into the thin, frozen air. He heard it whistle away, fade, and be lost. It fell down far enough that he never heard it hit, and that sat well with Kreig. Let it be lost.

If he was ever to be laid to rest here, it would not be

within confines which could be built by man—not even Keldon man.

* * * * *

Rough blankets draped most of the equipment in Gatha's labs, gray shrouds rank with colos sweat having been used as saddle blankets in the past. Gatha hated that scent, even after three centuries in Keld where the musk of that mountain animal seemed to permeate every facet of life. He wondered if the Keldons hated the large beasts as much.

He shrugged and shook his head, dispelling his speculation along with any lingering aversion to the scent. It did not matter anymore. Kreig had been to see him at the first of the week, carefully talking around the very point the witch king had come to make. It was something that couldn't be put into words. What Gatha had feared for fifty years—the Phyrexians were coming, and this time there would be no stopping them.

Standing still and silent, Gatha strained his hearing to catch the sounds of the battle being fought on the plateau below his laboratory. No fire crackled in competition. No slaves moved about doing his bidding, where their footsteps might have drowned out that distant ringing of metal against metal. There were only he and two guards who waited like motionless statues outside his main workspace while he prepared it. The fighting sounded as if it had moved closer. Gatha could hear the shrill cry of a wounded colos warbeast echoing up the mountainside, but it was drowned out immediately by the grating roar of a massive Phyrexian dragon engine.

Bloodlines

It was the sound of death knocking upon the gates, an Argivian saying which Gatha remembered from long before Keld or Tolaria. Strange, that deep down he had actually believed death would come politely, requesting admission rather than kicking down the barriers and falling upon its victim in a fury of fire and grinding metal.

Well, Gatha did not intend to quit without a fight. Where he had been forced to flee Tolaria, betrayed by those he had called colleagues even when they did not deserve such praise, here he knew strong allies and the strength of his own powers. Kreig had never failed him, never failed the Keldon nation, and Gatha knew that any chance for victory would revolve around them both: warlord and tutor. Witch king and wizard. Gatha remembered much of the Tolarian histories, of the battles waged with the dark forces. He knew many of their weaknesses. He could help turn the tide of battle, perhaps. In case he could not, the lab required preparation.

Moving around the room, Gatha continued to cover each piece of equipment with the rough, strong-smelling blankets as he wrapped them with magical energies drawn from the mountains of Keld. He pulled the mana from the land, feeling its raw power and knowing the destructive force such energies could bring about. Warmth flushed his skin pink, warding him against the room's severe chill, as he layered the magic into every device, every table, into each wall surrounding him. It pulsed at his temples, straining for release, but he held each strand tied into a simple knot at the center of his mind. He buried it down deep, and there he held it with an afterthought. So long as he lived his labs were safe, but at any moment he could bring them down. He would not allow his work to fall into the hands of such an enemy. Better that it go to Urza, who had appreciated Gatha's efforts for many years. He wondered at what Urza might be able to accomplish with the culmination of Gatha's three centuries of research—great things, certainly.

His previous casting completed, the mage stepped over to a large iron-bound trunk. The dark ebony paneling had been carved with scenes out of classic literature, each one depicting the gift or acquiring of knowledge from the gods or through man's own effort. Gatha had been known for both in his years in Keld. Inside the trunk was every scrap of information he had collected: early theories and experiments, two hundred years of refinements, his book of questions, as he called it, new paths of exploration suggested by his work, and many problems he had run up against or simply considered but had never possessed the time to pursue. Always time, his hated enemy, working against him. What he might have accomplished, eventually. Gatha smiled in the face of that consideration. What he *had* accomplished, *today*.

Thinking back on his time in Tolaria, Gatha felt for the magic inherent to the island and drew it for his use. It came in a cool, salt-laden breeze. He attached tendrils of the power to the trunk, and with a simple twist of his mind he transported the entire collection into a fissure deep within the ground. There it would await Urza, the only person Gatha knew who could possibly retrieve it and figure out how to unlock its contents without engaging the protective wards that would incinerate the research.

The lab dead and warded, the trunk hidden away with only a tether held in his mental grasp, Gatha picked up his staff from its resting place by the main door. Made of dark ebony, as the trunk had been, its headpiece a pair of crescent-shaped iron blades stained a deep crimson, it was no longer the simple walking staff he had used to enter Keld. A magical device he had imbued with powers over his long stay, it would aid him today in defending his home.

Passing through the door, he gathered his guards by glance alone and then added that final magical tendril, connecting his boon of knowledge to the knot of magical threads already tied within his mind. It was readied to search out and whisper a message to Urza Planeswalker. It would bring Urza here, eventually. What happened after, in the future, was not Gatha's concern.

It never was.

* * * * *

Kreig commanded his warhost from the left flank, near the edge of the plateau where the fighting was the most concentrated. Here there could be no quarter, no fallback—the opposing forces always aware of the precipice they could so easily be swept over. Already a number of Keldon warriors had plummeted to their deaths, dashed to crimson stains on the sharp rocks below. Kreig had led an assault which toppled a dragon engine to join them. His greatsword sliced apart treads while a white scar of lightning cast out from Gatha's fingertips slammed into the engine's enraged head.

The stench of oil and blood, scorched ground and burnt flesh, assailed the normally chill mountain air now warm with Phyrexian fires. Kreig registered the pain of his healing right leg. The witch king's armor had been burned away from a gout of a burning jellylike substance belched from one of the larger black creatures, that creature now destroyed and left in his wake. Armor-clad warriors, those stunted growths with their mechanical arms and legs, he left shattered by the dozens. They annoyed him, so small and insignificant compared to his expanded boundaries. His was the personal strength of a thousand men, borrowed piecemeal from the legion of warriors under his direct control. When he swung his gore-streaked greatsword, it struck with force enough to rip through armor plating and shatter metal supports. Flesh and bone where he found it among the dark soldiers, he cleft with ease.

How much more might he have become if he had brought the entire Keldon warhost under his banner? This was not the only battle being fought today. It was one of several, in fact, and the witch king never forgot his responsibilities. He was more than Kreig—immortal or not, the greatest of the witch kings or not—he was *Keld*. Even in the frenzy of battle the witch king never forgot his priorities. His nation would survive. The Phyrexians were here for him, testing themselves against the greatest warrior Dominaria had ever known. He and Gatha, they were the objectives. So long as Kreig did not put the whole of Keld in between the enemy and themselves, some—many—would survive.

The warlord was able to easily recognize the Phyrexians battle philosophy. They had apparently little use for subterfuge with what seemed to be inexhaustible resources to draw upon, and they had their god of pale flesh and black eyes that could place them for battle or withdraw them as necessary. They wanted to rip out the strength—what *they* perceived to be the strength—of his nation. They would learn that the Keldon strength was inexhaustible as well. It didn't matter whether the Phyrexians won today or next year. They could take all of Dominaria, in fact. One day the Necropolis would be full, and then nothing would stand before his nation and *him*.

A skeletal figure walked the battlefield toward him. Kreig knew of it immediately, sensing the approaching danger in the waning lifeforce of his warriors. It appeared only slightly more impressive than the spindle-limbed warriors in black armor—the only visible differences being its cleft skull and burning red eyes that sat back within hollow sockets. It carried a staff which looked to be a thin, twisted piece of wood, and it wore no more protection than a robe of tattered cloth bands, or so it seemed.

One Keldon warrior charged the thing, and it moved with blinding speed to eviscerate the man with one swipe of its thin, taloned hands. Another met an end with searing bolts from the creature's eyes. The one blow Kreig saw the creature take was shrugged aside as easily as the witch king himself might have done, hardly scratching through the tattered robes that writhed with their own life.

Rage gripped Kreig, watching his warriors so easily cast aside as if they barely merited a warrior's death. He kicked an impaled creature off his sword. The warlord shouldered his way past or through several skirmishes, trailing the smoke from smoldering colos horn back from his shoulder vents. A Phyrexian's clawed hand took off the bladed antler that guarded part of his helm's eye slit. He shrugged it aside, raking his armor's elbow spikes into the creature's midsection and tearing through several hoses acting as veins for thin, glistening oil.

The other creature finally noticed his advance and

paused to meet him. It screeched out an attack of tormenting sound. Waves of preternatural sound assailed Kreig with stunning force, as if he had hit an invisible wall which then toppled back over him. His armor shook, and small stabs of pain worked through his gut. He shouted his war cry, cursing his own muscles for their treasonous behavior, and then he was past the wall and set upon the Phyrexian.

His greatsword rose and fell three times in rapid strikes. The first two glanced off the bands of metal that rustled and rasped over the creature like living snakes, but the last connected solidly to the side of the Phyrexian's head. A few metal bands fell to the ground, writhing a moment before falling still. The vicious slash to the creature's face caused it to stumble and opened up a large cut in the taught, glistening-gray skin. Kreig moved to make a disabling blow but found his sword deflected by a flick of the creature's hand. A stiff-armed stabbing motion followed from the Phyrexian, allowing a pair of talons to pierce his armor and dig into his ribs.

Kreig backed off immediately, knowing to not press an attack after being taken unaware, and he watched the cut on the Phyrexian's face heal. Strands of fiber spun out from one side of the wound to the other, pulling the flesh tight again. Small spinning devices, fused right into the skull it seemed, spun and stitched the skin back together flawlessly. His own wounds burned painfully. He noticed a sludgelike black fluid dripping from the creature's two talons that had found his skin. Growling defiance, Kreig swung again. Another lightning flash of motion and the Phyrexian's poisoned claws scored again along his right shoulder.

Burning, the substance continued to eat away at him regardless of how much strength his warriors lent him. Kreig stumbled, going down on one knee, his swordpoint stabbed into the earth for balance. He hated the Phyrexian for humbling him in such a manner. He couldn't draw a breath, the burning now in his lungs. Kreig wrenched his helm away, drawing in deeply the steaming, smoky air.

Chattering a cacophony of squeals and hisses, the creature moved in to deal a death blow. A crackling, snapping arc of energy scored the air over Kreig. Gatha's lightning caught the Phyrexian in the shoulder, driving it back a step as two more warriors fell on it. One arm apparently fused into place, the beast clawed the throat out of one footsoldier and then threw him into his partner, driving them both over the cliff edge. It then worked at its shoulder, twisting it back into a full range of motion within seconds.

With a struggle to control his pain, Kreig levered himself back to his feet and brought his greatsword back up in challenge. He could feel his own blood trickling down his side, the wounds failing to close as that burning sludge worked deeper into his body. The Phyrexian advanced, striking out with long, skeletal arms that moved with blazing speed. Kreig countered, giving back a step under each blow but holding off the deadly embrace. More of his warriors leapt in to the fray—only to be thrown back dead or dying—and then the creature advanced again. Kreig knew that the space behind him was limited. There would be Gatha and then open air as the plateau fell away to the lower valleys. He would have to act soon.

The Phyrexian never gave him that chance. As if tired of the game, it simply grabbed his sword on a parrying stroke and wrested it from his grip. A razored claw shot out, piercing his armor and digging claws into his midsection. It lifted Kreig from the ground, its hollow sockets only inches from the witch king's tortured gaze, as it pumped more liquid fire into him, then it tossed both Keldon warlord and sword aside as if broken toys. Kreig slammed into the ground, and there he lay in wordless agony. So easily discarded, the greatest witch king ever known rolled over enough to see the face of his destroyer. He stared into the skull's lifeless expression.

The Phyrexian turned, no longer concerned with the broken Keldon, and its ember eyes found Gatha.

* * * * *

Hellfire scents of burning flesh and scorched ground rose to choke Gatha. Metal clattered against other metal. The grinding of gears at times threatened to drown out the orders passed among minor warlords and their witch king masters. A haze hung over the plateau, smoky and wraithlike, and from that haze the Phyrexians kept advancing. Warriors went down beneath physical weapons and blazes of energies, and some simply fell sick as if by sudden disease.

Kreig fell to the Phyrexian champion, and the shock value itself drove the Keldon army back several precious yards.

Gatha could not wonder if he hadn't somehow been responsible. The more magic he expended, it seemed, the greater the opposition brought forward by the Phyrexians.

His cast of lightning helping to topple a dragon engine, and then two more of the juggernauts rolled forward. He'd summoned a giant at one point, which had been quickly overwhelmed under a surge of black-armored warriors. Then came the particularly draining cast, drawing upon his entire store of mana to summon a rock hydra to block the lower pass, trying to limit the influx of more enemy soldiers.

The Phyrexians countered with their god.

The mage had glimpsed him in between castings while trying to marshal the energies at his control for another lightning strike. The image fit Kreig's description too well—pasty corpselike flesh and wide-set eyes of steel gray within black. The thin, hard line of his mouth grimaced under strain. Gatha did not believe the figure to actually be a god, no more so than he himself was, though the Keldons had for decades considered him and Kreig both as near-divine. He sensed the bridge form between worlds, saw briefly the dull tan landscape overlaid onto Dominaria. Planeswalker! The word shouted out in his mind from his earlier association with Urza. It was the closest he could come to naming the powers he saw demonstrated. From across the bridge stepped a new group of Phyrexian nightmares, the skeletal figure among them, bypassing the hydra.

Urza help us, was Gatha's first thought at witnessing the crossover. If he could have hoped to shout for the planeswalker's attention, right then he would have done so, but he had spent too much of his stamina already, manipulating heavy magics as well as maintaining his hold on the wards that protected his labs. Now he could only try and recover, witnessing the horrible passage of the new Phyrexian as it slaughtered its way quickly and effortlessly across the battlefield to put down Kreig. Even a solid strike of lightning failed to do more than slow it—and draw its attention. Right then as it looked to him, before its final confrontation with Kreig, Gatha sensed the hatred it felt. It froze the mage in his place for a moment—long enough for Kreig to fall—and then the dark creature was past the dethroned witch king and facing Gatha himself.

Backed against the plateau's precipice, his magical strength waning, Gatha began a sacrificial casting that would expend his own life in one final attack against the Phyrexian. One of the most powerful and dangerous spells he'd brought away from Tolaria, he held it in reserve for just such an occasion. With Kreig vanquished and the army poised at its breaking point, there was little else he could accomplish with his life. He could only hope to accomplish something more by his death.

Time betrayed him. The creature's red eyes darkened, becoming twin orbs of dark power within cavernous sockets. The black mana swept from it in a mind-rending wave—a banshee wail that drove the mage quickly to his knees. The spell he had held in readiness was lost to the chaos, torn from him in a painful struggle. It left him weak and defenseless. He rose back to his feet on shaky legs, his mind numb. He stared into the orbs, and they froze him to his spot. The Phyrexian reached its hands out toward Gatha's head—razor-sharp fingers on hands of metal framework and cable. One finger on each hand opened up to allow a short length of braided wire to escape. The ends probing the air in front of his eyes, searching. Gatha realized then that all his preparations to keep his research from Phyrexian hands were for naught, and worse, he was about to give up Urza's best-kept secrets—Tolaria, the *Weatherlight*, the Legacy and the bloodlines. He understood now. The Phyrexian was here for his mind.

In his entire life, Gatha had always lived by what could be done now, not tomorrow or the day next. Leaving his knowledge for Urza's recovery was in many ways an act of today, though it also prepared for the morrow when that knowledge might surface again. Seconds away from betrayal of Dominaria to Phyrexia, Gatha made the final commitment. Gauging his distance from the plateau's drop to a deep valley, Gatha released that buried knot of magical energy within his mind, collapsing the wards that protected his labs and held the call for Urza in place. Far up the slope from the plateau, fire blossomed as the destructive force of the mountain's stored mana welled up in a cataclysm of energy and raw power meant to destroy his labs completely. The roar of the explosion was matched with a magical shock wave which rode the recoil of such a heavy mana draw. The creature glanced away for a second.

That was all the time Gatha required.

* * * * *

Kreig had watched the Phyrexian advance on Gatha, his jaw clenched against the pain and refusing to give it justice through voice. His friend and advisor stood transfixed like a bird caught in the mesmerizing stare of a rock cobra. Kreig rolled to his stomach, ignoring the fire that burned within as he got his hands under him. His helm laying off to the side, Kreig's face pressed into the ground. It smelled of fresh dirt—no oil or blood to taint the ground of Keld here, no scorched earth, not yet.

The sweat of exertion runneling from his brow, Kreig levered himself back to hands and knees. He still maintained his hold on the warhost, still felt their combined strength and rage coursing through his veins as it warred with the foreign substance invading his body. He focused on the back of the creature that had laid him low. He saw the sky over the invader's shoulder deepening into purple as his bloodlust mixed with the normal blue. He rocked back to his feet as Gatha shrank to his knees—the two trading places. He stumbled for his greatsword, drawing it back from the dust where the Phyrexian had cast it. The Keldon nation was not finished. Neither was he.

The powers of a witch king were never without their limitations, even in him. He drew from his warrior nation that which he needed to make himself stronger and gifted back to them, in his exploits and energy, a lust for life and battle which would carry them through and home again with the spoils of war. Only here the spoils were Keld itself. He could feel the dark matter killing him. It certainly would have killed any mortal man already. Kreig had never known defeat before, but if it must happen, it would happen on his own terms.

The explosion of Gatha's labs did not distract the witch king's focus. He saw Gatha pitch himself backward, rolling for the cliff edge. The Phyrexian recovered quickly but not soon enough. Gatha was lost in the vast space that fell away from the plateau. Cheering his friend, defying death at the hands of Phyrexia, the witch king leapt forward sword reversed and poised overhead like a scorpion's stinger, the battle cry on his lips his own.

"Kreig!"

The skeletal creature spun quickly, arms flashing in on the attack. Kreig drove forward into the deadly embrace. Talons ripped through armor like a sword through old leather, digging deeply into each side. Pain blossomed— an agony unlike any he had ever known or imagined. Kreig retained hold of his weapon with a determination honed over one hundred fifty years of battle, and he felt his steel bite at the joint where the creature's thin neck met with armored bands covering its shoulder. Screaming his war cry, Kreig drove the blade down with his every ounce of strength and kicked forward.

The blade worked in and plunged deep, driven by the strength of every warrior who still survived and the raging will of one mortal who would never surrender easily to death. The Phyrexian screeched in pain and fury and then caught him fast, trying to hold Kreig in a final embrace. No physical barriers held a Keldon warlord, not even after death. Kreig drove forward, bloody spittle flying from his lips as he screamed his own name. His vision swam, and he stood at the entrance to his crypt facing out into the world, the drop before him leading down from the Necropolis. With his final call to battle, rousing those who woke behind him, Kreig leapt out into the space.

As he fell, he knew that somewhere, down below, Gatha waited for him again.

BOOK III

Natural Selection

(4013–4169 A.R.)

Life must endure. Urza said that to me once, and as usual there is just enough truth in it to suit the planeswalker's purpose. What he failed to recognize is that life will endure, often despite the best or worst intentions of individuals, no matter how powerful.

—Barrin, Master Mage of Tolaria

Chapter 20

Silence reigned in the Chancellor's Hall, the administrative work of the academy brought to a halt for the night and most offices locked up and darkened. Light spilled through the open door of the last occupied workspace. Timein approached it slowly.

Though he only held the official academy rank of senior student, Timein had passed through security with little trouble. The sorcerer had free access to Barrin or any chancellor on the master mage's own order. The island's night watch had not challenged him. The final doorway, however, was daunting enough to stop him cold. It stood open, inviting, and Timein could see Barrin working at his desk within. That last step across the threshold was one of Timein's most difficult accomplishments in all his time on Tolaria, precisely because it would signify the end of that time.

He stepped through into Barrin's office. The mage glanced up from his work, from reviewing the material he and Urza would be discussing no doubt. The mage had put out the word that he would be meeting with Urza for all those who might have business that needed to be brought to the planeswalker's attention.

"Timein," Barrin said in surprised greeting. His expression hovered somewhere between curiosity and suspicion. "It's been a long time since you've visited the academy."

In Barrin's presence, Timein removed his cap and shoved it into a pocket. "The academy is on my way to the docks," he said, mouth dry. He knew Barrin didn't need to be told that one of the academy's security-cleared trader vessels had docked there this week—and was leaving on the tide tomorrow morning.

The mage settled back in his chair, hands flat in front of him on the marble-topped desk. He studied Timein with guarded green eyes. "I see," he said. "You want papers for leaving Tolaria," he said. It wasn't a question. "What about your students? Your fellow exiles?"

"The colony refuge will sustain itself without me. But my own studies . . . " he trailed off. How much did Barrin know about the work he had done for Urza?

Most of it, apparently.

Barrin rose and offered the sorcerer his hand. "Your work these last years has been of extreme importance and help, Timein. Your refinements to the empathy magics couldn't have been accomplished by anyone else." Tolaria's master mage nodded slowly. "Are you certain you cannot be persuaded to stay?" he asked, a note of resignation present.

"Yes, I'm certain," Timein said.

The sorcerer had too much to work through on his own. While he'd begun to admit to a certain validation behind Tolaria's purpose—behind Urza's purpose—it was hard to balance that out against his lack of understanding for the lands and lives his work affected. Barrin might be able to make those hard decisions, balancing lives against the sometimes harsh necessities of the future. Timein did not yet possess such an outlook.

"I do hope to return, Master Barrin, someday, but I've gone as far as I can with the Legacy and Tolaria." He smiled a sad smile. "As far as I can, for now."

* * * * *

"It's been better than a century since the deaths of Gatha and Kreig, Urza. Still the Keldons haven't fully recovered." The mage shook his head. "I don't care for the idea that we may see that same kind of devastation in Benalia."

Barrin paced the *Weatherlight's* deck, trying to work off some of his nervous energy but feeling that in fact the reverse was true. Though the ship remained sea-bound, sailing emerald waters beneath a brilliant summer-blue sky, the mage sensed the large powerstone that was the vessel's heart pulsing from its protected vault. The magic charged him, a reminder of his part in the ship's design and construction, and of course, in its maiden voyage to Serra's Realm. That felt so long ago, the battle now just one more footnote in his never-ending life. Barrin's world seemed to shrink with each new year added to that span, lost among the incredible history.

Standing near the forward mast, pennants snapping in the rigging above him, Urza glanced upward for a long moment, possibly remembering the time he'd spent on ship climbing into the sails and mastering the ocean's temperament.

"I trust that Keld will survive," the 'walker said with regard to Barrin's first statement. "It has always been a strong nation. I doubt they will ever see another of Kreig's status, though certainly the witch kings wish for it."

The master mage conceded that point. Urza was right in that the Keldons had asked for Gatha and the rogue tutor's experiments, had *embraced* them. Their current difficulties, now that Phyrexia had moved on, stemmed from the witch kings trying to hold onto the power Kreig had once brought them all. Yes, that struggle would work itself out, eventually, but this was not the issue at hand.

"The Phyrexians stumbling over Gatha's work was unfortunate but not devastating," continued Urza.

Barrin disagreed. "It pointed the Phyrexians in our general direction. We have reports of infestations in Femeref, Sardnia, and especially in Benalia. They know of the bloodlines, Urza."

"*Something* of the bloodlines," Urza corrected. "But they seem to be focusing on them as warriors only and not on their future potential."

Barrin shook his head, then drew in a deep breath of the tangy sea air. "It doesn't matter. They *know*, and that's dangerous. It means they will keep looking, finding more of your bloodlines and placing the project in jeopardy."

Urza shook his head. His voice turned hard. "I will keep ahead of them. *We* will keep ahead of them. Even should the Phyrexians try, they couldn't find all of the bloodlines. Not near enough to make a difference, in fact." His voice softened, even as his expression followed suit. "We're getting so close, Barrin. There are so many promising lines, scattered all over Dominaria." He nodded a brief concession. "Yes, I'm concerned that the Phyrexians are stepping up to such an obvious level of interference. The invasion may not be far off, but I still need at least six generations. The Legacy is complete but for an heir to wield it." His eyes glinted hard against the overhead sun. "Barrin, I need that time. The infestations are being controlled. I expect that the Benalish can hold out a bit longer."

"We both know that if the Phyrexians want to take down Benalia or any other nation they will. Right now they are toying with the bloodlines, trying to gauge their effectiveness. You owe whatever time you have to Phyrexia, Urza, and betting on them is not a pleasant gamble to make." Barrin sighed in frustration. He knew he wasn't getting through. "We're lucky they have not discovered Tolaria," he said with a sharp glance to the planeswalker. "What's left of it," he added. The island was no longer holding up well to the centuries of mining and farming and general use by so many people.

"Gatha kept that from them," Urza said softly, ignoring the latter remark. "To the end, he was a loyal student."

Barrin could not allow *that* to go by unchallenged. "Loyal? If he were loyal he never would have left Tolaria. His work was a beacon to Phyrexia. We never should have allowed it to continue."

Urza slashed the air before him with a knife-edge hand, a human gesture of frustration, certainly chosen from the memory of his physical life and used now only to influence Barrin. "It *had* to continue. I needed the insight of his generation to accomplish sooner what might have taken me centuries of trial and error. I don't always have the answers, Barrin, and we don't have the time it would take me to find them myself."

His ears warm with the rebuke, the world swam in Barrin's vision as one particular turn of phrase stuck within his mind and set his hackles rising. The insight of Gatha's "generation." An eerie, prickling sensation crawled up Barrin's spine and spread over his scalp, squeezing in at his brain, which throbbed in painful response against his temples.

"Not possible," he finally said, voice hoarse with doubt. "You gave me the information on the bloodlines. Gatha was nowhere among them, and he's too old."

The mask frozen over Urza's face admitted to Barrin that the planeswalker had indeed given something away he hadn't meant to. His entire form an illusion of energy patterns, Urza could look as he wished. Gestures and expressions were entirely affectations he assumed for dealing with mortals. He simulated emotional responses as it suited him, most often preplanned to generate the effect he wanted. Caught unaware or in the grip of intense concentration, those were the first signs to slip away.

"I gave you the information on all *continuing* blood-lines, not every single bloodlines subject, and Gatha is not too old." The human mannerisms returned, and Urza allowed himself a small sigh of concession. "I began my first experimentation outside Tolaria not long after we discovered the mana rig in Shiv, when I knew the *Weatherlight* would fly, several decades *before* bringing the Legacy and bloodlines to your attention."

There was an uneasy pause, and then Urza continued. "I told you then that I had taken matters as far as I could *alone*."

The mage performed some quick math—thirty years! Just enough to raise one generation and breed the next, subjects that, if left unchecked, might have bred thousands, even millions, of descendents by now. Of course, theory never matched reality, but it was still staggering to contemplate.

"So you haven't kept track?" he asked.

The 'walker shook his head. "No need. These were prior to our official Bloodlines program, and the procedures were imperfect. I also relied on a heavier mix of Thran blood in the Matrix. Most of those early lines sickened, and I allowed them to simply breed my work back out. Only a few lines prospered, but they showed remarkable talents. Those I brought to Tolaria for their genius. I turned them over to you better than three hundred years ago."

For their genius. Barrin wondered at all those students over the years. Not Jhoira and Teferi, they fell outside the proper time frame. Gatha for certain, and how many others? How many remained in his classrooms and labs? In his life?

Barrin looked at the planeswalker. He remembered Urza's words spoken so long ago. "I certainly would not have chosen any other mate for you." He locked gazes with the true immortal, but Urza simply looked on, curiously now, which meant either he had no idea as to the question so close to Barrin's lips or was not about to volunteer the information. Barrin blinked, glanced away, and focused his gaze on the far horizon ahead. The wind cut sharply over the bow and welled tears in the corners of his eyes.

"Take me home, Urza."

* * * * *

It was a waking dream—a nightmare, actually. It was a clockwork world—a series of them—one shell world nestled around the next one. The ticking and grinding of gears sounded always at the edge of one's hearing, deep and pervasive as it threw the barest tremor into the ground. The air filled with the scent of hot metal and fresh oil, scents which Rayne knew well from her life as an artificer.

Rayne fought the vivid images, trying to clear her mind and concentrate on her work. A gyroscope belonging to a mechanical dervish rested in the clamps before her, held to a comfortable height such that she could inspect it while sitting on a workshop chair. She leaned in again, checking the wear and searching for tolerance deviations. Her gauge trembled in her slender fingers, and her wrist shook just enough to continuously spoil the focusing power of her wrist-mounted glass. Biting her lower lip in frustration, she tore the glass off her wrist and hurled it across the room. Hearing the glass shatter against the wall brought an instant of immediate gratification, followed quickly by a sense of loss and guilt for having taken her turmoil out on an inanimate tool.

"Rayne? Is everything all right?" Hurried footsteps came down the corridor and then the door of her workshop swung open.

Startled, Rayne stood quickly in the surprise of hearing Barrin's voice. She expected her husband to be gone for several hours yet. Catching her stool before it over-turned, she set it carefully against a table as he entered.

"You're back early." Watching him scan the shop with his quick, green eyes, she noticed their haunted look. Frowning, she clasped her hands together. A gesture of concern and meant also to hold them steady. "The meeting went as you suspected, I see." Rayne knew her husband too well. There was no missing his look of fear, quickly smothered under doubting eyes.

"I had Urza 'walk me back to Tolaria," he said in answer to her first statement. Taking passage back to the island should have cost him several days time, though only hours subjective to Rayne.

She noted the despondency in his voice, the too-casual shrug. Barrin was her entire world, always more important than her artifice. After so many years she could read him as she could no other, and she remembered better than he. She could compare her husband's moods and attitudes with previous years, and she noted the failing pattern. Something was wrong or going wrong. So far, though, Barrin had been unable or unwilling to share it.

Now he tried to change the subject. "What happened to your glass?" he asked, nodding toward the twisted frame and pile of glittering shards.

"A mistake," she said. That was truthful enough. "I will have to fix the frame later and order a new lens."

"I'll take care of the lens," he promised quickly.

Too quickly. He was definitely avoiding some problem. "Is something the matter?" she asked, knowing full well there was and wanting to draw him out—wanting also to avoid her own personal nightmares.

She noticed a glistening bead on her husband's forehead and reached out slowly to dab at it with delicate fingertips. Moisture. She almost expected the scent of glistening oil but shoved such thoughts back into the darker recesses of her mind.

"Something *is* the matter."

His eyes met her gaze, softened under the warm concern. Almost, she thought, he was ready to blurt it out. Slowly, almost sadly, he reached over and took her hand in his. "Rayne," he began, voice trembling only slightly. "Rayne, are you happy on Tolaria?"

An odd question, deserving perhaps an inconclusive answer. "I think I have been getting too close to my work," she said openly, her voice tight with the tension but feeling some of the strain draining away by speaking of it. "It does not hold the allure it once did. Not since . . ." she trailed off, uncertain.

"The negator?" Barrin asked, finishing the sentence. He asked it as a question, but something more rode his voice.

She nodded, feeling better for the admission. "Silly, I know, but we have been at this for so long." Her words caught as Barrin winced. "What is it, Barrin?"

Her question was insistent this time—worried. She couldn't remember seeing her husband so concerned. So *vulnerable*, that was the word. His fire was missing. Was the rock-solid strength that had guided the academy for over six centuries of relative time finally eroding under natural stress and the very unnatural pressures of dealing with Urza Planeswalker?

Barrin raised her hand to his lips. Kissed it hard, once. "It's not important." He called up a smile, tight and humorless but there nonetheless. "You're right, we've been at this for too long. But I don't think it will go on much longer, Rayne. Tolaria can't hold up forever. Urza's plans are near fruition, and the enemy grows bolder. Something is going to give and soon, then we can take a hard look at where the academy is and what *we* want to do." He nodded. "Then." The smile sparked briefly in the corners of his bright green eyes. "It's not important," he said again.

Wanting to trust her husband and believe in a brighter future that could arrive of its own accord, Rayne almost believed the lie.

Chapter 21

The seemingly endless plains of Rath were, in fact, not. There was a limit to the amount of flowstone the Stronghold had been able to produce in its millennium of operation. Here, at the edge of Rath, the sky boiled as if alive with fire—a riot of red and orange distorted ever so slightly like flames reflected from polished metal. It was a sight to twist the most sane mind into a terrifying shadow of its former self. The physical boundary of a plane was not meant for contemplation by mortal man.

Davvol, however, could hardly count as such anymore. He had been compleated to the point where he lived indefinitely, if at the sufferance of his Phyrexian masters. Six centuries of life, one in waiting and five more here on Rath as steward—evincar really, for in the last hundred and twenty years of his stewardship it could be said that he had truly ruled this plane. Since Croag had fallen beneath the sword of Kreig the witch king, the Phyrexian had been forced to slowly heal over the past twelve decades. He was in no shape to challenge Davvol, whose mastery of flowstone and the machinery of the Stronghold made him powerful. Davvol was finally powerful, out from under the shadow of the Phyrexian Inner Circle member. Croag rested in a place of darkness few knew of and where none could wonder at how the Phyrexian had almost been destroyed at the hands of a mortal Dominarian. Such was their new relationship. Croag was able to delay and heal rather than return to Phyrexia and face possible rending, and Davvol ruled Rath as evincar, with an unspoken but present guarantee that Croag's reports back to Phyrexia would never endanger either of them.

Davvol had come to this point today, the farthest reaches of his realm. Here would be the most difficult spot to attempt a transference, the forces controlled by Rath's great machinery at their weakest and so relying more on his own ability. Armored troops waited in formal ranks behind him, silently menacing.

Flowstone rippled as he made mental contact with the control machinery under the Stronghold, focusing it against the nearby ground. Tan-colored waves rose in the landscape, shallow troughs running between them, as the machinery first worked the larger features into the surrounding plains. It was a slow process and the pressure within his mind built to a steady ache. Simple vegetation followed in the transference, and then the homes and utility buildings so common to every Benalish village.

This was a Capashen settlement, the clan that had long occupied Croag's attentions until his accident. Davvol had decided to usurp those duties as well, the constant testing and probing, now that Keld was a forgotten experiment.

The village formed as he recalled it, the control machinery pulling it from his memories. The two worlds overlapped as the chaos that existed between planes was feathered aside and the final barriers weakened. He felt that final moment of transference. His mind lay open to the people of the Benalish village who now beheld the chaos storming about them as Rath intruded into their lives. Hundreds of humans—each a tiny flare within his mind as the great machinery seized his consciousness— heard the terrible wailing that encroached upon Rath from the chaos between worlds. He felt that moment, and held it.

On his gesture, the armor-clad troops raised their weapons high and moved into the village, fighting— slaughtering—at once on Rath and also Dominaria. Davvol felt each one's life added to the pattern the machinery forced upon his mind, a tangible weight pressing down on him. The tiny flare extinguished as another Dominarian fell before his troops. The warriors traveled dim streets, now only half-lit by sunlight. Davvol directed his soldiers toward specific people, wanting to bring over those who would represent a good cross-section of the village. Dominaria was his hunting ground. No one could hide from him.

Only, he was not about to get all that he wanted. The attack faltered in places. He found himself distracted by the rising wail of disembodied voices. He was distracted by the press of new wills acting against his own. The intruders interfered with his control over the Stronghold's machinery. This presence took on a luminescent, humanoid form within his mind as it wrestled into the pattern of transference in his mind. Davvol's mind swam, his train of thought barely able to hold control over the great machinery.

He tried to bring warriors against these apparitions plaguing his mind, but they possessed no physical form to attack. As he searched for ways to win the battle in his mind, he found the assault in front of his eyes going not as well as he'd hoped. Some Benalish held their own against the Phyrexian troops. Usually it was a single, leather-clad soldier, caught in the village during the attack or perhaps on permanent assignment, but others joined in as well. Here a blacksmith wielded his hammer and crushed through Phyrexian armor and skull alike. Over there a farmer employed his scythe to great effect, knocking legs out from under Davvol's troops and leaving them helpless upon the ground.

There was no meeting such challenges to his troops, not while the haunting cries continued to threaten his control. As his warriors began to drag back victims, stepping from Dominaria to Rath and leaving those Benalish no hope of return, Davvol slowly released the barriers and allowed them to drift back into place. He had his subjects, though not as many as he would have liked. They would be sent to live among the Vec, the Dal, or the Kor. His final live warrior returned. Straining, an acute pain shot through his mind with each strange haunting voice. Davvol reached out to the places where he had felt Phyrexian lives harmed or destroyed and latched onto their physical forms. He pulled them back to Rath even as the last barrier came crashing into place.

The intrusive forms slipped away as well, melting back into the chaos that existed between planes. The strongest of them faded away last, and Davvol reached out after that final alien presence trying to wrestle his mental touch over its mind. There *was* an intelligence there. He could feel it—a whisper just outside of his range of hearing. He pushed harder, rage over his partial failure today lending him strength.

Soltari.

Then it was gone.

A name? A place? Davvol had no way of knowing and no more strength left to pursue it. He stumbled to one knee, his weakness betraying him. Darkness swam over him, almost laying claim to his consciousness. He fought it off, refusing such a pitiful display in front of his warriors. Then he rose on shaky legs, dark eyes glowering at any Phyrexian watching him. Without a command given, he turned and walked with determined stride to the portal waiting several paces behind him. The gateway back to the Stronghold. He'd been given a lot to think about, and now he simply needed some time to put it all together.

If Davvol had any two resources on his side, they were his ability to think and the time to do so.

* * * * *

Shuffling out from the shadows with an odd hunching motion, Croag made himself known to Davvol with a screeching whisper. "You have news of Urza Planeswalker?"

Croag preferred to announce himself in such a way. It was better than allowing the steward to guess Croag's presence by the dragging foot he kept hidden beneath his banded metal robes or the rasping wheeze of his artificial lung breathing. Davvol appeared to take pleasure in the Phyrexian's damaged state, but like it or hate it—and Croag certainly hated it—the Inner Circle member was in need of Rath's first evincar. Croag required time for self-repair. Certainly he could not return to Phyrexia in such a state.

No, that would not do. Rath certainly was ahead of schedule now, but Urza Planeswalker still lived, and more, he was preparing Dominaria against the day of invasion. He was doubtful that the planeswalker could affect any meaningful widespread change before that glorious event, but admission of the attempt would be enough cause for an end to Croag's existence. Gix's failure had been nowhere near so severe, and he had still been cast into the furnaces of Phyrexia. Croag was of the Inner Circle. He was superior. At such a high pinnacle, second only to the Dark One, the fall would be all the more long and merciless.

He suffered the time spent away from his plans and power. Croag's body contained meat at such a minute level that every cell could repair itself or rebuild its neighbor, given time. However, without the use of Phyrexian devices and assistant operations the cells first returned to their simpler meat form. As interesting and at times as sublime as the return of pure meat might have been, Croag did not appreciate the feelings of helplessness and danger which had accompanied every moment. Davvol might have killed Croag, easily so, and claimed a right to further compleation through such an impressive act as to slay a member of the Inner Circle, except Davvol was apparently not so ambitious or was too infatuated with his self-proclaimed title of evincar.

Croag still could not be sure if Davvol was too simple, too stupid, or just more patient and crafty than the Phyrexian had ever credited. He had spent decades in consideration of such ideas while his body mended, unable to carry out previous designs with the strange subjects in Benalia or even attend to routine on Rath. Even Croag's temporary return to the state of being meat did not bring with it an understanding of Davvol's mind. Later, though, he would have such an answer. He would know Davvol's mind, all in its place.

He asked again. "You have news of Urza Planes—"

"No, Croag," Davvol interrupted, looking up from the newest batch of ruined corpses that lay at his feet. "No news of the negators currently hunting Urza. The 'walker has been very cautious these last several years." He glanced back, his lips pulled into a tight, wide-mouthed grimace. "I can't decide if Urza is worried for his own life for a change or if he has gone to ground in protection of his plans." He paused. "These," pointing at the mess in front of him, "were not sent after the planeswalker."

"If this is not Urza's work, who else has destroyed negators? Not the Vec." Rebellious they might be, but the Vec even in large numbers should not be able to kill a negator.

"Trees and flowers were mostly responsible for this," Davvol said, a frown pulling down the edges of his wide mouth. He brought his hands together, fingertips touching. "Animals. A few elves. The place is called Yavimaya, and it's dangerous, Croag, perhaps more so than Urza Planeswalker."

Nothing could be worse than Urza Planeswalker. Croag looked carefully at Davvol, searching his pale-skin face for signs of duplicity. The black skullcap Davvol wore still offered its inviting eye, the depression Croag had seen fit to design into that protective cap. That would be the only way to be sure, but Croag was not ready to dismiss Davvol yet. He shuffled closer, the few metal bands left on his covering robe rasping dryly for lack of glistening oil. Closer, Croag saw that the corpses had mostly been crushed or blown apart by explosion. Very little suggested magic, though perhaps artifice.

"Trees and plants do not stand in the way of Phyrexia," he screeched and hissed.

Davvol folded arms over his chest. "They do now. Yavimaya is completely hostile. The land itself attacks."

"Urza." The name escaped Croag before he bothered to consider. "This must be the 'walker's doing."

A shudder trembled through Croag's under-developed joints. How many ways could the planeswalker find to interfere with Phyrexia's return? Too many. Even once was too many.

"I don't believe so, Croag. A seeker found this place, and there is no evidence that Urza is involved. Plants that explode? Trees which turn suddenly supple and smash warriors between them?" Davvol kicked at the mangled leg of a negator, its hardened flesh shredded to the metal by some kind of shrapnel. A few wood splinters still protruded from the negator's areas of pure meat. "Too alien for the 'walker," he shook his head. "No, this is something different."

"Different is bad," Croag hissed, Davvol's soft speech beginning to wear on his patience. Croag should order

Davvol's voice compleated, able to speak in proper Phyrexian. "Different must be Urza. Destroy this place, Yavimaya."

Even the name caught in Croag's throat. A moment of silence stretched out, marked only by the irregular timing of Davvol's blinking eyes and Croag's rasping breaths.

"No," Davvol finally said, without preamble or qualification, a straight denial of Croag's order.

The Phyrexian drew himself up to his full height, cleft skull at a higher level than Davvol's head. His eyes glowed with the passion of molten steel as he leaned close to Rath's evincar.

"You will do as ordered." There was no room for denial here, or so Croag thought.

Croag didn't account for the negator that suddenly appeared at Davvol's side as if summoned by magic. Small and compact, it moved with fluid grace. It was one of the faster creations Davvol had developed over the centuries. Faster, perhaps, than Croag, even at the Phyrexian's strongest, which this time was not. It carried a saw-toothed shield. The other arm ended in a hand of oversized fingers all metal-tipped and backed by corrosive-fluid plungers. It had no armor to bind joints or slow its incredible response time. Croag noticed suddenly with a tremble of something akin to fear—it had no compleated ears. Would this creation even understand the Phyrexian language? Croag was certain it would not. This negator took orders in Davvol's meat-tongue language. This negator was present to kill Croag, and at this point it could do so. The Phyrexian never doubted that.

Davvol, to his credit, never bothered to threaten or even imply that the Phyrexian should feel threatened. Secure in his power, he simply repeated, "No." Then, only after a slow step away from Croag, he continued. "If you want to attribute every threat to Urza Planeswalker, Croag, you may, if you are that afraid of him. But we do not know enough of this Yavimaya to risk incredible resources. Yet. I refuse to underestimate an opponent. I will continue to press at this Yavimaya and find its weaknesses much as we did in Keld. And when I have its measure, then *I* will destroy it. As a present for the Dark Lord."

Croag shook, every fiber and component screaming for Davvol's death, but buried in the steward's refusal was a truth the Inner Council member recognized. Davvol was correct in that the Phyrexians had a habit of blaming Urza for any and all failures, because in three millennia of time, only Urza had orchestrated the defeat of Phyrexian plans. It could be possible that Croag now overlooked a new threat, and the Phyrexian could ill afford another mistake. That did not make his defeat here any easier to accept. He would know satisfaction, but not yet, not until he had healed.

Eyes blazing fiercely, casting red flickers before them, Croag turned away and moved from the room with his odd shuffling motion. His teeth clicked in exasperation. He still needed Davvol, and Davvol obviously believed that he still needed Croag, or the Phyrexian would have been killed. Croag would rely upon that for just a bit longer, then they would discover who was the true master of Rath.

Loren Coleman

* * * * *

Perhaps a visit to the newer attractors had not been the best of Davvol's ideas, not after the meeting with Croag, but his schedule called for monthly visits to inspire greater production of flowstone and that meant today. Rath's steward toured the complexes with brutal efficiency, executing workers if standards appeared lacking at all. By the time he reached the lower levels where the massive spinning blades drew glowing red lava up from Rath's molten underworld, the Vec had been alerted to their master's fury and were found climbing over machinery and coaxing every last ounce of effort from the devices—as it should be. Davvol took limited pleasure noting the steady rumble shaking the floor, his equipment holding up to stresses which would have caused the supports of the main attractors to buckle and give way.

A large room surrounded the spot where the encased blades penetrated Rath's flowstone crust to bore down into the lava beds far below. One hundred Vec worked furiously over controls, their blunt features bathed in sweat and soot. The heat pulsed at near-insufferable temperatures, the air hot, sulfurous and hardly breathable. Still, the machinery appeared to be well maintained, the joints greased with black sludge and most metal surfaces oiled for protection. He checked what few gauges he himself knew how to read and found the bladed dials rotating at full capacity, perfect, too perfect, in fact.

"Vec," he called out to the supervisor, ordering his presence. The humanoid ran over. "This facility is pulling up lava at the same rate as the main attractor,"

Davvol said, tapping the gauge. The supervisor nodded, eyes a pale but furious green and saying nothing. "But these facilities are better cared for!" Davvol shouted his fury into the smaller man's face. "Why are you not out-performing the main attractor by now?"

He flicked one hand toward a random worker, and immediately his negator leapt from the nearby shadows to seize the hapless Vec. With a violent motion it broke the Vec's back in three places. The worker was left laying on the blisteringly hot metal floor, crying in pain.

No Vec moved or spoke. Only the clanging and grinding of machinery spoiled a perfect moment of fear and loathing, then the supervisor barked out quick orders, and everyone fell to work with renewed energy. The noises intensified—a cacophony of metallic protests. The throb that shook the floor quickened perceptibly. Walls shook, and in places a few gauges cracked for the additional stresses. A sudden leak of sulfurous, yellow steam shot out from a ruined piping joint. Under such pressure, the thin stream sliced deep into one worker's leg like a fine blade and nearly amputated it. Everything else held, as Davvol had known it would.

"Better," he said aloud but not with anything resembling satisfaction. The increase in output would barely be felt in flowstone production. Rath's borders stretched out so far that to achieve a constant rate of growth was now impossible. The violence he had just committed had been simply a show of power, but it didn't help him shake the feeling of uncertainty he carried around with him. Casting a deformed shadow over Davvol's work here was Croag. The self-proclaimed evincar strode imperiously from the room, grinding his anger beneath metal-shod heels.

Davvol knew that he should have waited, not tipped his hand so soon to the Phyrexian, but the meeting had not been planned. That Croag had returned to the more active sections of the Stronghold did not bode well for the steward, who had hoped for another half-century or better. Five more decades of progress and Davvol might have accomplished just a little bit more. Perhaps he might have killed Urza Planeswalker by then, and Croag could have been safely disposed of so that Davvol alone reaped the rewards of such a victory.

Croag *had* returned now, and upon learning of Yavimaya he had ordered—to Davvol's mind—a poorly considered plan. Croag had pushed for obedience, so Davvol pushed back. He knew he could kill the injured Phyrexian, but he kept him around. If Croag were gone there would be another. It was better to have the devil you know—especially the one you know that you can defeat.

Even now Davvol sensed his personal guardian keeping pace behind him, the negator stalking shadows with deadly fluidity, ready to leap to Davvol's defense in a fraction of a second. It was of simple construction, very durable, and able to tangentially threaten Croag. Was it too soon? Would Croag now worry enough to move against Davvol or consider the idea that Davvol instead made a better ally than enemy?

It was a question with no easy answer. His echoing footsteps and those of his negator drove home the reality of exactly how alone he was here on Rath. Davvol stalked the Stronghold's lower levels and considered the possibility that today he had chosen wrong. Today, the first time in better than six hundred years, he had made his first major mistake.

Chapter 22

Lyanii hosted the meeting in Devas's cathedral, not a place of stringent religion—the Benalish definition of cathedral—but certainly a place of reflection and spirituality. An incredibly high vaulted ceiling rose overhead, alabaster arches opening up to covered balconies on the third and fourth stories. The Marshal wondered how many of her guests noticed that there was no access from the ground to those balconies.

A long, whitewashed oak table had been set for feasting. The delegation from Clan Capashen occupied one side. Representatives of Devas, most with the characteristic porcelain features that had been common to Serra's Realm sat on the other. The Marshal had placed herself in the middle, her best lieutenants to either side. Administrative diems and valued clerks also sat in attendance. Two former Benalish also sat among the Serrans, emigrants who had earned trust enough to share the secrets of Devas and also the table here tonight.

A table knife tapped on the side of a crystal goblet chimed a musical note repeatedly over the level of conversations. The low buzz faded, giving the man standing everyone's attention. Clan Leader Rorry Capashen placed the knife back on the table, nodded his thanks to all, and then looked to Lyanii. His brown eyes spoke of a calm intelligence. His strong face promised leadership. A descendent of Ellyn Capashen, Rorry had proven himself on the battlefield and at the bargaining table both.

Now he set his warm, steady gaze on Lyanii. "I was hoping we might discuss our business, now that we've finished your excellent repast."

Lyanii had wondered how long the Capashens' patience would last. The Serran Marshal glanced once to Karn—seated on a large stone block two positions down from Rorry Capashen—and then nodded her acquiescence. "By all means," she said calmly. But before he could begin, she shrugged and guessed, "You want our help in fighting the dark warriors."

Not one to be caught off guard for long, Rorry Capashen simply blinked his surprise while retaking his seat and then admitted it. "Yes. We've suffered their raids over years leading into centuries now, and they steadily get worse. This year it is particularly bad, and who knows what the next will bring? The Benalish court has refused our petition for organized involvement because most do not see a danger. Only Clan Blaylock is in agreement with us, having also met the raiders. But," and his eyes tightened, "I understand that your forces once took arms against them."

She couldn't help another glance toward Karn. He matched her gaze with a curious frown of his own, obviously not understanding the attention. He was certainly welcome in Devas and knew of the winged ones, though he retained no direct memory of the refugees' original ancestry. Karn simply knew that Urza vouched for Lyanii and her people—every ten to twenty years—and the golem would not gainsay the 'walker. More likely one of the students Lyanii accepted from time to time had let something slip. There were at least a dozen besides the silver man who had shared Devas's secrets. Karn would never betray Devas's trust.

The golem's presence, however, did speak for some pressure being brought to bear against them. A long-time associate of the Serrans, he often managed to win concessions that others might not have. Even if Karn didn't remember—couldn't remember—someone in Clan Capashen had noticed and likely wished to play off that connection here and now.

"You support this request, Karn?" It was a simple way of asking if Urza supported the request.

After a slight hesitation, the silver golem nodded. "I think you may want to consider it, Marshal Lyanii. People are being hurt." His pause answered Lyanii's real question.

"The people are frightened," Rorry Capashen spoke up again. "The legend that the Lord of the Wastes is returning has gained frightening acceptance among Clan Capashen." He tried to scoff at the old legends, but he was unable to purge his serious concern for his people.

"You don't believe in the Lord of the Wastes?" Lyanii remembered the first time she had heard of it herself. The merchant who had come upon the refugees their first year settling into Benalia had told her the story.

Rorry Capashen looked nonplussed at the question. "I do not," he said easily. "Are you saying that you do?"

Lyanii glanced to a few of her followers, noting their haunted eyes even now. "I think there is evil out there which we don't necessarily understand or even know about," she said cautiously. "Yes." Karn was leaning forward attentively, no doubt recognizing Urza's warnings in her vague statement. "There might be several so-called lords, and if I should someday find one, I would fight." She shook her head, strands of hair brushing the side of her face. "But I see no evidence of there being one here, Rorry Capashen. I'm sorry."

The Capashen leader took the refusal with proud bearing, though he could not hide all trace of disappointment from his voice. "As am I. My grandfather spoke of the training he received at Devas. He held you in high regard, Marshal. It would have been an honor to fight at your side." His brown eyes implored what he would not ask again in words. "I'm sorry you do not feel our cause is a just one."

Damn, Karn. Lyanii knew that last sparring attack was the golem's doing. Karn knew them well enough to realize that such a charge would not sit well. She gripped her hands into tight fists, stemming an outburst. Her eyes found the golem, and Karn had the good manners to shift uncomfortably under her non-blinking gaze. This meant something to the golem personally. That carried weight as well, but in this case not enough. This was not a training session. It would risk her people's lives. It might bring Phyrexia down on top of them again.

"Try to understand," she said, careful of how much she could safely say. "Our nation was once prosperous and content. Someone—" She paused, shook off that tack and started again. "We involved ourselves in a war that was not ours, and it cost us everything. That is not mine to risk again, not without better reason. We can't afford to be wrong." She slowly released her fists, wrapping her right hand instead around the stem of a crystal glass. "I'm sorry, Rorry Capashen. The heart to fight and a just cause are not enough."

The clan leader nodded, accepting her final answer.

Karn frowned, his silver face clouded with a dark expression. "That is not what you told Isarrk."

The glass's fragile stem snapped in her hand, cutting her palm and spilling dark wine onto the table. She fumbled with her linen towel but finally got it wrapped about her hand to stanch the trickle of blood. How had Karn remembered that? She had once told Isarrk that all a true hero needed was a just cause and the heart to defend it. Isarrk had eventually done so. Carefully she glanced to one of the Benalish humans sitting at the table on her side—a relative of Isarrk. The boy would not meet her gaze.

"Excuse me, Karn?" Rorry Capashen looked over at the silver golem, confusion apparent on his handsome face. The question was also in Lyanii's mind, and she silently thanked the Capashen leader for asking in her stead.

The golem appeared confused. He glanced from the clan leader to the Marshal of Devas and then stared at his own silver hand as he concentrated. Then he shook his head. "I'm sorry. Something I thought I remembered." His voice told of his own doubts. "A mistake."

The Capashen leader nodded, turned his attention back to their host. "My apologies, Marshal Lyanii, if Karn upset you."

Lyanii shook her head in response. "No, quite the opposite. He reminded . . . " she couldn't very well admit the entire truth, ". . . reminded me of another event. Let's say I will give your request further consideration, Rorry Capashen." She held up a hand at the clan leader's look of pleasant surprise. "Let's leave it at that for now, please." Not one to argue against a second chance, Rorry nodded at his fortune.

The Marshal lapsed back into silence as normal conversation resumed. She had more than an aversion to making the wrong choice again. Here was also the very real fact that after so many centuries Lyanii was finally beginning to understand something more than fighting and leading others in battle. She might want to avoid such things for both herself and her people. Was that wrong?

* * * * *

"Jhoira is my friend, my best friend. We met in the original academy, before the accident drove us from Tolaria. She named me Karn, for the old name of Thran metal. She said it meant strength."

That evening, alone in his apartments, the golem repeated his nightly mantra while pacing the floors of heavy timber. In times where nothing made sense, the repetitive statements allowed him some measure of focus.

Stopping at a bureau, the silver man placed one massive hand on the thick tomes he had filled with his own words over so many changing lifetimes. Why was he so preoccupied with the past when he knew that he could never hold on to it? Karn looked at the one portrait sketch he still carried with him in all his travels. Human she was, with dark hair and intense eyes. It was his oldest artifact from previous times, magically protected at some point in the past to preserve it. All he really knew was that her name was Jhoira, and that she had been a friend. He knew it from the nightly mantra he spoke. It was a promise to himself to never let the old memories completely fade, but they did, and they colored his current relationships, promising that they too would fade in time.

Slowly, Karn turned the picture down on its face. Not tonight. Tonight was for his current relationships, to consider them individually and together, because even as Karn admitted how important these relationships were to him, how they touched and influenced his life, he knew that he also touched upon theirs. How he remained in their memories, even after they passed from his, was suddenly more important to the golem than anything else.

Chapter 23

The sound was of splintering wood, like a hundred tiny explosions strung into long creaking strains, mixed with the shouts of battle and the snarls and growls of woodland creatures. The beleaguered enemy responded with roaring gouts of fire, the screech of wounded metal, and a cacophony of chittering and hisses.

For miles in every direction the canopy had shifted blue, a warning of intruders that continued to spread from treetop to treetop. The colors darkened the closer one arrived to the battle, the area of fighting shaded by trees—their foliage turned darkest black. Here Yavimaya's defenders met the small but lethal Phyrexian probe.

Leaves and thin branches whipped against Rofellos's face. The Llanowar moved too quickly astride his war moa for Yavimaya to shrug the limbs aside. Eyes clenched shut, he tracked his prey by sound and the growing scent of crushed marker beetles. Where most outside creatures found the scent offensive to the point of distraction, the elves knew it only as another piece of Yavimaya. They trusted its guidance just as they would movement reflected in their own eyes. Everything in Yavimaya worked together for the betterment of the whole, from plant to insect to animal to elf.

Now the elves were dashing in on their mounts to slash at the enemy flank, harrying the Phyrexians. They always withdrew before concentrated effort could be brought against them—only to show up in a new place on the offensive once again. Trees bent or shifted, twisting themselves atop their root system, to cover the elves' escapes. Brush would shrug aside, allowing access where before had only been a dense thicket of thorny vines and hardwood brush. Phyrexians who attempted to use such openings were destroyed by sharp brush and dart-throwing plants.

Yavimaya coaxed and guided so that not one of its woods-dwelling subjects was hurt by the forest's own hand. It rooted deep in Rofellos's thoughts, recognizing that here as nowhere else were the Llanowar elves supreme. The forest even allowed Rofellos to overrule a desire to recall Multani, the expenditure in resources and concentration unnecessary for so simple a battle. Their shared mind became the center from which Yavimaya structured its defense. His hand—*their* hand—clenched around the middle grip of his double-bladed sword. Rofellos sliced again at a footsoldier entangled in vines, splitting open its chest. The moa lashed out with its jet-black beak, taking an arm off at the shoulder. Then he—*they*—twisted about and leapt back into the gloom covering the forest. The stinging slaps of slender branches against Rofellos's face were easily ignored in favor of the freedom that came with fighting.

The Llanowar were warriors, but where Rofellos's

natural urge to bolt and run free pressed too sharply, Yav-imaya soothed him back into dormancy—a wild flower cultivated into a tamed garden. Rofellos found it hard to reconcile the different personalities that were now his: Rofellos the Llanowar, Rofellos the ambassador to—and *of*—Yavimaya.

No matter, Yavimaya promised. This eve he was at least acting Rofellos the Llanowar, and the night was golden in battle.

Rofellos yelled a Llanowar oath, taunting his enemies. The war moa he rode squawked a shrill call of its own, the warbling noise hard to track in the forests and hopefully leading to the enemy's confusion. Brush swayed before him, and he tucked his head down behind the moa's pow-erful shoulder as it leapt through a newly formed passage. He had circled to the Phyrexian rear, where their single, large war engine rolled forward oblivious to the trees shouldering into its armored sides. Its own demon head chewed at the roots of one tree, tearing through with mechanical efficiency. Rofellos rode along the flank of the juggernaut, taking the warrior picket by surprise. They barely knew he fought among them before his blade of living plantlife sliced deeply into armored carapace.

He whispered to his weapon, and the blades circled inward to reform as his staff, enabling him to hold his mount with that hand without worry about hurting the moa. His free hand dug into the leather satchel that swung at his side. He drew out a handful of acorns, toss-ing the collection of sharp points and rough caps into the jaws of the war engine as he rode past.

The mechanical leviathan shuddered, its internal gears grinding as they bent and bound. Armored plates, so impervious to outside attacks, split open as pressure from within surpassed its design tolerances. Roots worked their way out, digging for the ground and anchoring it in place. Limbs forced their way up through rents in the upper armor tree widening into thick boles. Rofellos paused in the safety of a thick steelthorn brush, his—*their*—eyes wild with delight at the run through the enemy force. They watched as—within less than a minute—a twisting stand of oak trees had burst from the innards of the giant machine. No mechanical animation left to it, its pieces littered the ground or were held in thick limbs high overhead.

Faster, Rofellos decided, a spark of his own mind flaring in their shared consciousness. The quick-growth acorns needed to sprout and develop faster. It would be even better if nearby trees could throw the little missiles themselves. He felt the twinge in the back of his brain as Yavimaya heard him and agreed.

The Llanowar leapt forward from the brush to race the moa around to a new side, his staff unfurling leaves which sharpened again into massive blades. He had other ideas. The elven mounts handled well enough, but Rofellos would prefer greater jumping ability so as to leap over an enemy line or onto the backs of their war machines. How about increasing the size of a dart-throwing plant for less range but more stopping power? Rofellos's thoughts separated again from the shared mind, briefly. He was surprised Yavimaya had not thought of such tricks on its own, but then the forest, while sentient, was not omniscient, and certainly not experienced at war, though it was learning.

Bloodlines

*   *   *   *   *

In the shadow of the Stronghold's volcano a small section of Rath and Yavimaya overlapped, but the raging sea of chaotic energy between planes worked to separate them. Davvol fought the Stronghold's machinery to retain control. Never before, not even at the edge of Rath's boundary curtain of swirling energies, had he known such a trial. Here, so close to the seat of power and control, the transference should have been easy. Not even the Soltari wailing could distract him here. Yet the weight forced on his mind slowly squeezed at his sanity, threatening to crush him for his temerity in challenging the laws of reality.

After so many years of receiving information from remote probes, Davvol required a first-hand account of how his warriors fared in the dangerous forest. Certainly he was not about to risk himself in that hostile setting. He felt the lands, the very nature of Yavimaya, shifting. Nothing seemed to remain static. Trees swayed, conforming to no natural patterns of growth or behavior. They even uprooted themselves, just to spite his efforts at holding the bridge. Now a new stand of oak, thick with intertwining boughs, erupted up from the bowels of his one war engine, decimating it and causing yet a new ripple of pain as a piece of the pattern slipped away and had to be rebuilt again. He felt as if he were in a contest against another mind for control of the machinery. Yet Croag was nowhere near strong enough to upset Davvol's designs, and the strange Soltari could hardly raise a distraction so close to the Stronghold.

Whatever the problem, it kept him distracted to the

point of being unable to properly evaluate the assault. He had time to note only a few points. Fire was, of course, a deadly weapon against plant and animal both, though the sap that boiled out of the bark of the trees squelched the flames rather than feeding them. While the compound released by his war engine would dissolve the wood eventually, these growths were proving resistant to immediate effect. At least the animals and elves still fell to blade, claw and tooth. If only the land itself were not so treacherous. How the elves had found mages of such caliber was beyond Davvol—for now.

As with anything, though, he had the time to observe and evaluate. His forces would improve for this battle, while nature was limited to such a slow progression that it could not hope to compete. It was a good thing, since the Phyrexians were not faring as well as he'd hoped. Davvol imagined the rage Croag might feel if he were to witness such a defeat in the making.

There was the elf warrior again, riding atop the large bird that he controlled with a skill that bordered on the two being somehow of one mind. This elf was different from the others Davvol glimpsed in those rare moments he devoted toward the battle. Apparently he was the only one of such size and marking. The elf rode deeper into the Phyrexian formation—a nimble dance frightening in its lethal grace. Davvol winced in pain as the Stronghold's control machinery fed back its effort in adjusting for a large stand of brush that finally succumbed to fire. That brush had separated Rath's evincar from the deadly elf commander. The dark-haired warrior glanced sharply in Davvol's direction.

Then with a blood-chilling cry, the elf spurred his

mount forward and stepped out onto the flowstone of Rath itself!

Davvol recoiled in shock, never before suspecting that as his own troops moved back and forth across the threshold so could others make the transference of their own volition, though it made sense. Stronghold's machinery held the bridge, reacting to the presence of any life in the area but not ultimately controlling who might pass through. This was not knowledge Davvol would want an enemy to return with.

The elf appeared just as confused for a moment, surveying his surroundings with a blank expression, then the warrior's fierce gaze locked onto him, dark eyes burning with hatred and rage. Davvol placed his mental touch upon the elf's mind, sensing for any connection to a leader or the mage who opposed the bridge into Yavimaya.

The elf, Rofellos *and* Yavimaya. The names came to Davvol, bleeding out of the elf's mind.

His concentration divided, Davvol was unable to hold the bridge between planes. Rofellos was torn between following the retreating presence and killing the stranger before him.

Like an artifice puzzle of gears and axles, the last piece was snapped into place, and Davvol understood. Yavimaya was part of the elf because Yavimaya was alive and aware. The forest manifested itself through its creatures and plantlife, and it controlled the very land over which it grew. Yavimaya opposed the evincar in holding the bridge. Even as Davvol challenged Yavimaya with the troops and machines under his control, so the forest was sensing at the boundaries of Davvol's control over the machinery holding the threshold. Davvol mentally recalled his warriors, reached out and pulled back what lifeless bodies he could quickly locate and grab. A quick hand motion summoned his negator guard from behind him and set it toward slaying the elf.

The elf was just fast enough to save his own life. Kicking off from the mount, placing the large bird between himself and the advancing blur, the elf pitched backward and rolled into the flowstone jungle that overlapped onto Yavimaya's forested land. Cursing, Davvol snapped after the elf, determined to sink mental teeth into him and drag him back over, but he was gone, cloaked no doubt by the blanketing intelligence of the forest.

His troops faded back across the threshold. Bodies of the fallen formed back up from the flowstone. As he severed the channel between worlds, Davvol cursed his pause, which had gifted that elf his life.

It wasn't until later, remembering the blood and oil dripping down from the elf's green blades, that Davvol wondered what else might have been—if the elf had not been given pause as well.

* * * * *

One half of the way around Dominaria, Multani had felt the changes take root. At the time, he was in the Burning Isles, where the renowned Shipbuilders' Guild was systematically destroying forests through logging. He worked among the villages and city-states who sold their timber off to the guild without thought to the future, teaching them care of the lands and trying to prevent their coming troubles. Already the rains fell less, drying up streams and smaller rivers on which many hamlets depended. Wind erosion cut scars into the land and dropped dust storms over some cities.

Multani's own work consumed him, distracting attention away from the happenings back in his parent forest. He had known of the Phyrexian incursion of years back, of course, feeling the forest's pain reflected as aches within his own body and mind. Alterations were to be expected, and as they progressed his appearance changed with the forest's. The nature spirit's bark skin already possessed the strength of ironwood armor. Multani recognized his improvements and approved as Yavimaya approved. Except the nature spirit did not take into consideration the involvement of Rofellos.

One day, Multani noticed the odd looks given him by his latest congregation. He followed their gaze back to his own shoulders. Growths extended from them in spiky fashion—ridged armor. The same growths sprouted near every major joint. He had gained length in his limbs, his toes thickening into sturdy stands and fingers extending now into the beginning of hardwood claws. Never before particular about his appearance, the nature spirit now looked and did not care for all he saw.

It was then he had heard the first whisper of Rofellos's voice entwined with the thoughts that were Yavimaya's. Multani mentally pushed his mind more in parallel with the forest's sentience to better understand the changes. It was a simple endeavor, usually, to bury his thoughts and intellect back into the stream of consciousness from which it had sprung, only this time he felt a resistance, so he pushed harder.

Rofellos pushed back.

Even as Multani felt at the boundaries now set within Yavimaya's consciousness, the nature spirit heard the forest's call to return. The nature spirit walked into a nearby stretch of forest—and disintegrated.

The nature spirit's physical body was actually but a shell—pieces of wood and bark and moss, shaped into a humanoid form—that allowed him to more easily interact with the various races of Dominaria. Now it fell away, raining to the ground as sticks and twigs and scale flakes of ironwood bark. His mind, all of who Multani actually was, faded back into Yavimaya's consciousness, but it was held distinctly apart from that which the forest now shared with Rofellos. Instantly the nature spirit was back within his homeland, the familiar feel of its high canopy and lush undergrowth. He sensed the incredible resources still buried in the land from the accelerated mulch cycle—so much strength yet untapped.

Multani stepped from one of the massive trees of a coastal forest, a watchtower tree, standing as high again as the surrounding woods. He peeled away from the bole like some new fast-growth, whole again in his bark-skin form and mossy hair. What the tree itself could not provide grew rapidly from his large frame. Yavimaya's incredible reserves fed him from the land through his contact with it.

The Llanowar elf waited in the shadows of a grenade plant, its bulbous growths much larger than the one they had inspected together so many years before. "Yavimaya wishes our physical presence," he said.

Unnecessarily, as Multani received the same knowledge even as the elf spoke it aloud. The ground to one side split and opened, the immense root system buried beneath Yavimaya welling up to allow a cavern into the forest's depths. The two moved toward it together.

Dwarfed next to Multani's larger frame, Rofellos never once showed any discomfort. His gaze had braced Multani immediately, as if sizing up a possible challenge and then turned elsewhere. He looked more the wild elf than before, as if in its latest cycle Yavimaya encouraged the reversion. Thin, thorny vines had been woven into a few of his braids. While not fully painted, the elf wore blue smudges under his left eye and a small circular design of red and blue decorated the right side of his neck.

"It has been a long time, Rofellos." Multani drew abreast of the Llanowar as the two moved along the dimly lit cavern. He noticed the bow, slung across the elf's back. A quiver of ash arrows rode against his left shoulder. "You fought well against the Phyrexians."

"I live to serve."

Multani did not disagree vocally, though inwardly he knew better. The nature spirit lived to serve—working Yavimaya's will in the world outside. Rofellos lived to war—the forest's weapon against its enemies, subsumed by Yavimaya for his knowledge and expertise. Multani tried to push such thoughts over to Rofellos, make the Llanowar aware again of his identity, but the fracture persisted that separated their minds from each other.

Seed torches lit the interior. Plants which sat high on a stalk and produced a phosphorescent pollen that burned cool to the touch. They sprouted along the wall as needed. Many were the color of Tolarian mage-lit stones, ranging from blue-white to lavender shades. Deeper, one burned a rare golden color that washed the wooden walls with an aureate shine. Rofellos and Multani paused here, knowing that the golden torch marked an end to their walk. A new chamber opened in the wall next to them, and they stepped into it as one.

In the center of the chamber, growing up from the floor, a branch of white-ash wood stood alone. Seven feet high, it was topped with a tapered frond that Multani knew was as rigid and sharp as any human-crafted blade. In his presence, Yavimaya gave the weapon its final living force. A green membrane grew up from the floor to wrap the staff in leathery chitin. That membrane connected the weapon to part of Yavimaya's force, making it able to bend itself into several different weapons such as the bow Rofellos wore or the double-bladed sword he had used to battle the Phyrexians. Multani knew this, though he still did not understand the barrier that now existed in Yavimaya's mind. That knowledge remained outside of his grasp.

"It is yours," Rofellos said, his voice soft yet filled with a mixture of awe and pride as if the weapon was a great honor. To the Llanowar, perhaps it was.

Multani, centuries spent working in harmony with the lands and people of Dominaria, did not look upon it with such reverence. "What if I do not wish it?" he asked, startled at his own words.

His voice rang out stark in the chamber, alone. Rofellos glared coldly. Yavimaya did not answer, did not encourage him one way or another. When Multani thought to push for the forest's mind he found it withheld, completely.

He was alone.

Yavimaya's nature spirit suddenly understood then what it meant to be his own creature. He would not be compelled, where once the choice would have been made by Yavimaya and simply accepted by him without question. Yavimaya was of two minds now. Rofellos and Multani would be allowed to choose their own paths, and if necessary, Yavimaya would then share a separate path with each. The nature spirit almost declined the weapon and left Rofellos to share such experiences with Yavimaya while he concentrated on healing and teaching, which had been his life for so long.

He almost declined, except he recognized that Rofellos required his help and healing more than any. Somewhere deep within the Llanowar elf's mind a tiny spark that was wholly Rofellos still burned. That part of the elf, Multani knew, likely struggled against the oppressive presence of Yavimaya's mind. It was the same spark that had pushed back, resisting Multani's efforts to share Yavimaya's consciousness. If the nature spirit was ever to reach in to help the elf, the two would need a common link through Yavimaya's consciousness.

Multani moved forward, slowly. He grasped the staff, accepting it into the crook of one arm as the base separated cleanly from the floor.

For an instant the barrier fell away. Multani felt it slip, brought down by Rofellos's own feeling of companionship as Multani accepted the weapon. That tiny spark still burned within Rofellos's mind. Multani breathed air to that spark in encouragement for the individual of Rofellos. He sent encouragement for the young Llanowar who had relieved the nature spirit of a portion of his burden and was now lost because of it. Personal identity was just as important as a sense of greater belonging. The nature spirit was just beginning to recognize his own balance between the two. He could only hope to do the same for Rofellos.

Chapter 24

The artificial thunder of hooves pounding the ground stormed across the battlefield as Devas's cavalry tore through a thin advance line of black-clad warriors. Sword and mace and lance rang against each other and glanced off metal armor. The screams of dying men and women, the shrieks of a wounded horse, all added to the cacophony of chaos that enshrouded the field. The air stank of sweat and blood and the gore spilled upon the ground. Beneath it all was the hated scent Lyanii remembered all too well from centuries before. It was the scent of glistening oil—the stench of Phyrexia.

Lyanii parried a slashing attack directed at her by one of the tall, spindle-limbed warriors. She turned its sword with ease, spinning into a riposting arc that severed the head and part of a shoulder from its body. Slime splattered onto her own armor, spotting its opalescent finish with inky foulness. She kicked over the creature and paused to catch her breath. A century ago she would not have even registered the fatigue—One more sign that age was finally claiming her.

"Therri!" The Marshal called out for her aide, a wary

eye on the large engines moving in the Phyrexian back-field. Therri Capashen swam up through a thick knot of fighting, moving with a grace that belied her relative newness to the field of battle. "Message to Gavvan," Lyanii ordered, naming Therri's brother whose Capashen forces held the center of the field. "We're holding the flank, but the enemy has moved both war engines oppo-site our position. If we are going to break the line, it will have to be done from his position. Go!"

Therri was off, but rather than race for the rear lines where she might hope to grab a mount, the young war-rior peeled away at a tangent and fought past a number of Phyrexian guard before breaking into open field where her legs carried her toward her clansmen. Lyanii could not help being torn between pride and frustration for the reckless maneuver.

"Remind you of anyone?" Karn asked, his voice easily carrying over the sounds of battle.

The golem carried a large shield in one hand and a huge mace in the other, his normally bright silver finish streaked with black foulness. Two armored Phyrexian warriors clawed and cut their way past one of the Serran Guard, bringing their long swords in at the silver man. The golem took one slash against his shield, stepped back from the other and then brained one warrior with the mace. The polished helm caved under Karn's great strength, and the warrior dropped lifeless.

The Serran officer ran the second Phyrexian through, her blade flat to the ground in proper fashion as it burst through the neck joint. The creature inside died with a gurgling screech. She stepped up next to Karn to take advantage of the natural shield the large golem presented

"Of any *one?*" she asked, changing the question. "Of every one. All of them. From Rorry all the way back to Jaffrey's first son. They're all in her and more." She felt a moment of pity that Karn could not remember Therri's progenitors, but then a spike of curiosity wondered at how he had come by asking such a question regardless. How many could he remember and compare her to?

There was no time to ask as Karn stepped forward into a new hole broken in the Serran line. A small, stoop-shouldered creature, more artifice than flesh, sprang for the opening and was slammed back hard by the golem's shield. It scampered back, hiding behind the legs of a guard elite. The golem thrust his mace forward like a spear, the large spike on its top piercing the slender ribcage area and winning only a thin trickle of oil.

The creature's slender arm shot out, raking scratches across the golem's near-invulnerable silver form. Its other arm, covered with a variety of blades, tubes and strange artifice, slashed inward as well but was fouled by a spear thrust from one of the Serrans. The Phyrexian turned against this new opponent, tearing past spear and shield and through the Serran's chain mail. It ignored Karn's attacks, determined to put an end to one of its enemies.

Lyanii leapt forward, shouldering aside her own man and taking his place before the onslaught of fast, lethal metal. Karn continued to rain sledgehammer blows against the Phyrexian's back and side. Lyanii's sword kept time with the creature, turning aside its hard-hitting blows with inches to spare. Then the Marshal missed.

The beast's slender arm sneaked past her guard, piercing the armor that shielded her right hip and digging slender talons in bone-deep. Lyanii fell back, rolling away from the creature's grasp. It bought her time, seconds only. She knew she wouldn't rise back up on the wounded limb. The Phyrexian followed, ready to finish her off. It would have, except for Karn.

The golem cast away his shield, wrapping his large hands about the reinforced shaft of the spiked mace. He came at the Phyrexian with an overhead rounding blow that caught the armored creature at the upper curve of one shoulder. The guard stumbled to its knees. Karn spun around, placing his weight and incredible strength behind another blow that buried several points into the Phyrexian's small face mask. It toppled back, screeching in a sound that reminded Lyanii of sharp claws drawn over a board of slate.

Karn helped the Marshal back to her feet, lifting her one-handed. Lyanii winced putting pressure on her leg. "Can you stand?" he asked.

Can *we* stand? That was the question haunting Lyanii's mind through the shroud of pain. For the second time in her long life—the first being on Serra's plane when her people had been subverted by Phyrexians and led against their own—the Marshal felt doubt in battle. This was what she had been created for by Serra. It was all she knew, and it wasn't enough.

Lyanii shrugged off the golem's help, anger at her own weakness making her abrupt. "I'll be all right." She exhaled a short exclamation of frustration. "We'll make it," she answered her own question, regaining control of her emotions.

Shouts of confusion and fear now erupted from the center of the Capashen lines. Lyanii grabbed up her main standard, planted nearby, ready to signal her next order.

Her battlefield experience whispered the reason behind the upset even before word finally reached the Serrans. Gavvan Capashen had fallen! Slain by a monster, the word said. The Capashen middle sagged, Phyrexians pressing forward. Lyanii paled, recognizing the beginnings of a rout and knowing the slaughter that would follow.

She remembered that she had sent Therri straight into its middle.

* * * * *

Therri Capashen had been close enough to see her brother fall, his personal guard holding the center of the Benalish line, the Capashen standard driven into the earth while Gavvan lent his own sword to the fight. Never one to sit back, he shared the danger and inspired those around him with his heroics. With sweeping arcs he took the spindly, mechanical arms off a Phyrexian warrior, the edge of his sword striking sparks against the black armor. Spraying oil, the creature fell back and one of the ornate-armored guard moved up into its place.

Gavvan wasted no time with this one, pulling the short rod from his belt and thrusting it forward. An ancient gift from Master Malzra, artificer and matchmaker, the rod was a Capashen heirloom. Malzra had promised it a defense against violent artifice, though it should be used sparingly. One of the Phyrexian guards, so much metal crafted toward lethal intent, seemed close enough to the old artificer's description. The creature's slender arm, slashing in toward Gavvan's throat, froze immediately as if the metal joints suddenly fused. The abomination shuddered to a stop. It became a frozen statue on the battlefield, and her brother simply shoved it aside. As it crashed to the ground, its animation stilled forever, the clan leader's personal guard shouted out a cry of, "Gavvan!"

Except her brother had not noticed the malformed, black-flesh creature stalking the lines and moving against his position. If he had, he ruled it a minor warrior due to its lack of metal armor. Its bloated chest rippled and pulsed as it moved forward on thin legs. Large, hook-shaped claws trailed near the ground at the ends of long arms. Glistening crystal eyes glowed a dull orange as it riveted its gaze on Gavvan. Therri simply knew that this creature *needed* no armor and that it hunted her brother.

"Gavvan!" she yelled in warning, pushing frantically past other Capashen warriors and laying about with her sword when the enemy pressed in too close. One long Phyrexian blade snaked through to slice away part of her leather armor, scoring a shallow cut along one arm. Therri ignored it. "Gavvan, no!"

In the other shouts of the Clan Leader's name, Gavvan missed the warning. The creature leapt forward over the last twenty feet, legs driving out as if it was some kind of titanic insect. Before landing it already began to spew a dark, sludgelike substance that stuck to Gavvan's arm and chest. The chain mail protecting his body held up, but the leather strips on his arm began to smoke at once. Gavvan had time for a single backhand slash at the monster. His blade hardly cutting the tough, wrinkled flesh over one shoulder, and then it stuck fast. Twisting violently to one side, Gavvan's sword was torn from his grasp.

The Phyrexian craned its head forward. Its chest heaved, and its throat expanded. A torrent of black sludge belched over Gavvan's face and shoulders. The young clan leader screamed, hands clawing at his own face as exposed skin began to blister and smoke. Blinded, thrashing about in pain, he made an easy target. The great, hook-shaped claws seized Gavvan, lifting him from the ground, and with a violent scissorslike motion left him in two large pieces, dead.

Therri stood in shock, the battle forgotten as she stared at the ruin of her brother's body. So close—she'd been so close to helping. If she'd taken a horse from Lyanii's flank . . . if she hadn't wasted valuable seconds in any of four different fights along the way.

The Phyrexian army pushed forward, now spearheaded by the monstrous beast that killed Gavvan. Suddenly, Therri realized how close they were to a full rout as news of her brother's death swept the lines and demoralized the Capashen. These black creatures, never skilled in working as a coherent unit, were pushing forward singly to exploit the sudden shift. Beneath Therri's doubts and recriminations she found a spark of rage, which she fanned until it warmed her entire body. She knew these things for the evil they represented, preying on a moment of weakness engineered by some kind of special monster.

Springing forward into the monster's path just as it set upon one of Gavvan's personal elite, Therri parried an attempt to fasten those hooked claws into the soldier and watched for her opportunity. She had recognized the nature of the creature's movements necessary to call up its terrifying weapon. There again was the bellowlike force of its bloated chest and expansion of the throat as it craned its head forward. Gavvan's sword was still stuck in its shoulder, a warning against any slashing attack. Instead she ducked into the creature, risking its claws as she drove her sword forward with all her strength into its throat. She left it there. Sludge leaked out down the blade. She danced back, avoiding the claws that suddenly flailed about as if possessed of their own mad intelligence. No weapon, Therri wrenched the nearby Capashen standard free of the ground. Reversing it, she bore it back at the Phyrexian like a spear, its ornate tip aimed unerringly for one of its crystalline eyes. The dull orange gem shattered, and she drove through into the head. Leaping up behind the attack, she rode the creature backward and into the middle of the Phyrexian line.

Therri counted herself dead. Perched atop the creature's bloated chest, disarmed and surrounded by the enemy, she expected a finishing stroke any time. She didn't care, having avenged Gavvan, having blunted the Phyrexian advance. Then a black-armored warrior to her right stumbled and fell—one arm missing and its chest pierced by a sword. The sword was still held by the Capashen warrior she'd saved seconds before. Only a fraction behind were two more of Gavvan's personal guard, driving in on her left and pushing the enemy away from her. She took quick stock of the battle. The four of them were a tight knot in the midst of the Phyrexian line.

Wrenching Gavvan's sword free, her own covered by too much of the burning sludge, Therri also took hold of the Capashen standard and pulled it from the creature's head. She waved it crisply back and forth, the white and gold ensign fluttering and snapping. Three men to her force and clan still in danger of rout, Therri accepted the only option left to her.

She led them forward, on the attack.

Chapter 25

A sea of raging energies broke over Urza in a kaleidoscopic wash. It permeated his mind and nearly drowned his consciousness. As certain as Urza was that there must be a fundamental pattern to this chaos, underlying everything, it remained of such a magnitude that even the planeswalkers could not comprehend it. Propelling his mind through the chaos on will alone, the 'walker was trailing a Phyrexian. He followed a dark beacon—the characteristic pattern left by a Phyrexian portal device. He pursued a trail left by the creature he now pursued—and would destroy.

The negator had ambushed him. Its teeth were blunt, unusual for a Phyrexian, and set at wide irregular intervals. With every breath those teeth rang out with energy-disrupting force. The hisses and screeching that made up Phyrexian speech formed partially translated in Urza's mind, drawing a shadowy lethargy over the 'walker's thoughts. Urza still remembered how he had stood there, only vaguely aware of the mounting problem.

With a voice able to whisper a numbing darkness into his mind, the thing had been on him with little chance to prepare. Except for that strange new power, the negator had relied on physical assaults and an old system of burning fluid. The storage tanks were not even protected by the desiccated flesh covering the rest of its deformed body. The skin was simply split open in three places, and tanks were buried partway into its frame. Metal-braided tubing connected the tanks to a shoulder-mounted weapon. It was an older negator, set after him long ago. Hardly a match, especially once Urza had used his staff to knock away half of the creature's lower jaw. Without its siren's sound, the negator had chosen flight—to report its partial success back to its masters, no doubt.

Urza was not about to allow that to happen. His mind piercing the veil, Urza drew his body into form and set foot down upon a strange plane. For a moment he thought he remained partway into the chaos between worlds, the steel-gray skies cascading with the same energy as did the void. The clouds were real enough, roiling in strange winds, and the ground firm beneath his feet—though he sensed its potential for treacherous footing. The dull tan stone stretched in seamless perfection over a rough plateau and then fell down an impressively long and steep mountainside into the deep valley below. The mountain ended only a few hundred yards above him at a sharp ridge. Halfway up that slope the negator had paused, dark eyes staring back at the enemy who had trailed it.

Urza drew in the winds, striking them by will to fit his own pattern. The wall hammered into the Phyrexian, driving it back downslope. Its progress thwarted, the creature spun and leapt for the 'walker—and died midflight, a summoned phantom snatching it up in a large mouth of teeth and shredding desiccated flesh away from a metal-reinforced skeleton. Black, decaying meat clinging to few metal cauldrons and a few dull gray bones rained to the ground.

Yes, it was an older creation of Phyrexia, not too dissimilar from what he might have seen in the days he traveled with Xantcha. So many worlds traveled then, he explored the planes of the Dominarian Nexus and out to the fringe of the multiverse itself. Now this world—a world he had never 'walked before. The chaotic sky lacked a sun, and the ground, this strange stone, was not true soil but manufactured.

Welcome to Rath, planeswalker.

Distracted at the importance of his discovery, Urza did not immediately question the appearance of a new voice. This was a created plane, like Serra's Realm—like Phyrexia.

"Rath is an artificial plane," he said, answering aloud.

That is correct.

Urza now realized that the voice sounded within his mind, not his ears. He guarded his thoughts, wary once again. His expanded consciousness identified the intrusive thoughts as a simple voice, unable to read his mind but "heard" through the same function that allowed him to speak in anyone's language. "Where are you?" he asked, finding no places a body could hide.

Lost. And not even you can redeem our bodies, Urza, if Urza Planeswalker you are. Look above you. Look beyond.

Above him Urza saw only the sharp ridge and heard the cut of wind slicing over it. "Look *beyond*," the voice had said. The powerstones burned within his eyes, replacing the illusion of mortal blue as he concentrated his preternatural senses. He saw their outlines, spectral dances of energy, sometimes twisting into a simple globular pattern but more often holding a humanoid shape with arms and legs and head. There were three of them, then ten, then fifty. Similar to his own form of pure energy, but they were so much more basic in nature. They swam along the ridge, unthreatening.

"I am Urza," he admitted cautiously, continuing to tap the mana of traveled lands should he require the power. "How do you know me? And who are you?"

Who else would bring war to Rath rather than await Rath to bring war to him? We are the Soltari. One of the patterns of energy pulsed. *I am Lyna.*

The Soltari. From the depths of his memory Urza recalled the name, a small city-state of Dominaria, which mysteriously disappeared back in the days when he and Xantcha had worked to free Efuan Pincar from the Phyrexians, over two hundred years before his founding the first Tolarian academy. Lost, Lyna had said. Lost between worlds!

Urza had no need of bending to the ground. His contact with it allowed his consciousness to work against the strange stone—to test its properties and sense its purpose within the plane of Rath. He could feel the movement far below, spreading outward to the distant horizon. It was a flow of malleable stone, able to hold back the energy curtains and force a new plane into existence—able to penetrate the veil and rip pieces of Dominaria away. What had Lyna said? Rather than await Rath to bring war to him? The planeswalker leapt into the air, flying above the ground as he rushed for the summit—the direction from which the strange stone flowed.

He found himself on the volcano's rim, staring down into an incredible caldera. The base of which was spanned by an incredible fortress tower. Dark metals gleamed beneath eerie lightning. This place was obviously Phyrexian in architecture, and it had to be the nerve center of Rath in that the stone radiated outward from it as it continued to push in all directions. Urza reached down through the fortress, testing the production of the strange stone. He felt the tremors shaking beneath.

It can overlap Dominaria. Lyna again. *Such has been done many times. We were the first, and the only failure that cost so many lives, though with any transfer some are lost. They wander Rath or their own lands, always apart. You will destroy this place?*

Though he had contemplated just that, now the 'walker shook his head in a silent negative. "No," he finally said. "It doesn't feel as if I can." He looked hard at the fortress below. "Different from Serra's Realm," he said, thinking aloud. "It will not collapse so easily. The stone holds the curtain back—it would take massive destruction of the land itself, of the world." Then the purpose of Rath hit him—a hard cruel blow to his mind. "This is their staging area for the invasion. No portals. From here they hope to set entire armies across the world."

You must destroy this place—the Stronghold. We have worked to distract the overseers here. We have pushed at the equipment over great amounts of time, but our work is too slow. They will finish soon.

"No," Urza said, offering a grim smile. "Not soon. I felt your work beneath the fortress. The equipment is weakened and being run too hard. Artifice requires more care—a lesson the Phyrexians will learn without my help. It would be better if they never knew I was here."

You will simply leave then? This was no judgment, just a clarification from Lyna.

"I will, but you are welcome to return with me." Urza felt again at their energy forms, certain his strength could pull them across a short 'walk between planes. "I cannot give you back form, but I can return you to Dominaria. And when the time is right, I might be able to give you revenge." How many years had these people waited? A millennium?

We would like that. Phyrexia has much to answer for.

Urza couldn't have agreed more.

* * * * *

The lingering scent of dinner, grilled swordfish from the leftovers that Barrin had walked past in the kitchen, told the mage he hadn't missed the meal by more than thirty minutes. That was subjective, of course. Having just come through the timelock, Rayne would have actually finished hours before Barrin ever left real time for their shared home. The wonders we have done here on Tolaria, he thought, not a little bitterly. For the sacrifice of one meal, Barrin had been able to spend a full day with Urza.

A poor substitute, he decided. If only there wasn't so much to do and now so much more, after Urza's revelation.

The house was silent except for a crackling fire, which warmed the main room, occasionally tossing out a small spark, which glowed dull red on the hearth before fading to a cinder. Rayne waited on the couch, legs tucked beneath her and lost under the folds of her silken robes as she stared into the dancing flames. His wife did not greet him.

"You are still not working?" he asked, lacing concern heavy into his voice.

Barrin couldn't remember the last time Rayne had gone into her workshop. He was concerned, of course, but he also did not want Rayne to hear the doubts crowding his thoughts—doubts for her, for them. Every day he hoped she would solve her problems, uncertain how he might help.

"I didn't want to get involved in a new project just now." Rayne put little feeling behind the excuse. She studied her husband with haunted eyes. "I had hoped you would be home early, that we could talk . . ." She trailed off, waiting.

Barrin paced over to the couch and sat wearily on the opposite end. Usually Rayne would have asked after Urza's reasons for an emergency meeting, especially since the 'walker had simply shown up this morning and pulled the mage away. She was obviously beyond caring about academy business this night. The short stretch of fabric and cushion that separated Rayne from him seemed at once a great chasm with sharp rocks waiting below. He ventured a foot toward the edge, dreading where it might lead.

"We can always talk, Rayne." His spirits lifted slightly as he discovered he actually meant it. The shock of Urza's news, about the artificial plane of Rath, left the mage with a new perspective. Suddenly he saw the avoidance of their problems over the last few years, and he felt the worse for it. "We should've talked some time ago." He heard the regret in his own voice, hoped Rayne read into it as well. "If ever I wished that Urza's time travel machine was still functional to be able to relive a period of my life, this is it."

The time machine. How many problems could be traced so far back? The shattered temporal zones, the constant threat of Phyrexians discovering Tolaria, then Urza's second academy, and the projects developed— when was the last time Barrin had truly considered any of those projects?

Rayne shifted uneasily. "The world has passed us by, Barrin. And we're," she paused and then put it in terms more familiar, more comfortable, "we're winding down. This is a problem we've avoided for too long. Yes or no. Stay or go."

"Easily asked," Barrin said with a heavy sigh, feeling every day of his eight relative centuries of life. Rayne had started with the one problem on which he knew he would have to fight her. "I walked around Tolaria," he said by way of edging into the discussion. "All around it, which is why I'm so late. The island is not in good health." It was a euphemism for the ruined lands now blowing dusty tendrils out over the ocean, the failing crops, and now worries over the water table. "The island is suffering but still the academy goes on, teaching and learning and building. How much more might we have accomplished, Rayne, without the Legacy, the bloodlines and Metathran wasting so many valuable resources?"

"Were they wasted?

"I don't know. And maybe that's the trouble." Barrin smoothed his cloak flat, ran fingers back through his graying hair. "It cost us Gatha, Timein, and dozens of others over the years. The Phyrexians claim their price, even when they aren't attacking, and the Legacy . . . " He paused. "It finally seems we've put all our hopes into one plan, into Urza. If he's wrong, again, or if he simply makes too many mistakes along the way, then it's all over."

Rayne wiped at her eyes with the heel of one hand. "I have to leave," she said simply.

"I know, and I have to stay."

There, it was said. Her admitting her decision freed him to admit his. Living in slow time for so long with only brief vacations back into the real world had left them both drained, but where everything else paled, still Barrin could hang onto his duties. Those duties would be impossible to run from anywhere but here—for now—for as long as it took to complete the Legacy and discover its heir. Urza's revelation had convinced him that he must see this through to the end. He was always the outsider, never at peace with the world, his family or himself. He breathed a heavy sigh and proceeded to slowly tell Rayne about the meeting with Urza—about Rath and why he was needed in slow time now more than ever before.

Rayne had her own private demons to dispel—he knew—from listening in on her nightmares some nights. He knew from the truth Urza all but admitted at their meeting the subjective year before. Trapped inside a slow-time cage with the darkness, her every moment suffused with Phyrexia or the preparations against them, she could never come to terms with that black side of her nature. She could never come to terms with being a child of Phyrexia—whether she recognized it as such or not it was true. She was one of the bloodlines—Urza's child—one of the thousands touched unknowingly by the 'walker.

To his surprise, Rayne shook her head. "Then I stay as well." Not the same emphatic statement she might have made at the project's beginning, but a weary acceptance of the circumstances.

Barrin hadn't expected that, though inwardly his hopes sparked that the two of them could see this through to the end together. "Are you sure?"

"No." She stretched a tentative smile over her face, apparently found that it didn't cause her any new pain. "I can't leave you behind. I refuse to let Tolaria, Phyrexia or even Urza separate us." She stood, one hand catching Barrin's and pulling him up after her. Standing there, both his hands around both of hers, they stared into each other's eyes. "I do not want you lost to me, Barrin, my husband. Do what you must, what needs doing." She released his grip, stepping away in a whisper of silk and the light whisk of leather sandals against the wooden flooring. "I'll be waiting. Always." She backed her way from the room, eyes tearing only slightly but her confidence in her husband never wavering. In that, Rayne obviously possessed no doubts. She turned at the entryway and walked toward their private chambers.

How long he stood there, lost in his own thoughts, Barrin wasn't sure. The fire hissed and popped, the flames offering a small measure of company and solace though never so warm as the touch of Rayne's hands against his. His conscience and sense of duty both nagged at him, finally prodding him from the room and moving him along as far as the long hall. There he paused, staring in the direction of his private offices, knowing there was work to be done, but putting off Rayne who had sacrificed again for their common good. He turned away from the offices, heading instead toward their chambers. Perhaps he couldn't solve Rayne's problems, but he could be there for her as she so often had been for him.

His work could wait one more evening.

Chapter 26

Croag had waited for this day.

A tremor rumbled through the floors of the Stronghold, and in places metal bracing squealed under new stress. Such quakes were commonplace these last several years, the result of running the machinery so hard for so long. With each day the purpose of Rath came so much closer to being fulfilled, then only the task of the Dark Lord would remain, and Dominaria would belong to the Ineffable. Pushing for that day, Davvol had decided on another inspection. He would try to find a way to silence the tremors, but at the same time he pushed the Vec and the machinery all the harder. Guards in tow, he started his routine. He left his negator behind.

For better than two centuries now, Croag had worked to heal himself, a slow and even painful process, though at times the pain had been rather exquisite to feel: the culture and growth of new meat, the slow infusing with artifice, mixing his blood with fresh glistening oil. His strength had taken decades to rebuild, bringing back his powers even as he learned to alter and improve on his old design. Now came the time of testing himself—of reversing the shift in Rath's power that occurred the day he had been struck down by the witch king Kreig. Today he would destroy the first of Davvol's supports.

The negator waited in its alcove near the throne, a saw-toothed shield in one hand and its other tipped in both claws and corrosive-fluid plungers. It shifted when the Inner Circle member entered the room, setting itself into a state of preparedness. Croag would not allow it to turn more on guard. The Phyrexian's eyes blazed a hard red, and searing beams of energy lashed out to split the hardened, wrinkled flesh that covered the negator's face. This would be Croag's second battle for Rath's throne room, and he had every intention of victory.

The negator's movement was a dark blur. Springing from its resting place, shield blocking Croag's attack as it swept in with its claws. Croag could never be so fast, though he came close. The Phyrexian master relied on his armored bands to make up the difference, the metal strips fully repaired as well and equal to the task. They turned the claws of the beast, though a few were spattered by the corrosive sludge. Croag struck back, but already the negator was past and pulling up short on the other side of the room. It stalked back carefully, watching for its opening.

Sampling the corrosive material the negator used had been part of Croag's plans. Knowing his body capable of withstanding any of the older chemical attacks, he had doubted Davvol's latest was too different. Radical leaps were not part of the Coracin's way. He preferred slow, methodical improvement. Such was the case here. The sludge burned into Croag's bands but failed to cause much more than a mild distraction. A rasping slide of metal and new coat of glistening oil, and the annoyance was gone.

Now it was Croag's turn. He leapt for the negator, offering it a deadly embrace. The saw blade shield slammed into his side, cutting past several metal bands and damaging the compleated flesh beneath. More of the claws scored deep wounds, but now Croag had the measure of the corrosive and his body was already working to negate its effect. One of the Inner Circle member's skeletal hands shot out to dig razored fingers into the negator's chest. They cut deeply then began to vibrate with a new life.

Where Croag's artifice-blended flesh pierced the negator a new process began. The negator's flesh reacted with Croag's, merging. The Phyrexian master's entire hand slid into the negator, then his arm up to the elbow. The negator began to twist violently now, feeling the invasion but unable to react as its own flesh and artifice turned against it. Croag reveled in his triumph, knowing instantly that he could consume the negator's entire being in this way. Such an expenditure of power for so simple a creature was not necessary. The negator was fast, deadly in its own right, but could never stand against a fully operational member of the Inner Circle. It would add so little to him, and Croag could wait for a better opportunity.

With a wrenching pull, Croag ripped his arm free and so brought with it the negator's flesh and machinery already consumed. He left behind a hole that bled oil and thick black blood.

The negator was well built, keeping to its feet though all the fight had gone out of it. Croag lashed out with both taloned hands, raking off large swaths of flesh and gouging into bone and metal support. The shield came up, and Croag ripped it from the other's grasp, hurling it with all of the Phyrexian's force so that it actually stuck into the armored walls of the throne room. The clawed hand rose sluggishly, and the member of the Inner Circle caught it and used searing whips of energy from his eyes to sever it at the wrist. Still the negator remained standing.

Just how long could it stand up under such damage, Croag wondered. With something very much akin to physical pleasure, the Phyrexian set to work.

* * * * *

A violent quake shook the Stronghold, as if the plane's flowstone foundation had shifted under the weight of the towering fortress and its processing equipment.

Davvol slowly paced the short aisle that ran between both lines of negators. Four of the Phyrexians to a side, each was a deadly instrument. They were the result of his centuries of effort, tailoring the best of the negator abilities into ever more-efficient creations. If not for the unknown strengths of planeswalkers, Davvol might have thought any one perfectly suited for the task of killing Urza. As is, they were his best—and last—gamble.

A particularly sobering thought, Davvol was now forced to gamble his hard-won power in this bid against the 'walker's life. Still fresh in his perfect memory was the day of several months prior when he came into the Stronghold's throne room. The oil mixed with blood was pooled in the middle of the room and splattered in streaks and splotches against the walls. He remembered the scent of flesh—meat—spoiling in the fortress's warmth. He found his own guardian negator shredded, fouling the throne room. It was not defeated, not dead, but shredded—rent down into pieces so small that it could only be done with a deliberate and determined effort. It could only be credited to Croag. It was a message, no subtlety at all, that Davvol's immunity from the Phyrexian Inner Circle member had expired.

For the first time in many centuries Davvol remembered a trace of the fear he had once felt for the Phyrexian—the cold touch along his back and the metallic taste of a mouth suddenly dry in nervousness.

Fear, as would forever be the case, was a wonderful motivator. Davvol brought the production of flowstone up yet again, pushing his workers and the machinery well past their limits. The secondary attractors shook with constant tremors, at times twisting against the Stronghold itself, but the counterbalancing torque built into their design allowed for such abuse. Today's earlier visit, in fact, set a new threshold for the equipment. He also stepped up other projects, readying a private army capable of killing the land of Yavimaya once and for all.

Of course, he bent himself strongly to the task of killing Urza. Destroying the 'walker was the one act Davvol knew could assure his continued position as evincar of Rath. It could bring him closer to the compleation he desired. His body was already strengthened to the point where aging and routine damage could not hurt him, yet Davvol still knew many of the physical limitations of flesh: Heat and cold, pain and discomfort. The evincar looked only toward protecting his mind, allowing it an immortal existence free of such encumbrances.

For now, however, he could only imagine the benefits of such a form while the threat of Croag hung over his present life. That threat colored everything darker in an already black land. It interfered with Davvol's ability to think straight and to plan.

One final nod completed the inspection. Nothing seemed amiss, and the evincar could think of no other refinements that might make the difference—none he had time for at any rate.

"Find Urza Planeswalker," he ordered. The floor shook again, causing him to stumble to a wall rather than be cast to the ground. Cracks showed in one flowstone wall, then reformed to a smooth surface under his mental direction. "Find and kill him. Go."

Each negator turned away, stepping for their own portals, which already stood open at the back wall, then they were gone, tracking. Davvol stood alone in the throne room, trying to sort through so many mental notes and decide on his next action. Another quake worked its way up through the floor and along the walls, a grinding tremor that seeped up past the armored soles of his boots to churn inside his stomach. This time it did not fade immediately, setting off a sympathetic shaking that reflected back from other directions.

Something was wrong. Davvol sensed it. The Stronghold was by no means a sentient entity, but he had known it for so long that he sometimes felt a connection to it that had nothing to do with the flowstone properties or the great machinery at his command. That connection spoke of danger.

Now the walls shook but not the floor—decidedly unsettling. Davvol called for guards, led them toward one of the bridges he had ordered built in his first century as steward, a construction which held one of the secondary attractors. Even through half a kilometer of flowstone and metal, Davvol felt the grinding of metal tearing into metal, of gears stripped or screeching as the joints threatened to bind. Before he had crossed the bridge's expanse Davvol was running. Why this day of all others, he wondered briefly, allowing his emotions to color his thoughts. Why not tomorrow or the following year? More precise logic returned. Why not last week or the last decade? Whatever the problem, it happened now. To solve the problem was paramount, not to make matters the more difficult by dwelling on his own frustrations.

The upper chambers were frantic with workers running about trying to bring machinery back under control. The sealed shaft that housed the large driving screws twisted against its mountings. Machinery rattled, and a pipe ruptured to pour cold lake waters over the floor. The water flashed to steam where it washed up against hot steel, raising an instant steam bath. Davvol ordered the local supervisors captured by his guards, stopping them to put questions forward. Frantic work degraded into chaos with the workers suddenly bereft of leadership. Davvol grabbed one by the shoulders, lifting it off the floor and shaking it like he might a rag doll.

"What is happening?" he yelled at it, not thinking to place the touch upon its mind. In this hectic environment, he likely would have failed regardless. The entire bridge shook, throwing half the workers and even a few Phyrexians to the ground. "What is it?"

One worker leapt for Davvol's face, its gaze wild and

panicked, swinging a sharply-tapered tool. A Phyrexian soldier skewered him on its sword, held the Vec dangling in the air while blood seeped out around the edges of the blade, and then cast it down to the floor. The Vec supervisor waved down other workers who looked about to snap under the stress and sudden violence. The superviser then pointed down, jabbering at Davvol in its own speech. Whatever the problem, it came from below, in the complex mechanisms of the bladed dials that pulled lava up from the furnaces far underground.

Davvol wasted no more time with questions. He kicked at the lifeless worker, venting rage and frustration. "Kill them," he ordered two guards. "All but that one."

As per his standing orders, the supervisors were punished in watching their people die. Then he was running again, his steam-sodden cloak trailing behind him, and his armored boots ringing against steel decking. The bulk of his Phyrexian escort followed. They found stairs and spiraled down into the depths of the machinery—into the main gears room.

The room curved about the central shaft, immense in the open space contained within the walls but made confining by an array of steam pipes, clockwork gears and various machinery. A hideous screeching filled the space, machinery worked too hard and tearing itself apart under the stresses applied. The room was out of a nightmare— awash in an orange glow, the light cast through large portals in the shaft's shielding by lava as it spilled upward, driven by the spinning blades. Yellow steam spilled from cracked valves and warped piping. The scent of sulfur was heavy in the room's jungle dampness.

Dozens, possibly scores, of Vec leapt from overhead

concealment or from under deckplates suddenly loose and sliding over hiding holes built into the flooring. They had been driven to the limits of their endurance, and now with the Stronghold apparently collapsing about them, they did all they had left in them to do. They struck out at their tormentor. As other doors opened to admit more into the large theater filled with steam pipes and an incredible array of clockwork gears, they numbered better than a hundred.

Against a dozen Phyrexian troops, such ill-trained warriors were at the disadvantage. The black-armored soldiers hewed their way through the wave of bodies. Blood spattered the floor and machinery, drying quickly into rustlike streaks against the dark metal. The floor trembled and continued to shake longer than it had previously with the earlier tremors. Machinery tore loose of mountings, tumbling about the floor and indiscriminately crushing Vec and Phyrexian alike. A gear arm shattered and came crashing down in a ringing clatter. The screeching wail grew louder until it seemed tangible. This was likely the cause of the violent vibrations. The great complex machinery—Davvol's design—was tearing itself apart under high speeds and stresses.

The evincar screamed his frustration, attempting to find some way to bring it back under control. He didn't know the machinery like the Vec, had relied on them to maintain it, and this group was beyond even acknowledging his demands. They would need dispatching, and new workers brought in to shut down the system. Except there was no time for such a change out of personnel. He spared one thought for the workers in chambers above, before remembering he had ordered them slain. Events had conspired against him in a way even Croag could not have. Davvol made up his mind then to flee—able to recoup his losses another day.

Barely was the decision reached, however, when the floor suddenly pitched up sharply as if struck from below with a mountainous fist. Walls bowed and crumpled, and the ceiling caved downward raining shafts and toothy gear wheels. While still airborne, Davvol felt a metal pinion impale him. He came down hard, spitting blood from between thin, pale lips. Another gear fell across the backs of his legs, crushing them and pinning him into place. Pain flared in his mind, cloaking any thought of saving himself with a panicked desperation. A hideous rumble of stressed and avalanching metal overrode the noise of the overhead gears, still spinning wildly and trying to complete their function. The floor dropped out from beneath them all, as the entire bridge and shaft collapsed down into the lower caldera.

Davvol, evincar of Rath, fell with it.

*　*　*　*　*

Scorched metal and molten rock, the scents of hell.,Davvol knew only those scents and pain, never-ending pain, as the mountain of collapsed metal struts and supports, machinery and gearwork, continued to shift and grind. The molten glow of the lava had faded some time before. He could not say when. He didn't think it had touched him, the scent of charred flesh being that of others and long since cleared from the scalding air. Now darkness reigned, broken only by the occasional spark as metal shifted and struck against metal and flowstone. It was light enough to show him that his head and one arm remained free in a small space. The rest of him had been caught under an avalanche of gear-work—toothy wheels, pinions and shafts.

He faded into and out of consciousness, praying for rescue, rescue or death—either one after so long. This was the curse of near compleation. His body was simply unable to die, keeping his mind alive but not strong enough to allow him to free himself. With no voice for calling out, his restricted air intake was not enough for speech. It was barely enough to feed his brain and perhaps not even that. The veil clouding his thoughts threatened a slow torturous death of his mind. It was the only thing Davvol had ever possessed of true value, so he fought, trying to stay alive. He focused on the brimstone scents of his prison and the sound of grinding metal as the avalanche continued a slow fall toward entropy. He listened to the drip of water pinging against steel plates and the rasping whisper of steel bands rubbing together.

Croag.

Twin sparks of flame, hovering in the black, artificial night, flared up to offer a dim light to see by. Davvol noticed the dark doorway of an open portal behind the Phyrexian. There were no Vec laborers, no guards, just Croag, making his way carefully to Davvol's position. No humping walk or raspy breath, the nightmare had been reborn. Davvol remembered the way in which Croag had dismantled the negator set to protect the steward. The Phyrexian could likely free Davvol from this misfortune. Davvol would do anything for release. If he'd been able to speak, he would have promised whatever was asked of him—would have pledged the rest of his life to Croag's service.

Except, the rest of his life was exactly what Croag intended to take.

Extending one clawed hand, Croag set a single finger against Davvol's black armored skullcap, right where the circular depression would be, the evincar knew with a sudden wave of fear. He felt the sharp stab of fresh pain as Croag physically dug into his mind and began to drain the steward's memories, sifting knowledge from experience and taking both for himself. The Phyrexian was heedless of the damage this procedure caused, never planning to release Davvol and always having planned to drain the other in this way. Davvol felt his mind slipping away, leaving only the knowledge that he remained trapped, alone, and in pain. He had been given a long existence of suffering, robbed of the one thing he had ever treasured.

Croag was gone, having taken what he had come for—finished with Davvol, once and for all.

* * * * *

Croag paced the small plateau, feeling with every step how the surface might bend and reshape itself to his will, *his* will, but bent by the skill of Davvol.

Never before had the Phyrexian drained so much from a single subject. Several lifetimes worth of experience and accumulated knowledge were all at Croag's disposal now: the ability of flowstone, the evolution of negators, the trials Davvol had fought in Yavimaya, and the hatred, undeniable and uncompromising, for Croag. Everything was there, including how Davvol had planned to dispose of the Phyrexian, and when Croag circumvented those plans by destroying the negator, how Davvol would have used the death of Urza Planeswalker to elevate his position in the Dark God's gaze.

Urza Planeswalker had found Rath. There was no denying the evidence. The ruined shell of a negator lay upon the flowstone, tortured metal and some desiccated and petrified flesh was all that remained. Croag could see the creature fighting Urza and then escaping back to Rath, leading the 'walker right back to Phyrexia's most secret plan. Why not? Davvol had never thought to instruct them against such a feat. Urza had tracked the negator back, finished it off, and then escaped with knowledge of Rath's existence. Urza would have recognized the nature of this plane—and its ultimate purpose—at once. It was the staging ground for the coming invasion. The planeswalker would sense it, and in the voices of the Vec or one of the other races brought across he could find confirmation if necessary. There were no doubts. In the back of his mind, where Croag had stored the mental essence of Davvol, the Phyrexian heard the evincar's dark laugh.

Could Urza Planeswalker be killed? Davvol had thought so, but Croag no longer felt sure. Perhaps only the Dark One would be able to destroy the 'walker, but no doubts remained now that Croag would have to try. He would have to do it himself personally, and that required drawing the planeswalker into the open, a feat not accomplished in the assaults on Keld or in any fighting since—but Benalia—that seemed so much more likely. Benalia or Yavimaya, either should do. Both of those would have to be dealt with before Croag could ever face the Dark Lord again, even in his dreams.

The negators and troops would be called into battle then—a preliminary strike to herald the coming invasion. The planeswalker would show, and he would fight. Croag would be ready to meet him—to kill him. He would do the job himself rather than continue to trust failing subordinates. He would test his own mettle and metal, as he had once already, proving that he remained Croag, favored of the Ineffable among the Inner Circle of Phyrexia.

Epilogue

The heir

Barrin watched as the last student filed from the slow-time end of the timelock. They would be carting out records and other files today, cleaning out the last of his personal effects on the morrow. The final evacuation of the buildings might take weeks, cataloging every scrap of paper, but nothing would be lost in this move. Eventually the buildings would be torn down for their raw materials. Even the paving stones would be pried out of the ground, and the fresh soil possibly excavated for healthy landfill.

The necessity of such scavenging only underscored his resolve that Tolaria had been left unmanaged for too long. The master mage paused at the timelock entrance for one last look about his home, at the slow-time envelope that had been his world for so long. It was just another lie or a half-truth, once believed for the sake of convenience but no more. Dominaria was his home, his world, and he would not remain isolated in his self-inflicted exile any longer. Recent events had finally driven through the need for his return, the need for Tolaria's return.

The misted slow-time waters were damp on his skin as he passed into the first chamber, the fog seemingly alive in the blue glow of mage-lit stones. It swirled about him reminding of monumental events in his life, and Barrin's mind formed patterns out of the chaos. He could see— constructed of tiny beads of water—the fortress compound of the First Academy, torn apart by magical upheavals brought on by their temporal experiments, the same catastrophe that had shattered Tolaria's temporal fabric and created the pockets of slow and fast time. There in the corner, formed out of mist, was the *New Tolaria*, the ship that had hosted the academy in those years following the destruction of the first school and crashed through the waves until making landfall once again on the island shores. Above his head, near the ceiling in a swirling spire of fog, was the rise of the second academy and the mist wraiths which were of course the Phyrexians come to tear down all they had built. One larger swirl of misted waters sparkled against a mage stone—the *Weatherlight*—smashing through the rest just as it had helped to carry the day on Serra's Realm. Yes, he remembered those years well enough—the dark and the light of them.

The breeze of his passage shredded the mist images. He remembered back on times and events that stood out visibly in his memory. He recalled the early days, acting at times as surrogate father along with Urza and Gatha in creation of the Metathran warrior simulacra, even as he started his own family and locked both he and Rayne away behind temporal doors. He thought about the bloodlines, in their many incarnations, tearing at the unity of the academy and then moving in force out into Dominaria. He saw Keld cast into ruins, its people only now recovering from their several centuries of Phyrexian *testing*. He felt for the Capashen Clan of Benalia—desperately wounded, along with a half dozen other strong centers of the bloodlines. And now, Karn was missing. The master mage shook his head, so many lives disrupted, so far yet to go.

A warm tropical sun shook the chill from Barrin's skin as he passed from the final chamber and back into real time. The deep-blue sky might have been a reflection of the ocean waters except for a few snowy clouds that drifted lazily overhead. He blinked against the bright day and took a deep draw of the salt-tang ocean breeze. No more mistakes, he promised himself.

"Care for a stroll about the island?"

No mistaking that soft, beautiful voice, though Barrin still noted its hesitant approach. He turned to one of the stone benches that sat to either side of the timelock. Rayne sat there, her silk robes gathered about her, each hand tucked into the opposing sleeve. Long, raven hair cascaded down over both shoulders. Brown eyes studied him in a mixture of concern and hope.

"Been waiting long?" he asked.

"Not long," she admitted. "A few hours. I heard that you were closing down all the slow-time offices and labs. I saw the students go in earlier and hoped that you might be coming out with them." She stood, as graceful as ever, though she kept her arms crossed protectively in front of her.

Barrin nodded. "However long we have left," he said slowly, "I'd rather spend it on Tolaria, the *real* Tolaria." He paused, at a loss of where Rayne intended to take the conversation. "The *Weatherlight* has not left, has it?"

"No, though Multani and Rofellos hope to continue on their way soon. Did you want to talk with them? I already arranged for a group of scholars to interview them on what happened in Yavimaya."

"I wouldn't mind speaking with Multani. I also want to send the *Weatherlight* toward Argive. I hope to arrange a new trade of scholars with the Argivian University. They might have knowledge of ways to repair some of the damage we have done to Tolaria. It might give us a chance," he said, the various meanings warming the mage.

Rayne smiled then, bright and wonderful. Her eyes gleamed with a hint of mischief. She took his hand in hers, guided it to the slight swell of her abdomen. "Give us *all* a chance, then. I'm pregnant."

The revelation shook Barrin to his core. A smile in answer to Rayne's own spread across his face, a reflection of the warmth he felt inside. "What better omen to begin with than the start of a new life?"

"Shall we head for the new offices then?" Rayne asked. "There is so much to get done."

Barrin shook his head, enjoying the brief spark of confusion that flashed on his wife's face. "I'll take you up on your first suggestion, a stroll about the island." No more mistakes, he had promised himself. No matter the demands placed on him, Barrin would not—could not—allow himself to ignore the very reasons for which he fought. No one could, not if they were to believe in a better life after the battle.

"The Legacy and the heir—if there ever will be one—can wait until tomorrow." Someone else would simply have to watch over Dominaria today.

* * * * *

Jamuraa's mountain peaks were barely a smudge over the line of the horizon—a promise of the distance still to be traveled. Behind Karn, the sun fell low over the Voda sea. Sunset crimson splashed against the heavens. A sailor's good omen, Karn had learned in taking ship across the Voda, but it reminded the golem of nothing more than the blood spilled behind him in Benalia. The lives lost in protecting Urza's plans were not lost for nothing. Karn made sure of that.

A wind touched already with evening's chill raked the grass. The full Glimmer Moon rose low on the eastern horizon, promising some gray light by which to travel this night. One heavy step followed another—the same tireless pace that had carried the golem away from DeLatt and finally out of Benalia. He had stopped at villages only when necessary, once to engage a silversmith for repairs to his body, four more times to complete at least part of his mission as tasked by Urza Planeswalker. In the water crossing he kept to his cabin and away from prying eyes. He had been brought ashore by longboat, away from any port city, and of a necessity, far from his final destination.

Therri's face still haunted the golem, pale and drawn after the narrow battlefield victory that cost her her brother and landed the responsibilities of Clan Capashen upon her shoulders. Karn had not forgotten her, but again his conflicting loyalties called for compromise. Stay with her or follow Urza's order. Life versus Legacy.

The planeswalker still worried more for his collection of clockwork, sculpting, and magical devices than he ever would the people whose lives he touched. His only words to Karn, after the death of the Phyrexian incursion in Benalia, had been to direct a recovery of Legacy items.

"The Legacy," he'd said to Karn. "Collect what you can and take it away from Benalia. You will find protection in Jamuraa. I will locate you there," and he grimaced, "when I can."

He had smiled with a grim sort of self-satisfaction, and winked from existence—stepping in between worlds. Perhaps it was better that Urza kept his words so simple. The 'walker would never be convinced of anything other than his own genius—his own plans for the future of Dominaria.

Life versus Legacy. For Karn, the choice came easily. Therri Capashen would remain in his memory—for as long as Karn could keep her there. Karn might not even remember this day when the invasion came—if the full invasion ever came—but he would live the next two decades at least secure in the knowledge that the Capashen heroes lived on through at least one child. One more life, then, might someday make a difference. Carry the Legacy from Benalia, Urza had charged him. Protect it until found again by the planeswalker. Karn did carry several artifact pieces of the Legacy, and in his arms, swathed in new, thick blankets, he carried another part of the Legacy—what might well be the last surviving Capashen hero—the infant, Gerrard, Therri's orphaned grandson and her final request of Karn that the silver golem take him somewhere safe.

Bloodlines

Urza Planeswalker focused on his *human components* as his path to an end product rather than for their own special talents and abilities. Living among them, caring for them as children and often befriending them as adults, the golem instead recognized in each the spirit that defied Phyrexia and promised any form of salvation. Urza had been wrong in that. Perhaps they would not wield the Legacy in its final form and discover how to defeat Phyrexia once and for all time, but one of them survived. How many more might be critical to the future? This was a simple truth, which Karn in his limited memory had recognized where Urza Planeswalker and his millennia of experience had not. Every one of them, bloodline subject or not, was a separate hope for Dominaria—could make a final difference that might stand between life and loss.

This one Karn would keep safe, so that in his own life, Gerrard Capashen might hope to make a difference, the mark of a true hero.

Get the story behind the world's best-selling game.

The Brothers' War

Artifacts Cycle Book I

Jeff Grubb

It is a time of conflict. Titanic dragon engines scar and twist the very landscape of the planet. The final battle will sink continents and shake the skies, as two brothers struggle for supremacy on the continent of Terisiare. And one alone survives.

Planeswalker

Artifacts Cycle Book II

Lynn Abbey

Urza, survivor of the Brothers' War, feels the spark of a planeswalker ignite within him. But as he strides across the planes of Dominia™, a loyal companion seeks to free him from an obsession that threatens to turn to madness. Only she can rescue him from despair and guilt. Only she can help him fulfill his destiny.

Time Streams

Artifacts Cycle Book III

J. Robert King

From a remote island in Dominaria thousands of years after the Brothers' War, Urza tries to right the wrongs he and his brother perpetrated against their homeland. His task is immense, and his enemies are strong. Only a mighty weapon can turn the balance of history.

Bloodlines

Artifacts Cycle Book IV

Loren L. Coleman

Urza's weapon lacks but one component: a human hand to guide it. As the centuries slowly pass, he patiently perfects his plans, waiting for the right moment—and the right heir. The heir to his legacy.

www.wizards.com